MESSA
"THE S

The Shadow Game is
  The rules must be followed accordingly . . .

When all points are gathered and there's but
  one player,
  The loser shall shout, "All hail the mindslayer!"

LOSERS WEEPERS

A brilliantly chilling game of psychological terror
by Deanie Francis Mills, author of the acclaimed
thrillers, *Spell Bound*, *Free Fall*, *Dead Line*, and
Dark Room . . .

Titles by Deanie Francis Mills

DARK ROOM
DEAD LINE
FREE FALL
SPELL BOUND

LOSERS WEEPERS

DEANIE FRANCIS MILLS

JOVE BOOKS, NEW YORK

Grateful acknowledgment is made for permission to use excerpts from the following material:

DANDELION WINE by Ray Bradbury. Reprinted by permission of Don Congdon Associates, Inc.

THE HOBBIT by J.R.R. Tolkien © 1966. Reprinted by permission of Houghton Mifflin Co. All rights reserved.

THE FELLOWSHIP OF THE RING by J.R.R. Tolkien © 1954, 1965 © 1982. Reprinted by permission of Houghton Mifflin Co. All rights reserved.

THE LION, THE WITCH, AND THE WARDROBE by C.S. Lewis. Reprinted by permission of Lions, an imprint of HarperCollins Publishers Limited.

"Tandy" from WINESBURG, OHIO by Sherwood Anderson. Introduction, Malcolm Cowley. Copyright 1919 by B.W. Huebsch. Copyright 1947 by Eleanor Copenhaver Anderson. Used by permission of Viking Penguin, a division of Penguin Books USA Inc.

LOSERS WEEPERS

A Jove Book / published by arrangement with
the author

PRINTING HISTORY
Jove edition / September 1994

ISBN: 0-515-11461-8

A JOVE BOOK®
Jove Books are published by The Berkley Publishing Group,
200 Madison Avenue, New York, New York 10016.
JOVE and the "J" design are trademarks
belonging to Jove Publications, Inc.

PRINTED IN THE UNITED STATES OF AMERICA

10 9 8 7 6 5 4 3 2 1

For my children,
Dustin and Jessica,
who bring magic to my days
and
sunshine into all my shadows.

Mayhem has gone mainstream.

"Violence in our Culture"
Newsweek, April 1, 1991

LOSERS WEEPERS

PROLOGUE

The whirlwind funneled forth from a black and brittle sky without warning. Weather forecasters said later that it was a true phenomenon, that the little country cemetery had seemed to have been selected for destruction with some sort of cosmic malicious intent. No buildings, houses, or trees were damaged by the delinquent winds. The only witnesses were fireflies, brightening and dimming like ghosts taking drags on cigarettes in murky corners of the graveyard.

The wild and howling winds descended on the serene and lonely little cemetery with an undeserved fury that sent the fireflies scattering like sparks. Tombstones, set in place a century before by hardy pioneers, were yanked up and flung about haphazardly, some landing in a crumpled heap a half mile away.

When the heavens' rage subsided, an eerie quiet settled over the gravesites. Starlight gleamed softly along the jagged edges of the broken tombstones, sharply etching partial names and dates.

Most of them belonged to children.

PART I   SHADOWLAND

Douglas walked through it thinking it would go on forever. The perfection, the roundness, the grass smell traveled on out ahead as far and as fast as the speed of light. The sound of a good friend whistling like an oriole, pegging the softball, as you horse-danced, key-jingled the dusty paths, all of it was complete, everything could be touched; things stayed near, things were at hand and would remain.

It was such a fine day, and then suddenly a cloud crossed the sky, covered the sun, and did not move again.

—RAY BRADBURY
Dandelion Wine

Some there are among us who sing that the Shadow will draw back, and peace shall come again. Yet I do not believe that the world about us will ever again be as it was of old, or the light of the Sun as it was aforetime.

—J.R.R. TOLKIEN
The Fellowship of the Ring

ONE

Jeremy Scott knew he should have gone straight home from softball practice, but his mom wouldn't be home for another hour yet, so he decided to hang out in the park for a while instead. Randy Brubaker's mom had offered him a ride home, but he only lived a couple of blocks away, and anyway, coach's words were still stinging in his ears. He was in no mood to share a ride with the World's Greatest Outfielder.

It wasn't his fault he missed that fly ball! He thought Mark Mason was going to get it! Geez. Guy makes a few little mistakes and next thing you know, he's sitting on the bench. *Plus*, as soon as Dad found out, he'd get *another* butt-chewing. Like it was his *mission* in life to grow up to be another Darryl Strawberry or somebody.

Jeremy poked down one of the park's numerous nature trails. Still, even his baby cousin could have caught that last one.

"*Hey.* Jeremy!"

Jeremy stopped and looked behind him. He could have sworn the voice came from behind that big juniper tree, but he couldn't see anything.

"*Over here.*"

The tree moved, and a guy stepped out, wearing the coolest camouflage fatigues Jeremy had ever seen. Instead of being splotched with blobs of color, these were covered with intricately drawn twigs and leaves. He'd never have seen the guy if he hadn't have moved.

The guy was older than Jeremy, but it was hard to tell

5

how much older. Maybe high school age. He had mud-colored eyes and hair, and was very pale and thin.

Jeremy thought he'd seen the guy before, but he couldn't remember where. Maybe at McDonald's or the Pizza Hut, or playing video games somewhere. Jeremy was still trying to place him, when the guy held out Jeremy's missing backpack. A cry of joy popped out before he could stop it.

"Did you lose this?" the guy asked.

"You kidding? I thought somebody stole it!" He ran his hand over the bright red waterproof surface, with the initials "J.C.S." in the corner. "I lost it two weeks ago. Man, I thought I'd never see it again."

"You wouldn't believe where I found it," the guy said.

Jeremy pawed through the backpack's contents. Shoving aside his Cub Scout Bear book, he suddenly yelped, "Oh, *cool*! They didn't rip off my baseball cards. My mom about had a cow when I told her I'd lost them." He turned the cards over in his hand. They were still wrapped in cellophane, marked, Chris's Collectible Comics & Cards. "I had just bought them. Hadn't even had a chance to look at 'em yet."

"There's a whole pile of missing backpacks where this one came from," the guy said.

"Really?"

"Yeah. C'mon. I'll show you." The guy turned and went walking back into the park.

Jeremy hesitated. A little kid had disappeared from a construction site just a couple of weeks ago. Jeremy's parents had given him all sorts of dire warnings about going anywhere with a stranger. Still, this guy wasn't exactly a stranger. Jeremy *knew* he'd seen him around. More than once, too. Besides, Jeremy figured, this guy didn't look anything at all like a kidnapper.

"You go to Tom Daniels Elementary, don't you?" the guy asked over his shoulder as he walked. Jeremy wasn't sure what to do. He didn't want to be rude, and the guy *had* returned his backpack. Tentatively he began to follow.

"There's all kinds of stuff where I found your backpack," the guy said. "Clothes and toys and stuff. You could help me return those things to the kids who lost them."

"How did you find *me*?" asked Jeremy.

"Your name and school were written in the Cub Scout book."

Jeremy nodded.

Behind another tree, they came upon the coolest dirt bike Jeremy had *ever* seen. *"Oh, wow!"* he said.

"No need to walk when I can take you on *this*," the guy said.

"I don't know," said Jeremy. "I'm not sure if my mom would like it."

"You'd have a helmet. See?" He held up just about the most totally rad helmet ever made. It was glossy black and had a smoked visor that completely covered the face.

"Like Darth Vader," Jeremy gasped. *"Cool."*

"I'm a very careful driver," the guy said, "and I'll take you right home. Oh, and you could wear this, to protect you from the wind." He handed Jeremy a red Jurassic Park windbreaker and smiled. From a pouch at the back of the dirt bike, he withdrew an oversize Levi's jacket, which he put on over his camouflage fatigues. He also traded his camouflage cap for another black helmet with visor. He gestured toward the helmet Jeremy held. "Try it on."

Jeremy couldn't resist. Oh, it was *so* neat! It made everything look shadowed. He wished he could see himself in a mirror.

As if reading his mind, the guy said, "Check it out," and pointed toward the rearview mirror. "Wait. Try on the jacket first."

Jeremy shrugged on the windbreaker and bent over to see himself in the mirror. *"Oh, wow!* I wish Randy Brubaker could see *this*!"

"We'll take you by and show him on the way home, if you like."

"Really?" This was just too awesome to believe. Wait'll

he told his best buddy, Moose Derrick. Moose had never ridden on a dirt bike before. But then, neither had he.

"Ready?" the guy asked. "When we make turns, remember to lean into the turn."

Jeremy nodded, but his stomach did a little flip-flop. He was beginning to have misgivings. His mom probably wouldn't want him to ride on the dirt bike. Still . . . maybe they'd get back before she got home from work. He felt a little queasy. He'd never done anything behind his mother's back before. Well, nothing *big* anyway. (She didn't know about his secret candy stash.)

On the other hand, she'd never actually *said*, "No, Jeremy, you are not allowed to ride on dirt bikes." (Of course, he'd never asked, either.)

The guy started the dirt bike, and it gave a satisfying little growl. "How far is this place?" Jeremy asked, still doubtful.

"Not very far," said the guy. "If you want, I can drop you off a block from home and you can walk the rest of the way. That way, your folks won't give you any hassle about riding a dirt bike."

That did it. With a gleeful grin Jeremy climbed onto the back of the dirt bike and wrapped his arms around the guy's thin waist.

This was going to be the ride of his life, he just knew it.

As soon as they left the city limits, Jeremy knew he was going to get into big trouble. The guy had told him they weren't going very far, but the longer they rode, the more Jeremy's anxiety grew. He even thought about jumping off the dirt bike, but they were traveling so fast he was afraid to. He kept asking the other guy where they were going and when they were going to get there, but the guy just ignored him.

Finally they turned down a country road near the river. Eventually they left the road and took a half-hidden trail through the brush. Jeremy had no idea how long they'd been going. His mom was going to be so mad.

At last they pulled over at the base of a tree-shrouded rise. Jeremy got off and looked nervously around while the driver hid the dirt bike behind a large boulder.

Jeremy bit his lip. Something was definitely not right. He thought about running, but where would he go? There were no houses around, and he was already lost anyhow. He thought about the boy who had vanished, and his hands began to sweat.

"It's up here," the guy said. "Come on." He started the steep climb up the hill.

Jeremy hesitated. The guy stopped and looked over his shoulder. Jeremy thought, *Okay. I'll go along with him. If he tries anything funny, I'll just kung-fu him.* He clambered behind the fellow through gnarled tree roots and rock slabs in a zigzag path up to the top of the hill. After that, they descended into a glade thick with tree-shadow and followed a narrow path into a natural grotto.

For a long moment they both stood, panting, drinking in the sheer wonder and beauty of the place. Ancient trees arched overhead like the Great Hall of a king's palace. Butterflies and birds flitted about, bright flashes of color against the backdrop of rock and trees. Greenery of all kinds laced together below like silken emerald draperies.

As if it were a long sigh, Jeremy whispered, "Coo-o-o-l." He glanced at the other guy. He had a strange expression on his face. It frightened Jeremy a little, but he couldn't say why. It was spooky somehow. With a ghost of a smile, the guy said proudly, "Welcome to Shadowland."

Then he headed through the trees toward those leafy green "curtains," which he parted with a flourish. Jeremy followed him into the most incredible place he had ever seen.

"A cave!" he cried.

The darkness was cool and moist and had an unfamiliar acrid smell. "It's dark in here," said Jeremy. His voice shook a little and seemed to echo. Something fluttered nearby in a rustle of wings. Jeremy jumped.

"I have a lantern," the guy said. "Down here." He led the way down a tunnel until he came upon a kerosene lantern, which he lit. The walls of the cave sprang to amber life. The lamp made giant shadows of miniature mineral formations which hung from the ceiling and extended sometimes to the floor.

Jeremy was beginning to wonder if they were going to go on a great adventure, like in the movie *The Goonies*. Maybe it wasn't anything to be afraid of after all. He was excited by the idea and a little nervous. "Awesome," he said. "I never been in a cave before. This is so cool."

"Yes, it is cool in here," said the guy, "even on the hottest days."

Jeremy quirked an eyebrow at him.

The guy turned to Jeremy. The lantern gave his face an otherworldly glow. "I am Shadow," he intoned. "Shadowland is a place of mystery and danger, a place which guards its secrets jealously."

Jeremy nodded. This was kind of fun.

"Shadowland has allowed me to stay because I have the power, the gift of *not-being*. Therefore, Shadowland understands that Shadow respects secrets and would never divulge to anyone the presence and place of Shadowland."

"Oh, I won't tell anybody!" blurted Jeremy. "But what's *not-being*?"

"*Silence!*" With almost hypnotic movements, Shadow peeled off the Levi's jacket and began unbuttoning the camouflage fatigues.

"What are you doing?" asked Jeremy. *Wait a minute,* he thought. This was getting too weird, and he was beginning to feel uncomfortable and a little scared again. "Where are all the backpacks and things you were going to show me?"

"All in due time," said Shadow and turned his back to undress. Quickly he pulled on a loose overshirt with blousy sleeves, tights, high-topped suede boots, and finally, with a flourish, a purple velveteen hooded cloak. Around his waist he strapped on a scabbard with dagger.

He swirled to face Jeremy, who had stepped back a few paces, just to the edge of the lantern's light. Jeremy regarded him warily. "You're not going to try to touch any of my private parts, are you?" he asked in a quavering voice. He'd meant to sound forceful, but his whole body seemed to be betraying him. He couldn't seem to remember any of the kung fu he'd seen in the movies.

Shadow laughed, and his voice echoed with a resounding ring off the walls of the Secret Caverns. "I have no use for any of your parts," he said scornfully. "Now, do you want to see the journey-pouches or not?"

Journey-pouches? Jeremy wondered what the guy was talking about, but he was afraid to ask. He wasn't so sure anymore that this adventure was going to be fun. "I don't know," he said. "I just want to go home." He glanced around. Outside the protective circle of the lantern's light, the cave was completely dark. From somewhere deep within its mysterious recesses, Jeremy could hear dripping water.

Shadow was staring at him with gleaming eyes. Jeremy squirmed uncomfortably. "It will only take a moment," said Shadow, lifting the lantern and striding on down the tunnel with a batlike flap of purple velveteen. Jeremy, not wanting to be left behind in the cave blackness, hurried along just in the circle of the light.

They entered a large room within the cave. Shadow held the lantern high. "This is the Treasure Trove Room," he said. "Observe what the power of *not-being* can do."

Jeremy's mouth dropped open. A large pile of backpacks, toys, windbreakers, and the like occupied the center of the room. He crouched over the pile, sorting through other children's belongings. After a moment he looked over at Shadow. He knew now that he was in very serious trouble, and that it had nothing to do with his parents.

"You stole these things, didn't you?" he asked.

Shadow smiled. "The trolls are no match for Shadow."

"Trolls? What trolls?" Jeremy peered into the cave shadows. What was this weirdo *talking* about? The adventure had lost its appeal. All Jeremy wanted now was to get out.

Still smiling, Shadow said, "Even the dragons can't protect you here. Shadowland is secret. The Secret Caverns are hidden. You'll have to rely on your little dim troll wit to escape."

Jeremy had heard enough. "I want to go home!" he shouted. He dashed down a dark tunnel, but it only took him a few steps to be eclipsed in blackness. He stumbled to a halt and looked back at Shadow. With that same strange smile Jeremy had seen earlier, Shadow withdrew a parchment scroll from the folds of his cloak, unfurled it, and in a commanding voice, began to read:

"The Shadow Game is simple for all to see;
Three rules must be followed accordingly:
Trolls must be taken one by one.
Once a fortnight may the deed be done.

"The Secret Caverns will make a labyrinth fine
For Shadow to chase trolls until they decline.
A torch and a head start will be given free
To provide trolls a fair battle's chance to flee.

"For each turn of the maze that is completely mastered
By troll or by Shadow, whichever is faster,
A twenty-point award will be given—
Ten points more for the true terror-stricken!

"Those with special powers shall surely use them,
But those who have none will face quite a problem!
When all points are gathered and there's but one player,
The loser shall shout, 'All hail the mindslayer!'"

When he was through reading the poem, Shadow rolled up the scroll with a flourish and put it back into his pocket.

Jeremy began to cry. He didn't want to, but he couldn't help it. This was like nothing he had ever known, not in his worst nightmares. He'd played video games before that featured trolls and dragons and labyrinths, and in a way, this was like being trapped in a giant video game. And Jeremy knew what happened when you messed up in a video game.

You got killed.

Shadow gestured toward the pile of backpacks and things. "My treasure trove," he boasted. "Stolen from beneath the noses of you stupid trolls. Not even your dragons knew!" Grinning gleefully, he reached behind the pile and withdrew a sturdy tree branch. Rolled around the tip of the branch was a woman's clean sanitary napkin, soaked in kerosene. Shadow lit the torch. It flamed high, making macabre shadow figures of him and Jeremy against the cave ceiling.

For a moment he held the flickering torch high. "I will call you *Darth*!" he cried.

Darth? Oh, yeah, Jeremy had said he felt like Darth Vader in the motorcycle helmet. Jeremy's heart was pounding. There was something about having his name changed—his identity stripped from him—that chilled him. He shivered. This guy was crazy. Really crazy.

Shadow extended the torch toward Jeremy. "Your torch," he said solemnly. "Take it."

Jeremy snuffled. "P-plee-e-z-e," he begged. "I want to go home. I won't tell anybody about this place, I swear!"

"Take it!" commanded Shadow.

"I won't tell anybody about the backpacks and stuff, honest!"

"Take it!" shouted Shadow, thrusting the torch toward Jeremy, who was now quaking from head to toe.

"Why won't you cooperate, you fool of a troll?" demanded Shadow. "By the goblins, I'm giving you a fair chance!"

Hesitantly Jeremy took the torch. It wobbled crazily, light dancing back and forth from cave ceiling to walls. He didn't know what kind of game this crazy guy was talking about. All he knew was that he didn't want to play, not at all. All he wanted to do was go home!

A wild hope took root in his trembling heart. Maybe somebody saw him leave the park with this guy, and they told his dad, and his dad called the cops, and they were on their way! On TV they always found the kid just in time. Yeah. They had to be on their way.

Shadow lit a torch of his own. Pointing it deep into the bowels of the Secret Caverns, he said, "You will have a head start into the labyrinth. For each turn of the maze, you will be given twenty points; ten more if you display courage and valor. If you should find a way out of the labyrinth before I reach you, you will be allowed to escape unmolested and the victory goes to the trolls. If I should catch up to you, the game's over and the *mindslayer* wins."

"W-what's a mindslayer?" Jeremy stammered, struggling to follow the rules.

"Ignorant, blubber-brained troll!" shouted Shadow. "It's *me*, you piece of bat guano. I used the power of the *mindslayer* to get you to come with me to the Secret Caverns."

"Like a spell?" Jeremy was trying to make sense of things.

"No! Not like a spell! I'm not a magic user, you dragon shit! The power of the *mindslayer* allows me to enter into your mind, to think and talk like you, so that you would not know I was Shadow—until it was too late." His chest swelled with pride.

"Then . . . what's *not-being*?" Jeremy was desperately trying to buy time. Maybe if he acted interested in this guy, he'd let Jeremy go.

Shadow smiled. "The state of *not-being* enables me to blend in so completely with my surroundings that I am never seen. Not even dragons can see me."

Jeremy thought of the strange camouflage fatigues and

nodded. But *dragons*? He started to roll his eyes and stopped himself just in time.

"Now. Let us get on with the game." Shadow picked up an hourglass he had stored with the troll treasure. Torchlight gleamed softly off the glass. "You will have ten turns of the hourglass."

Jeremy's torch dipped and swayed, the light casting ghastly silhouettes on the cave wall. "How long is that?"

Shadow turned over the hourglass and set it down firmly beside the kerosene lantern. White sand began spilling rapidly through the glass. Transfixed, Jeremy watched until the glass was empty, then looked at the young man, his face tight with fear. Now he knew. There was no way he was going to be able to get out of this. "B-but I've never played the game before," he said, stalling. "I don't know my way around the ca—labyrinth."

"You see? That's the genius of it! I've never navigated the maze, either! This way we will have a fair contest."

"You mean, you don't know if there's a way out?" Jeremy's body went cold.

Shadow hunched his shoulders and laughed. "Of course not! Where would be the challenge in that?" He turned over the glass. "Nine more times. There are two tunnels. Take either one. You may not return the way we have come." He gave Jeremy a long, steady look with his strange eyes. "Oh, and don't think your protecting dragons will find you here. *Nobody* knows where the Secret Caverns are." Sand streamed through the glass. He smiled.

Jeremy ran.

The torch flared, casting a huge, deformed Jeremy shadow on the cave wall. The tunnel was narrow—barely big enough for him. Save for the flickering yellow glow of the torch flames, it was black as the parking lot tar that stuck to the bottoms of his sneakers in summertime.

The tunnel narrowed to a crawl space. Stumbling to a halt, Jeremy dropped to his knees and began to crawl, struggling not to drop the torch from his trembling hand. His own whispers echoed off the barrel walls and came back to him, mocking him. Tears blurred his vision. If only he'd accepted that ride from Randy Brubaker's mom. If only he hadn't climbed onto the back of that dirt bike. If only—

The tunnel closed itself around Jeremy's body. Torch extended out in front, he squeezed along on his stomach. His wrist was aching; his hand shaking so hard he nearly dropped the torch. Pulling himself along, he switched to the other hand. An overpowering odor assailed his nostrils; that same cave smell as before, only much, much worse. Jeremy sneezed.

The crawl space widened and suddenly ended. One moment Jeremy was reaching in front, and the next he was dangling downward. He felt himself beginning to slide on the slick cave-tunnel surface. He resisted, holding up the torch desperately as he slid inexorably into space.

A strange, high-pitched squeaking sounded in his ears.

Jeremy stumbled forward and landed on a flat surface just a couple of feet below the tunnel, torch—miraculously— still in hand. Something fluttered near his face. Jeremy jerked away. Holding his torch up high, he looked around.

The roof of the cave room, while still solid black, was moving.

The squeaking noise multiplied, became a shriek.

Thousands of tiny black figures swarmed and swung into each other and, without warning, seemed to move as one. The air was suddenly filled with screaking, fluttering black monster-creatures, swooping and dipping into the torchlight with skeletal wings extended, great hooded eyes glaring at Jeremy.

Horror-struck, too petrified to move, Jeremy froze as the room thickened and howled around him. Something black and velvety struck him on the face. He slapped his hand over it and pulled it, struggling, squeaking, and biting, into the light of the torch.

A bat.

Another hit him on the back of the head, and another, his shoulder. Jeremy jumped to his feet and began slapping at himself.

The torch fell to the ground, and the light was extinguished.

His high, long scream melted into the total blackness with all the others, echoing off the cold cave walls.

TWO

It had been a bad day for Dylan Tandy.

She'd lost a hot tail on Interstate 35 in Austin. It made her feel like an idiot. She should have had two tail cars all along; Matt loved doing it because it got him out of the house and away from the computer and the telephone for a while. But he'd been busy on a report, and she'd hated to ask. Besides, she didn't feel comfortable leaving the kids home alone in the summer all day long, even though they were getting old enough to look after themselves. In some ways she was still getting used to rural living. It wasn't like there were neighbors right next door to run to in an emergency.

Losing a tail meant chalking up a whole day's work. Nothing to do but go home a failure. Nurse a beer and kick herself awhile. Stretch out on the couch and think how to phrase the client's report so she wouldn't look as stupid as she felt. Start all over again the next day.

Long afternoon tree shadows laced the van as Dylan turned down the winding drive to her country home. The sight of the white limestone house with its dormer windows, dual chimneys, and wraparound front porch never failed to lift her spirits. It always brought to her a feeling of safety and belonging.

She only wished her grandmother had told her that she planned to will this Texas Hill Country place near the Guadalupe River to Dylan *before* she had died so that Dylan could have put her head in Gran's ample lap one last time and whispered, "Thank you."

18

In a lonely childhood scarred by divorce, emotional upheaval, and frequent moves, Gran's home on the banks of one of the many creeks feeding into the beautiful green river was Dylan's refuge, her sanctuary, her solace. She spent most summers there, and never wanted to leave, particularly since it nearly always meant starting another new school in the fall.

The house had fallen into a shocking state of disrepair since Gran's long illness and death, but Dylan had never hesitated. She was determined to get her children out of the city and raise them in this place of innocence and beauty. She and her husband, Matt Armstrong, and the kids had driven down almost every weekend and vacation time for a year, working on the place, before hiring carpenters for the more complicated jobs and moving down the summer a year before.

Dylan pulled up behind the garage and parked the van. Actually, they no longer had a garage; they'd converted it into a home office for Tandy-Armstrong Investigations, Inc., where Matt took her illegible scrawls and turned them into comprehensive, tightly written client reports. Matt also handled most of the investigating that could be done by computer modem and telephone, while Dylan took care of most of the fieldwork and surveillance.

Dylan began gathering up her equipment. Her leg was bleeding from an earlier run-in with a dog, and her ankle throbbed where she'd twisted it while scrambling under a fence. She glanced in the rearview mirror. Her glossy auburn hair was dusted with dirt and grass, her creamy, freckled complexion was grimy, and her green eyes hidden behind the sunglasses she always wore on the job.

Laden with surveillance paraphernalia, she plodded up the short steps to the broad wooden porch and banged her way into the front door. The delectable smell of one of Matt's roasts wafted toward her, along with the sound of her daughter's shrill *Stop it, you stupid twerp! I hate you!"* followed by her son's piping, *"Make me, rabbit-face!"*

Dylan crossed polished parquet floors of the main room, glancing around as she did so to make sure the kids had done their required chores and straightened up. Just walking into the house still excited her. For years she and Matt had scoured flea markets and estate sales, picking up antiques and country collectibles, never dreaming they'd have such a natural showcase for them one day.

She lay the tripod and videocamera on the blue gingham-checked sofa with its antique quilts tossed over the back, which flanked the fireplace, and set down her backpack on the nineteenth-century trunk that served as a coffee table. A blue graniteware bowl on the trunk was heaped with shiny red applies. Dylan picked one up and took a big, satisfying bite.

"Sticks and stones may break my bones, but nerds can never hurt me!"

A fluffy calico cat blinked lazily at Dylan from "her" chair— a hickory twig rocker that had belonged to Dylan's grandmother. "Hi, Pandora," Dylan said, leaning down to scratch the queenly throat. "Has it been like this all day?"

"Shut up, stupid!"

Dylan sighed. Even the thick limestone walls and heavy timber crossbeams in the ceiling couldn't muffle a twelve- and nine-year-old at war. Resigning herself to the role of peacemaker, Dylan headed through the wide archway into the dining room and through a similar archway into the kitchen, frowning as she did so at the cereal bowl that sat in a pool of milk on the eighteenth-century hutch table.

"Whose cereal bowl is this?" she demanded.

Both kids gave startled little jumps and began accusing each other in loud, angry tones. Dylan took another bite of her apple and regarded them. Aidan, the youngest, was a strawberry-blonde with her mother's freckles and green eyes. A high spot of color always flooded her cheeks when she was outraged, which was often. Her name meant "little fire," and she came by it naturally. Caleb had the beginnings of his father's rugged blond good looks. Already he had the feet of a Great Dane puppy and the clumsiness of a boy not quite ready yet for adolescence. His favorite sport was tormenting his little sister.

She interrupted their tirade. "Caleb, you clean up the cereal bowl mess, please."

"But that's not fair!" he erupted.

"Don't shout at me," she said calmly. "Just do it. I know good and well that Cocoa Crispies is your favorite snack."

"How do you know it was Cocoa Crispies?" he challenged.

"Because the milk in the bottom of the bowl is chocolate."

A smile tugged at the corner of his frown. "It's tough having a PI for a mom," he mumbled, and she ruffled his hair as he brushed by her. When had he gotten too big to cuddle? She just could not remember.

"Mom, are you okay? You look awful," fretted Aidan, Dylan's little worrier. Dylan held out her arms, and Aidan crossed the room to burrow herself into her mother's embrace.

"I had an adventure today," Dylan told her, kissing the soft upturned forehead. "A dog chased me across a field."

"Cool," said Caleb, mopping up the spilled milk with paper towels. "Did he catch you?"

"Almost." She held up her leg for their inspection.

They were dutifully impressed. "I don't know anybody whose mom does the kind of stuff you do," said Aidan proudly.

"Mom, do you miss being a cop?" Caleb asked, dumping the cereal bowl unceremoniously in the sink and taking a step away.

"Stop right there! Go back and wash that bowl."

"Aww, Mom." He turned with infinite slowness to the task.

"In answer to your question," Dylan said, "yes and no. Yes, I miss my friends on the force. The work your dad and I do now is kinda lonesome at times. But no, I don't miss the bureaucracy or the city traffic hassles or all the dead people."

"Yuck, Mom," said Aidan with a shudder.

Dylan shrugged. "Sorry, but that's what a homicide detective sees all day."

"Why didn't you stay on patrol?" her son asked.

Dylan pursed her lips. "You know why, honey."

He nodded and headed for the dining room. She caught him on the fly and gave him a rough hug.

"Now. You guys go clean up your rooms." They protested loudly all the way, begging for mercy, which she ignored. Mainly, she just wanted a few moments of silence and solitude in her kitchen.

Her country kitchen was the heart of their home. Hanging from the crossbeams were nets of garlic, chile peppers, and onions, dried flowers and herbs, copper pots and wicker baskets of all shapes and sizes. The cabinets were covered with weathered planking she and Matt had stripped off a tumbledown shed out back. Lining shelves were little treasures they'd collected through the years—old jars, antique tins, advertising signs, and more graniteware. Flour sacks served as dish towels, and a pair of ice tongs held the paper towels. Extra storage was provided by an old pie safe and an antique washstand, which they'd chosen not to strip and refinish, but to leave as they'd found them. Even modern appliances were hidden behind boxes Matt had made from old boards. This room, more than any other, said "home" to Dylan.

She finished her apple and left the core on the cabinet for Aidan to take outside and leave for some wild critter. Deer, raccoons, and rabbits routinely came up close to the house or drank from the rambling stream with its miniature waterfall out back. Walking past the breakfast nook with its bay windows decorated with stained-glass flowers around the edges, Dylan opened the door that once led to the garage and entered their office.

This room was more sparse and utilitarian than the rest of

the house. They'd left the limestone floor uncovered. Dylan would have liked to scatter rag rugs over the floor, which could be cold in winter, but it was easier this way. As she had figured, Matt was working at the big rolltop desk, oblivious to noise from the kids or anything else. His fingers clattered deftly over the computer keyboard. The hairs on the back of his neck, leading into his thick hair, were downy and blond. In that moment of vulnerability, the sight of them, as he bent over his work, always made her ache for him as he had once been; something, of course, which she could never tell him.

"How's it going?" she asked.

As if he had known she was there all along, he continued to type for a moment, then pivoted and gave her that smile which never failed to melt her heart. "Tough day at the office?" he asked in return and rolled out to meet her.

With an answering smile, she crossed the room, kissed him on the lips, and settled herself in his lap like a child, laying her head on his shoulder.

Adjusting the lock on his wheelchair, Matt wrapped his arms around her, and they sat for a moment as they did every day, glad to be alive and together.

Dylan sighed.

"What's wrong?" he asked.

"It's just so hard to build up business as a private investigator in a small town," she said. "Especially when you're not from around here. I get tired of having to drive to San Antonio or Austin to investigate cases. I was hoping to get more work in Kerrville."

Kerrville was a town of eighteen thousand nestled right on the beautiful banks of the Guadalupe River. But it was not typical of most towns that size. Located in an arts and tourist resort area, Kerrville's population swelled each summer and again with hunting season. It was surrounded by dozens of dude ranches, private resorts, summer camps, church camps, day camps, and wildlife ranches. Many wealthy people maintained homes in the area. The Point

Theater, located in the nearby tourist village of Ingram, and overlooking the river with its outdoor amphitheater, was a launching pad for much young and local talent (Tommy Tune was said to have gotten his start there), and attracted people from all over the state all summer long, as did the numerous artists' colonies scattered throughout the various riverfront properties.

City born and bred, Dylan and Matt had underestimated the slowness to trust outsiders that characterized small-town people, even in a town so cosmopolitan as Kerrville. Another problem neither of them could have anticipated was how slow some people are to pay a private investigator for his services—which is one reason they did as much insurance and corporate work as possible. Dylan was deeply worried that the money from the sale of their city home and her retirement funds from the Dallas PD—which they'd collected in a lump sum to help start the business— would run out before they could make enough to support the family. Matt's disability checks only went so far toward paying bills, running a business, and maintaining a country home.

"If we have to move from this place, I swear," she murmured against his neck, "it will surely break my heart."

"Hey, Red." Matt ruffled her hair. "Don't look so gloomy. We're not going to have to move anywhere. Something will break, you mark my words. We'll get the case to end all cases. I can feel it in my bones."

THREE

Nine.

Nine turns of the hourglass! Shadow watched the sand streaming through the bottom of the glass, shifting his weight impatiently. He couldn't wait for ten whole turns!

No, he *wouldn't* wait! After all, this was Shadowland! It was *Shadow*, after all, who made the rules in this game, and he could change them any way he liked.

Flinging a corner of his cape over one shoulder, Shadow held his torch high and began hurrying down the tunnel after the troll. Wouldn't that stupid creature be surprised! He still thought he had ten turns of the hourglass! *Ha!* That would teach those trolls to trust the *mindslayer*!

Shadow's heart pounded. This was *so* exciting! Here he was, chasing a troll through the labyrinth. It was just as he always knew it could be! He would give himself twenty extra points for cunning.

He was nervous as well as excited, and even a little frightened. After all, he had never explored the Secret Caverns before.

No one had.

Shadow ducked. The tunnel was getting lower. He couldn't stand up completely straight.

What was that? Coming to a halt, Shadow strained his ears. He could hear nothing. He wondered how far the troll had gotten in nine turns of the hourglass.

A new thought sent little needles of fear through his stomach. *What if the troll had found a way to escape?*

Shadow had told Darth that if such a thing happened, he

would be allowed to escape unmolested and would be declared the winner of the game. But *what then*?

Would the troll bring back dragons to Shadowland?

He would. And they would destroy Shadow.

A cold sweat broke out over his body. Shadowland was in great danger! He must catch that troll. He *must*! It was a matter of *survival*.

Shadow hurried forward, crouching now to fit in the narrow tunnel. A sound came to him. A whisper, like the rustling of the wind through grain in a pasture.

A shiver clutched at Shadow. His torch trembled.

Were the Secret Caverns trying to tell him something?

Perhaps . . . by the goblins, he hadn't considered this! Perhaps the Secret Caverns were . . . *enchanted*!

Shadow could feel his own pulse throbbing in his throat. The tunnel narrowed around his body. He dropped to a crawl, holding his torch carefully. The whispers drifted over him again.

Shadow halted, listening carefully. If only he could understand what the Secret Caverns were trying to tell him!

Perhaps they were *warning* him!

That *had* to be it. They were warning him of something horrible, something unthinkable, just ahead.

Shadow hesitated. Should he turn back? Should he heed the warning of the Secret Caverns?

Extra points for courage and valor. He had said it himself. That decided it. He would press on.

Stretching out on his stomach, Shadow began pulling himself forward, the torch wobbling uncertainly.

Suddenly he could go no farther. Narrow as his shoulders were, he couldn't squeeze them through the opening.

By the goblins! What was he supposed to do? The troll must surely have been able to fit through. What now? He turned his body sideways but it made no difference.

He would get no points for losing a troll in the Secret Caverns, of that Shadow was certain. He had to think of *something*. Panting, he rested for a moment, trying to think if he had any powers that could work magic on the tunnel.

A new sound invaded the tunnel—high-pitched squeaks that grew more and more frantic, echoing off the narrow cave walls and assaulting Shadow's ears like fingernails on a blackboard. He recognized the sound instantly, but he'd never heard it in such incredible volume before—waves upon waves.

The Secret Caverns began whispering again, as if trying to drown out the bat noise. Shadow's heart began to pound, but before he could make out what the Secret Caverns were trying to say, the scream came to him; high, long, and terror-filled.

Shadow's breath caught in his throat. The Secret Caverns *had* warned him! There *was* something horrible, something unthinkable, beyond the tunnel!

The troll had not heeded the warnings of the Secret Caverns, and now . . . *he was being killed in some terrible, awful way!*

Shadow began scrambling backward. He had proved his courage and that was enough. But he was no fool. And from now on, he was going to listen very carefully to what the Secret Caverns had to tell him.

Dylan received the phone call from Campbell Scott the day after Jeremy disappeared.

"I've heard some good things about your agency around town," he said. "I want you to find my son."

The voice at the other end of the line was forceful, energetic, used to having its way. Dylan hesitated. "But Mr. Scott, surely you know that the police are forming a task force. They think your son's disappearance may be related to the Castillo boy's kidnapping," she added, referring to a similar child disappearance two weeks before. Timmy Castillo, eight years old, had vanished while playing with friends at a construction site near his home.

"I'm well aware of that, Mrs. Tandy. The Texas Rangers are assisting, and they may bring in the FBI."

"Please call me Dylan. I guess what I'm trying to say is that there are hundreds of man-hours going into this investigation. What makes you think we could do any better?"

"I don't know that you can. But I do know this . . . The police are restricted by procedure, by rules and regulations. There is so much they are prevented from doing, by law. A private investigator has much more freedom of movement."

"Surely you're not suggesting we go beyond the law, Mr. Scott."

"I'm suggesting you do whatever it takes to find Jeremy. You will be well compensated for your time."

Dylan felt herself bristling at the man's tone of voice, but she kept her own calm and courteous. "I wouldn't expect you to pay any more than our usual fee."

There was a long pause. When Scott spoke again, his voice was hushed, struggling with emotion almost too powerful to bear. "He's our only son, Dylan. My only child. Surely you can understand our desperation."

"Of course, Mr. Scott. I have children of my own. I can't imagine anything worse than what your family must be going through right now."

"Then, please . . . help us."

"Give me your address," she said. "I'll be right over."

On the way to the Scotts', Dylan reflected on the missing Castillo boy. Nothing like this had ever happened in this peaceful river community. She had noticed that small-town people tended to take their safety for granted, as if random crimes only happened in the Big Bad City. Hell, she'd done it herself.

After Timmy Castillo vanished, parents watched the news each night with a shudder and warned their children not to speak to strangers. But the truth was, there were so *many* strangers who came each hot summer to fill up all the big hotels lining Sidney Baker Street / Highway 16 and Highway 27, or to stay in the cabins and RV hookup sites at the state park along the river. There was even a spot right there in downtown Kerrville where anybody could bring their coolers and inner tubes and frolic in the ever-cool waters of the Guadalupe River. Anybody at all.

Then there was San Antonio, only an hour's drive away, and the state capital, an hour and a half in the other direction. The highway arteries leading to those major metropolitan areas led right through the heart of Kerrville.

It was an ideal stop for anybody on the road.

Dylan had taken the news of the boy's disappearance particularly hard. Perhaps even more than the locals, she had convinced herself that she had moved her children out of reach of such senseless crimes, that they were safe, living in the country near a small town. Now she knew that crime had no boundaries, and that she could not always protect her children from its threat.

And it saddened her.

"Did you ever stop to think," she'd asked Matt in their big warm waterbed one night a week after Timmy Castillo vanished, "that ours was the last innocent childhood?"

"Whatd'ya mean?" he mumbled sleepily. Matt never had insomnia.

"I mean, those of us who were children in the fifties and early sixties . . . We knew a time of innocence. We had free run of the neighborhood and played outside till long past dark. We never had to worry about child molesters or abductors. We never had to have our Halloween candy X-rayed for needles."

"Oh, kids were being molested then," said Matt, adjusting his body over to his stomach, the position he needed to sleep in each night to improve the circulation in his legs after sitting all day. "It's just that nobody ever talked about it."

"I know. I know. It's just . . . kids have to be so street-smart nowadays. Even if they don't live in a ghetto, they get exposed to so much misery on TV and in movies. They don't ever get a chance to be *children* anymore."

"Well, that's up to the parents," he said, his voice muffled by his pillow. He didn't say any more, but Dylan lay awake for a very long time.

There was something about the Timmy Castillo situation that had haunted her from the beginning. From the time she'd heard the news, a sick, anxious feeling had insinuated itself into her consciousness, a feeling of dread and foreboding.

That night she'd slipped out of bed and padded through the quiet house to her children's rooms. Caleb slept like the comatose, his blankets draped smoothly over his shoulders, hiding the bear he clutched underneath. She'd smoothed back a strand of his hair and listened to the soft sound of his breathing in the room until her troubled soul was quieted.

Aidan's bed always looked like a pack of dogs had slept in it. The quilt always wound up on the floor and the sheets usually tangled themselves beneath her restless little body like seaweed. Aidan was the one most likely to still be lying awake when her parents went to bed, the one with the most vivid dreams and nightmares, the one who, as a toddler, often got up in the middle of the night and played alone in the living room. On that long night Dylan had gathered up Aidan's quilt and her stuffed mouse, Squeakers, and tucked them both close.

Love sliced her heart then and laid it open.

Now Dylan wondered the same thing she'd wondered then. . . . How . . . *how* . . . could the Castillos—and now the Scotts—bear it?

Dylan knew she needed to remain objective in order to do the best job on this case, but as a mother, she found it impossible. And there were other factors that made it more personal. She conceded that her own childhood insecurities were possibly making her overprotective of Aidan and Caleb. How many nights in her youth had she lain awake in the darkness, listening to her parents' shouts and name-calling? How many times had she gone to bed, not knowing if her mother or her father would be gone by morning? How many times, after the divorce, had she said good-bye to a new friend when her mother decided to move yet again? How many times had she clung to Gran in this very house and wept when it was time to go home?

She had tried so hard to make her children feel safe.

Timmy Castillo's face, frozen forever in a school photograph, flashed into her mind. She wondered what had happened to him, where he was, if he was alive or dead, if he was suffering.

And now another little boy was lost . . . maybe forever.

And the sick, anxious feeling of dread and foreboding came back all over again. It was all she could do not to turn the van around and go home. Instead, she braced herself for what she knew would be an emotionally draining confrontation. As a homicide detective, she'd dealt with grief-stricken parents before. It was always difficult—for all of them. Dylan knew she had the experience to fortify her, but for some reason, this case was different.

Perhaps she was dealing with her own loss of innocence. After all, small Texas towns were supposed to be quiet and sleepy places seldom touched by bloodshed and street violence. In a sense, the Killeen massacre at a Luby's cafeteria had changed all that for all small-town dwellers.

Still . . . it had happened somewhere else, not *home*.

As a mother, her heart agonized over the question: Was there no place safe to raise her babies in peace and innocence?

And as a detective, she already knew the answer.

FOUR

Shadow was restless.

The rush he'd had from playing the game in the Secret Caverns with the troll had been cut short all too soon, leaving him with a suffocating feeling of frustration. It had only taken that stupid, dim-witted troll nine turns of the hourglass to get himself killed!

What kind of fun was that?

It made Shadow angry.

He'd given that goblin-brained troll every advantage. A torch. A head start. A promise of freedom if he found an escape tunnel. And for what? Darth had managed to show himself every inch the coward, blubbering about going home; then he'd ignored a clear warning of danger from the Secret Caverns and gone and gotten himself killed!

If all trolls were that thick-witted, then what kind of challenge would they present to the *mindslayer*?

Somewhere out there, Shadow knew, there had to be a worthy opponent for him. It would take all his powers to be able to confront that worthy opponent. And not just those powers he already possessed. Shadow believed he had shown enough courage, valor, and cunning to have developed more powers along the way. He was just going to have to discover for himself what they were.

As well, it was time to change the rules of the game again.

After all, it was *his* game, wasn't it?

Yes. It was his game; it was his Secret Caverns; it was his

Shadowland. He had *total* control, total power. Nobody could tell him what to do in Shadowland.

So. First rule change: He could not wait an entire fortnight to find another troll. After all, that rule had been made back when he thought a troll could actually provide him with a challenge and a good game of skill. The stupidity of the trolls themselves had changed that rule!

It wasn't *his* fault they couldn't stay alive long enough to make it fun.

The Scotts' upper-middle-class home was located in a well-kept neighborhood just a couple of blocks from Tom Daniels Elementary School and the lovely, spacious Singing Winds Park, with its Olympic-size swimming pool, three baseball diamonds, and various scenic jogging and nature trails. The Singing Winds development was relatively new. None of the houses was over twelve or fifteen years old. A perfect small-town neighborhood in which to raise a family. The last place from which you might expect a child to be snatched.

Dylan drove slowly past the park, which was busy with summertime activities. She spotted a few cruisers and at least one unmarked car. She knew the officers were canvassing the neighborhood, questioning anyone and everyone they could find, asking if anybody, anywhere, had seen anything. She also knew that in the days to come, they would follow up on hundreds of leads flooding the police department switchboard.

The city limits skirted the edge of the park. Mounted sheriff's deputies had joined in the search, just to the other side of nearby Highway 534. In the distance she could hear the thrumming beat of a DPS helicopter, still crisscrossing the area. And she wondered, yet again, what she and Matt could possibly do for the Scotts that law enforcement was not already doing.

The Scott home was choked with cars. Dylan parked two houses down and walked past a small knot of family or friends, speaking together in hushed, funereal tones. Dylan felt completely inadequate. She pressed the door chime.

The man who answered the door was about thirty-five, wiry of build, and had thinning brown hair. He kept running his hand through it as he peered at her with dark, haunted eyes.

"I'm Dylan Tandy," she said. "I was called by Mr. Scott."

"Yes," he said. "Come in. I'm Scott." He extended his hand and encased hers in a firm grip. "If we're going to work together on this, you'll have to drop the 'Mr. Scott' stuff. Call me what my friends do—Scotty."

She smiled and followed him into a handsome den littered with people, all wanting to help and all probably feeling just as useless as Dylan did. Scotty led her over to an overstuffed couch, to a haggard, once-pretty woman who sat, blindly staring at a Kleenex as she slowly shredded it in her hands. She had short brown hair, and her ravaged face was very pale. The eyes she turned toward Dylan pierced her to the core.

They were vacant with grief, filling with longing, shock, and fear. . . . They were a mother's eyes.

"This is my wife, Colleen," said Scotty. "Honey, this is the private investigator I've hired to help find Jeremy."

The reddened blue eyes filled again, and Colleen dabbed at them with the tattered tissue. "Do you think you can find him?" she pleaded. "Do you think there's any hope? Oh, God . . ." She pressed a trembling hand to her eyes.

Dylan knelt down in front of the woman, blinking back tears of her own. "Mrs. Scott—Colleen—I have a daughter the same age as Jeremy. And I have a son. I swear to you that I will search for Jeremy as if he were my own child. I won't stop until I can find *something*, one way or the other, to tell you." She reached out her hand, and Jeremy's mother clutched it.

"They never found the Castillo boy," Colleen whispered.

"I know," said Dylan, "but I think there's hope."

Colleen sucked in her breath. Scotty sat next to his wife

and put a protective arm around her shoulders. "Why?" he asked.

"Because if the two kidnappings are indeed related—if the same guy took both boys—then he's got to live somewhere in this area. In other words, he wasn't a transient passing through. He's got a residence here, maybe a job. Maybe even a police record. We've got a much better chance of tracking him down. And if we find him—who knows—we may find both boys alive."

Colleen stifled a sob. "Do you really think so?"

"It's possible."

The woman groped for another Kleenex, and someone pressed one in her hand. She blew her nose. "What I don't understand is what anybody would possibly *want* with little boys."

Dylan glanced at Scotty. He ducked his head and looked away. Clearly, he knew as well as Dylan did what somebody could want with a little boy.

Years as a homicide detective had taught Dylan patience, doggedness, and a certain eye for detail. The other searchers, she knew, were looking for something relatively large—a missing boy. She left that job in their capable hands and began a slow, methodical search of the park, her sharp eyes taking in every footprint or broken branch.

No one knew exactly which direction Jeremy had taken, but those who'd observed him leaving had told his parents and the police that he seemed in no great hurry to get home. One of the women at the Scott home was Mrs. Brubaker; she was so awash with guilt that she had not insisted that Jeremy ride home with them that Dylan had a hard time getting her to talk of anything else. But she had admitted that, according to her son, Randy, Jeremy had not had a good day at practice and he'd wanted to be alone to think about it for a while.

So Dylan started there, at the softball field, before any scheduled practices. She sat right down at home plate, cross-legged, and pictured it: being a nine-year-old boy, having a bad day at Little League practice. She imagined the coach yelling at her, the other players taunting her, which of course, only made things worse. She could see how she might have tried too hard then, tensing up, making more mistakes, feeling humiliated and angry.

She stood up, head down, feet shuffling, and headed away from the diamond in no particular direction, relieved that it was over, remembering each dropped ball and missed pitch and wincing. No, she would not like to ride home with Randy Brubaker—Jeremy's own father had said he was just about the best player on the team.

In fact, she would not like to walk too close to the street at all, because surely other moms or dads would offer her another ride home, when all she wanted was to get away from the other players for a while. So she headed into the park, toward a nature trail. She walked very slowly, taking in every branch, every tuft of grass.

Park sounds receded behind her. Birdsong filled the air. The wind soughed through the trees. She felt herself unwinding from the miserable practice. After all, she was nine years old. By the time she got home to a few cartoons, softball practice would be a distant, unpleasant memory. She began to dawdle.

Crunching footsteps approached her from a bend in the trail. A man came around and walked toward her. He gave her a preoccupied nod, passed her, and went on his way. He looked like a cop and probably was one.

Around the bend in the trail, Dylan came upon a particularly large juniper tree. Juniper trees made great clubhouses. Their gnarled trunks always split off into several directions, and their limbs bent forward as if at the waist, reaching down their evergreen boughs almost to the ground. Deer often made snug little beds in the soft earth beneath, sheltered from cold and wind by the encircling branches.

This would be a good hideout. A just-right place to plop

down and hide from the world for a while beneath cool, flickering shade. Dylan crouched down and duck-walked under the boughs to the little hideaway. At the center she could stand up to her full height. Junipers were good climbing trees, too. What little boy could resist?

Dylan examined the trunk where it split into various limbs, looking for a good handhold.

That's when she saw the paper.

It looked like a little scroll, rolled up and tied with a purple satin ribbon. It wasn't the sort of thing a kid would be carrying home from softball practice. Did it have anything to do with Jeremy? Maybe not. Maybe so.

Handling the document delicately, she removed the ribbon and rolled out the message, holding it by its edges. Written with a fountain pen in careful calligraphy was a poem:

> *Trolls must always beware of*
> *the Shadow,*
> *For e'en in sunlight trouble may*
> *follow.*
> *The state of* not-being *will defeat*
> *dragons bold,*
> *And the* mindslayer *will triumph—*
> *be it foretold!*

FIVE

Shadow sorted through the journey-pouches, toys, and other things from the Treasure Trove, flinging each item aside in mounting frustration. While he could remember the faces and locations of each troll from whom he had stolen, none of the items had names in them, as had the last (stupid) troll's journey-pouch. He was going to have to be very shrewd indeed. It would not be easy to lure a troll to Shadowland if he could not call the troll by name.

For a moment he sulked, and then he remembered. It was not *supposed* to be easy! That was the challenge of the game! He was going to have to use his (superior) wit and cunning, and the state of *not-being* and the power of the *mindslayer* and all his other skills to capture trolls.

And the dragons. He would have to be *particularly* wary of them. Dragons could be deceptive. At times it appeared as if they didn't care what the trolls were doing, but as soon as they perceived a troll as being threatened, they came roaring out, blowing fire and brimstone. He would not like to be burnt by dragon's fire, no indeed.

Cunning. This is what he would need more than anything. He would not be able to find another troll as easily as he'd found the last. He'd have to select one, find it, and then stalk it until he could separate it from the dragons and lure it to Shadowland.

One misstep could bring dragons from all four winds, descending upon Shadowland, taking back his treasure, and destroying the Secret Caverns.

A shiver crawled down Shadow's spine. If he brought

dragons to destroy the peace of Shadowland, he felt certain that the Secret Caverns would punish him. They would lure *him* into the bowels of the labyrinth, and they would not warn him of impending danger.

So. He would have to be extremely careful and depend heavily on the state of *not-being* to find and capture the next troll without alerting the dragons.

Excitement jittered in his belly. He couldn't *wait* to begin!

Dylan had no idea whatsoever what the little scroll meant. On the surface it seemed to have nothing to do with Jeremy Scott's disappearance. In fact, she couldn't even be sure that Jeremy had come this way. She almost put the scroll back. Almost.

But once a cop, always a cop. She could not bring herself to leave something behind that might prove to be important somewhere later on.

She reread the scroll. Trolls? Dragons? *Not-being? Mind-slayer?* What on earth?

Maybe the Point—the community theater in nearby Ingram—was doing a play, and this was a prop which had somehow gotten misplaced. The Point's schedule of summer plays was widely publicized, and she couldn't remember what was on the bill, but she *had* been awfully busy this summer.

Dylan felt a pang of guilt. The kids would love to attend a play at the Point. She'd been too busy to think about it. And she did seem to remember that they were doing C. S. Lewis's *The Lion, the Witch, and the Wardrobe*—in fact, Aidan had begged to be taken to see it, and Dylan had promised her. . . . She felt a little stab of panic. Maybe the play had already come and gone!

Pretty rotten, to be so busy that you couldn't manage to find time to take your kids to such a marvelous production as that.

Okay. She'd go to Ingram and talk to somebody, buy

tickets for the play (if they hadn't already done it), and ask about the scroll.

Still . . . *The Lion, the Witch, and the Wardrobe* was Aidan's favorite book. Dylan hadn't read it—her tastes had never run to fantasy, but more to murder mysteries—but she didn't think there was such a thing as a *mindslayer* in that story.

What about trolls and dragons? She'd have to check with her resident expert on that.

Next step. What if it wasn't a prop for the play?

Part of a school project? Not likely in the middle of summer.

Part of a game?

A game. What kind of game involved the exchange of handwritten scrolls in a park? And how in the world would Jeremy Scott be involved?

Dylan concluded that she was wasting her time on a red herring. She had so little time! This was not a typical missing persons case, an adult who was eluding the law or wanted to get lost for some other, more personal, reason. This was a child who'd been snatched from a friendly public park in broad daylight and whose life might be ticking away at this very moment.

She didn't have time for games.

Just to be on the safe side (once a cop . . .), Dylan showed the scroll to the Scotts, who assured her that it couldn't possibly have anything to do with Jeremy's disappearance. He was all boy, they said, too busy with sports and skateboarding and swimming and playing outdoors in summer to fool with fantasy games. He didn't even like to read. Yes, he liked to play Nintendo, but he favored the sports games and the Super Mario games to the games of strategy. (He had no patience for those, they said.)

A search of Jeremy's room confirmed what the Scotts had told her. This was a boy with feet planted firmly on the ground, who had no time for dragons or trolls. A tree-climber and fort-builder and Little Leaguer. A boy like Caleb.

She visited the Point Theater, a large and lovely outdoor amphitheater located on a bluff overlooking the Guadalupe River, near the small and trendy tourist town of Ingram. Lush green lawns sloped down to the river's edge. Twice the building had been swept away by floodwaters. This theater was built with large doors which could open to allow floodwaters to pass through, and thus leave the building standing. So far, they'd never had to use the doors.

In the adjacent building which housed a small folk art museum, Dylan found a tiny birdlike woman with sharp features, short, crisp dark hair, and huge overpowering preppie-framed glasses. Dylan showed her the scroll.

"I found this scroll in Kerrville and wondered if it might be a prop for one of your plays," she said.

The woman adjusted her glasses and peered at the scroll myopically. "Not that I know of," she answered. "We are offering *The Lion, the Witch, and the Wardrobe* this summer, but there's nothing like this in the play. I mean, there *are* trolls in the play, but no dragons and certainly nothing like a 'mindslayer.' And I don't remember seeing a scroll."

Baffling.

Dylan bought four tickets to an upcoming performance, and the woman gave her a list of summer plays.

It had taken Dylan a considerable amount of time to follow that particular dead end. A feeling of frustration and creeping panic dogged her heels—as it must surely be dogging the heels of all the searching officers, she knew—and she hardly knew what to do next.

How did you search for a phantom?

How did you track down a softball-playing, skateboarding, tree-climbing, Nintendo-loving nine-year-old boy who took a walk down a park trail in broad daylight and simply vanished?

A boy that big could not have been snatched against his will, not in the middle of the park. It would cause too much of a ruckus. Somebody would have seen something. So, he had to have gone voluntarily. That meant he had to have walked down a trail and gotten into a car on his own with *somebody*.

Most modern kids knew better than to leave with strangers.

Could it have been someone he knew?

Possibly. But there had been no messy divorces in the Scotts' past, no dirty business rivals, no enemies that they knew of. And there had been no ransom demands.

That left only one possible motive that Dylan could think of. If she were still a cop, she'd be checking the records right now, making a computerized list of all known sex offenders in the area, particularly child molesters.

If she had a suspect name for Matt, she knew he'd be able to find out any criminal history on that individual that they needed to know, but a broad search such as this was not something he could call up on a modem. Law enforcement tended to guard those facts pretty jealously.

Which left her one alternative. She was going to have to talk to somebody on the Kerrville PD. She knew she could expect one of two reactions: Either they would appreciate her help and would cooperate with her as long as she cooperated with them; or they would resent her outside intrusion and block her every step of the way.

The dinner hour had crept up on Dylan; the hours since she first met the Scotts had flown past in a blur. She hadn't even called home to check in with Matt. Still, she knew a cop or two who might appreciate a free meal in exchange for a little chat about the case. It had to be done delicately. Dylan had to assure whomever she met with that she had no intention of showboating or getting in their way. She had to make him feel that, as a former cop, she was part of the team, so to speak, and that the most important thing was that Jeremy be found. Diplomacy and mutual respect were the key.

But the Scotts took all that out of Dylan's hands. Before she had even had a chance to meet with one of the officers,

Campbell and Colleen Scott gave a press conference to the media, just in time for the six o'clock news. They announced to the world that they'd hired Dylan Tandy, of Tandy-Armstrong Investigations, Inc., to find their son.

"The police haven't found Timmy Castillo," they said tearfully, "so we decided to move right away and hire Mrs. Tandy, before any more time gets wasted. She has a child just Jeremy's age, and we knew she'd understand. It's been two weeks since the other boy disappeared. He might be dead by now. We just can't wait around for the police to fumble the ball on this one. Mrs. Tandy assured us that she'd search for our boy as if he were her own, so we trust her that she won't stop until she finds him."

Shadow didn't normally waste time in front of the magic box; nothing it displayed ever really appealed to him. But he had decided to check and see if it had anything to say about the troll he'd stolen. He had to know if the dragons knew anything about Shadowland or the Secret Caverns, or even the fact that the troll had ridden away with Shadow on Moonlight, his trusty unicorn.

Shadow's heart quickened when he saw the two dragons who protected Darth. There they were, in full disguise, blubbering out of the magic box just like their miserable little troll. Then something they had said caused Shadow to sit straight up and pay close attention.

They had hired a Master Dragon Queen to find the troll; a Dragon Queen with trolls of her own, apparently, who wouldn't stop, they said, until she'd found him.

Who wouldn't stop until she found him.

Until she found . . . *Shadow.*

His breath began coming out in little gasps. He took a couple of gulps to calm himself.

No. She couldn't possibly find Shadow. The Secret Caverns were too well hidden. Shadow laughed softly to himself. Then his eyes grew rounded as it dawned on him: *This* was his worthy opponent! He could tease her and taunt her and bait her to his heart's content, because she would *never* find Shadow! The state of *not-being* would protect him!

Oh, this was an unexpected boon, indeed!

Just *think* of the games he could play with the Dragon Queen while he kept thieving trolls right under her very nose!

Shadow jumped up, silenced the magic box, and began to pace, thinking furiously. He knew he would not sleep on that evenfall. No indeed. He had far too much planning to do.

SIX

Dylan's car phone rang just as she was headed down Main Street toward the police department. She picked up.

"Dylan Tandy."

"Where the hell are you?"

She blinked. This was Matt at his angriest, and she couldn't begin to imagine why. "I'm headed toward the police department."

"So you weren't at the press conference?"

"What press conference?"

There was a long pause. Finally he said, "Park somewhere so we can talk without you wrecking the van."

Dylan bit her lower lip. Not good. She whipped into a large parking area and stopped next to a collection of multicolored recycling bins with cartoon faces painted on them, grinning mouths waiting to gulp down glass or cans or whatever. "Okay," she said. "Shoot."

"Let me ask you something first. You didn't ask the Scotts to go public about our involvement, did you?"

"Of course not! What's going on, Matt?"

He told her.

Dylan groaned and leaned her head against the steering wheel. Her neck muscles were beginning to tighten up, and the movement started her head hurting. She leaned back again. "This is the worst possible thing they could have done."

"You got that right. It'll be much harder to conduct a discreet investigation once the whole world knows we're in on it."

"I wasn't even thinking about that. I was thinking about how insulted the Kerrville police are going to be. I know they're working their butts off, probably continuous shifts, trying to find those boys, and this makes it look as if we've come sailing in to save the day. *Dammit.*"

"Tell the Scotts not to mention us again if they do any more press conferences."

"I can't believe they did it this time. It just never occurred to me that they might do something like this."

"Dylan—hold on a minute. There's a call on the other line."

Dylan rubbed the back of her neck with one hand and stared glumly out the window at the people bustling into the nearby Hastings Bookstore, running errands on their way home from work. She couldn't imagine a single cop on the Kerrville PD who wouldn't resent her inquiries after the Scotts burned them on the evening news. They would think she was using the Scotts' and Castillos' personal tragedy to get publicity and more business for Tandy-Armstrong Investigations, Inc.

Well, are you? asked a nasty little voice from deep within her weary mind.

"No," she answered it firmly. "I'm just trying to help these people find their child. I didn't ask them to go public about it."

"What?" broke in Matt.

"Nothing."

"This going public might not be such a bad thing, after all."

"What do you mean?"

"We just got a call from a guy who says he thinks he saw the Scott boy leave the park."

Dylan sat bolt upright, all fatigue vanished. "Wait a minute. I think my notepad fell to the floor." She groped around for it. "Okay. Talk to me."

"He says he saw a guy and a little kid leave the park on

a dirt bike at about the same time that Jeremy was thought to have disappeared."

"Did he get a good look at Jeremy?"

"Well, no, and that's a problem. The guy says both of the people on the dirt bike were wearing black helmets with dark visors, but he insists the kid on the back of the bike was about Jeremy's age, and that he distinctly noticed him wearing a bright red Jurassic Park windbreaker."

"Got it. Huh. It didn't occur to me that people would call *us* with leads."

"He says he already told the police."

"He must be pretty sure of what he saw, then."

"Seemed like it."

"Okay. I'm on my way to the Campbells'. I need to have a little talk with them anyway."

"Right."

"Matt—did the guy happen to notice which way they were going?"

"Unfortunately, no. He says a truck pulled out behind them and he couldn't see the dirt bike anymore after that."

Dylan felt that little thrill of the hunt that she always felt whenever a good lead came down in an investigation. She took down the man's name, address, and phone number so that she could interview him further if necessary.

"This is the eighth anniversary of the shooting, you know," added Matt quietly, as if they'd been discussing it all along.

Dylan sighed. It explained his irritability.

"I know," she said. "I was hoping that, well, since we moved out here . . . you'd forget."

"How can I forget?"

She pursed her lips. "That's not what I meant."

"I know." He paused. "Sometimes I think, you know, if I hadn't tried to be such a hero . . ."

"They asked for volunteers. I can't imagine you doing otherwise, Matt."

"I've gone over those few moments of my life a thousand times," he said quietly. "I've *dreamed* them."

"I know. I was there, remember? Listen, would you have felt any better about it if it had happened to your partner or one of your buddies? That guy was so hopped up on PCP, it was just a matter of time before he decided to blow away his wife and baby. So when he offered to give up the baby—"

"Yours truly to the rescue," he said gloomily. Matt always grew depressed on the anniversary of the shooting. "So this guy who's doped to the gills insists I come in shirtless so his paranoid little fried brain can be assured I'm unarmed. Jesus."

"Matt, nobody could have dreamed that he was going to shoot you in the back with that baby in your arms."

Matt was silent.

"I'm just saying. Would you have felt any better if Ryker or Garza or Thompson had gone? Would you have felt better if *I* had gone instead of you?"

"No, of course not."

The sounds of traffic filtered down around her. A baby cried while its mother tried to strap it into a car seat, and the sound brought that day back in a rush—gunsmoke and blood and the screams of the other baby.

"You know that baby would have been hit, too," she said, "if you hadn't had the presence of mind to hold him out of the way as you were falling. You saved his little life."

He sighed. "I've always been sorry that you had to be on the scene when it happened. If you hadn't been a cop, too—"

"No. There's nowhere else I'd have rather been that day. At least I know that it was nobody's fault. It was just one of those things that happens on the job from time to time. There was nothing you or anybody else could have done to change your fate."

They were quiet for a moment, reflecting, as always, about how individual and family lives could be shattered forever in one blink of an eye. Most people took their daily existence, and their family relationships, for granted, never expecting anything to change, never appreciating what they had. Dylan had done it once—they both had—but neither of them ever would again.

Matt was given the Medal of Honor, made Officer of the year, and retired from the force with full disability and retirement benefits. He was thirty-three years old at the time—eight years older than she. They'd had two small children.

Dylan took herself out of the line of fire then and went plainclothes, joining the Crimes Against Persons division, working first sexual assaults and then homicide, where she remained for the next seven years.

But that first year in CAPERS was sheer, raw hell.

She and Matt didn't talk about that time much anymore, and Dylan wisely chose not to bring it up now. During those dark days Matt sank into a bitter, hopeless depression. The new limitations on their sex life made him feel inadequate and emasculated. Not being able to do the work he loved made him feel worthless. Not being able to walk filled him with rage.

He tried every way he knew how to drive Dylan away from him. Many times he almost succeeded. The only thing that kept her with him during that bleak period was the children. She was absolutely determined not to wreak on their lives the havoc she'd had in her own childhood. And deep down beneath the late-night fights and early-morning despair, she still loved her husband deeply. Somehow, she always knew that kernel of courage within him would reemerge, and they would be able to build a new life together.

In the end it was the children who saved them. After losing the third baby-sitter in as many months, Dylan was raving around the house, filled with frustration over every single aspect of her life, when Matt, to her shock, said,

"What the hell. I can be Mr. Mom. What else have I got to do with my life?"

Almost overnight the new sense of purpose invigorated him. The children thrived. The household settled down. And Matt began stretching his limitations ever further, finding creative ways to do things he thought he'd never be able to do again. They visited a urologist and looked into ways to develop a more normal sex life. His confidence increased. Bouts of depression still came and went, but never again so crippling as before.

Dylan never loved Matt more than when watching him go tubing or canoeing down the river with the kids, or dragging himself up a long flight of stairs while she followed with the wheelchair, or doing any number of things that most people wouldn't even attempt. He was an active member of P.O.I.N.T.—Paraplegics on Independent Nature Trips, and had participated in mountain climbs and sailing regattas. This was *her* Matt, the man who would think to save a baby even as his own life might be ending. She figured he did more to teach his kids about courage in any given day than some men did in a lifetime.

"What are you thinking about?" he asked, breaking her reverie.

"Oh . . . just about how much I love you."

"I love you, too," said Matt. He paused. "I guess you won't be home for dinner."

"How can I," she asked, "when I know that little boy may be still alive out there, somewhere, desperately hoping somebody will find him?"

"We'll find him."

Dylan wanted, with all her heart, to believe that; but they both knew that with each hour that passed, Jeremy's chances of being found alive diminished.

SEVEN

Shadow stood very still, took deep breaths, and entered into the state of *not-being*.

Only when he had completely entered into the state of *not-being* could he become invisible. Then he would become a part of all that was around him.

Entering into the state of *not-being* was Shadow's most important skill, his magic, in fact. *Not-being* was power. *Not-being* enabled him to move about freely in the land of the trolls without being seen.

For the land of the trolls was fraught with danger. Trolls were adept at disguise and often pretended to be kind while harboring hearts black as a dragon's eyes. While in a state of *not-being*, Shadow had often observed trolls behaving in a wicked manner amongst themselves, and he had felt, firsthand, the sting of a troll tongue-lashing when not in a state of *not-being*; had suffered, in fact, more than one physical torment from a vengeful troll.

But then Shadow discovered his magic. And with it came revenge.

Even now, as Shadow entered his state of *not-being*, he became one with the trees and moved about within their own flickering shadows with complete freedom.

From there he watched.

Trolls often enjoyed various games, many of which mystified Shadow. For even in their games they had a strange habit of cursing or shouting at one another. Some trolls were more skillful than others and so excelled at the games. Other, clumsier trolls were often excluded from them.

But, overall, trolls were so amazingly stupid. Not only did they never see Shadow when he was entered into the state of *not-being*, but they never even suspected that anyone— certainly not him—could be watching them. And so they never guarded their treasure.

Which made it quite easy for him to steal.

Always before, when he had stolen troll treasure, or even when he had captured the troll, Darth, he had not had to do it beneath the very snouts of the dragons! He had come upon them in their game-playing areas, where the dragons were often at bay, trusting their trolls to safety in numbers and the warmth of a midday sun.

But this was different.

Dragons and trolls alike frolicked along the river's edge, fishing or floating past on big round bladder-type devices. In this situation the dragons generally kept a sharp eye on the trolls, but Shadow was trusting that they would relax their vigil somewhat while taking their ease on the sun-spangled water.

Shadow believed that the cleverness and cunning he had displayed in capturing the troll and defeating him in the Secret Caverns, without so much as a dragon squeak, meant that he had acquired the skill of the *mazemaster*. After all, most anybody could find their way out of a maze, given enough time and not too many monsters lurking about; but to actually *devise* a maze so difficult that there was no escape from it required true genius. Shadow had displayed that genius, and so Shadow had earned the title of *mazemaster*.

This newly acquired power would enable him to snatch another troll without his protecting dragon even knowing it!

There was one particular troll Shadow had been watching for some time, hidden, as he was, in the state of *not-being*. Now, as the troll drew near, his heart began to pound and his mouth to grow dry. Assuming the power of the *mindslayer*, he shook off the state of *not-being* and arranged himself carefully, back just enough from the water and into the trees so that the dragons couldn't see him. He prepared himself to enter into the mind of the troll.

The troll drew near.

Shadow opened his lure and waited for the troll to take the bait.

The troll crossed his path. "Hi," said Shadow. With casual indifference he turned a page of the comic book.

"Oh, *cool*!" cried the troll, drawing nearer.

Shadow held up the comic book in front of his face.

"*X-Men Number One!* I can't believe you've got it already." The troll stood directly in front of him, practically drooling over the bait.

Shadow began to reel him in. "You mean you haven't found this one yet?"

"Naw. And I've looked *everywhere*."

"The first edition of a new comic book is supposed to be worth a lot of money someday," said Shadow. "The original *X-Men*s cost something like fifteen thousand dollars now. This is a revival of those."

"Do you collect comic books?"

"Sure. Don't you?"

"When I can. My mom doesn't like them much."

"How come?"

"She says they'll turn my mind to mush."

Shadow nodded. "Moms are like that. Wanna see it?"

"Oh, *yeah*." The troll sat down so close to Shadow that he could smell him. He almost gagged.

He handed the troll the comic book. "Don't get it wet."

"I won't." The troll flipped through it.

"I've got a bunch more back at the campsite," said Shadow.

The troll glanced up. "I didn't know people camped around here."

"Oh, yeah. We know a special place. I brought some of my comic books. I've got a first edition *Spiderman*."

"Are you kidding?"

"Come on. I'll show you." *This was going to be so easy, truly befitting a* mazemaster.

They scrambled to their feet, and the troll followed him through the trees to where Moonlight stood waiting.

The troll stopped.

"Come on," said Shadow.

"I didn't know you had a motorcycle."

Shadow shrugged. "It's not really a motorcycle." He picked up one of the helmets. "You can wear one of these for extra safety."

The troll shook his head. "I don't think my folks would like it."

"It's okay. I already asked your dad."

"You did?"

"He said it would be all right as long as we were careful and didn't go too fast."

"I don't know. . . ." The troll eyed Moonlight doubtfully. "I could fall off."

Blubbering coward! "You can hold on to me. I won't let you fall." Shadow could hear the edge to his voice. This was going to be more of a challenge than he thought. He had to be careful. If he slipped back into the language of Shadowland, he might frighten off the troll. Fortunately, the power of the *mindslayer* would enable him to speak in troll-language.

He dangled the comic book before the troll. "I've got a whole box back at the campsite. They've got cardboard backing and individual slipcovers and everything."

The troll peered through the trees. "How far is it?"

"Not far."

"Can't we just walk?"

Stupid-goblin-brain! "Wouldn't you rather ride? It'll be fun. You'll see."

The troll stepped back. "Nah. That's okay."

"C'mon. Don't be a baby."

"I'm not a baby!"

"It'll be fun. Like a ride at a carnival, you know?"

The troll's eyebrows pinched together. "We-ell—"

"Danny! Where are you?"

"Over here, Dad."

Dragons!

"Tell you what. I'll go get some of my comic books and bring them back," said Shadow hurriedly, clambering onto Moonlight's back.

The troll said, "Okay," but Shadow was already taking off, flinging dirt and leaves behind him.

By the time the dragon got there, Shadow had vanished.

Dylan could not remember ever being so tired.

It was late and dark, and like the ground searchers, she had to concede that there was very little she could do except try to get some sleep and start over again early in the morning. The emotional drain had taken a tremendous toll on her. And if that wasn't enough, they'd had to put all their other cases on hold, which wasn't fair to those clients. Just thinking about it was exhausting. As she dragged herself in the front door, home wrapped itself around her like a warm shawl.

Matt was in the living room, Pandora in his lap, watching the late-night news. The kids, who hadn't gotten to see Dylan all day, were waiting up with Matt. Aidan, as usual, was reading. She was a voracious reader, gobbling down a book a day during the summer. She had recently discovered the marvelous fantasy worlds of C. S. Lewis and J.R.R. Tolkien, and was reading everything the library had to offer on Narnia and the land of the Hobbits.

"I'm worried that she's using books to escape reality," Matt had said recently. "Somehow it doesn't seem healthy to read so much."

"You wouldn't have said that to Robert Louis Stevenson or Ray Bradbury," she'd countered. "There are worse addictions for a child than reading. Don't worry. As soon as she discovers boys, all those books will start gathering dust on the shelves."

All the same, there were times she wished Caleb would read a little more often, and Aidan would get more fresh air outdoors.

Caleb was stretched out on the floor on his stomach, folding up sheets of notebook paper into convoluted triangular contraptions that he would thump toward his sister, who steadfastly ignored him.

Everyone smiled at Dylan in greeting, and both kids started talking at once.

"Mom, you should see the dam we built at the waterfall. It's so cool!"

"Mom, did you get the tickets for *The Lion, the Witch, and the Wardrobe*?"

"Shut up! I was talking first!"

"You're always interrupting me. You're so rude."

"Like I care."

"*Guys, please!* Caleb, I'll look at the dam tomorrow. Aidan, the answer is yes, I got the tickets."

"Oh, *thank you!*" Aidan flung her arms around her mother's neck and hugged her so tightly that Dylan almost choked. She hugged the strong young body back and then released her daughter, leaned down to kiss the top of her son's head, and crossed over to her husband. He held out his arms, and after de-lapping a protesting Pandora, she sat in his lap herself, nestling her head on his shoulder.

"While you were out, I got another lead on Jeremy," Matt said.

"Oh? What?" She rubbed her tired eyes.

"His mom says he had a backpack stolen a couple of weeks ago. She scolded him about it at the time because he'd just bought some new baseball cards. Of course, now she feels awful about it."

"What does this have to do with his disappearance?"

"Nothing, maybe. She just thought of it and figured the more we knew about Jeremy, the better."

"That's true."

"Anyway, he had just bought those cards that afternoon, down at Chris's Collectible Comics and Cards."

Dylan shook her head. "Never heard of it."

"Well, every kid who collects baseball cards or comic books around here has, apparently. Caleb told me about it. It's right downtown, near Pampell's."

Dylan yawned. "I'm so tired, I've completely forgotten what Pampell's is."

"Oh, you know. It's that antique soda fountain place in that restored historic building down on Water Street. It's got antiques and collectibles and folk art and stuff. We browsed around there when we first moved out here."

"Oh, yeah. I remember now. The kids loved that soda fountain."

"Right. Okay, just down the street from there is this little hole-in-the-wall place that sells and trades baseball cards and comic books and the like. It's one of Jeremy's favorite places."

"Good. I'll go as soon as it opens in the morning and check it out."

"Can I go, too, Mom?" Caleb asked.

"Me, too?" enjoined Aidan.

"Aw, she always copies everything I do."

"I do not!"

"Do so."

"Do not."

"Do so."

"Guys, if you don't mind? I've got a headache."

"Well, can we go?"

Dylan hesitated. On the one hand, she wanted to say no, should, in fact, refuse, because she would be on the job and didn't need the distraction of the kids. On the other hand, she'd been so busy lately she'd hardly had the chance to see them at all. Thinking aloud, she said, "How would I get you home? It'd be a lot of trouble to bring you all the way back here, and I just couldn't take you with me all day. This isn't a simple missing persons case, guys. Jeremy Scott's life may be in danger."

They were silent a moment. "It's all right, then, Mom," said Caleb sadly. "We'll go another time."

The disappointment in his voice made Dylan want to cry.

"Tell you what," said Matt. "Why don't you guys go on with Mom in the morning to the card shop. You can mess around while she asks a few questions. I can meet you at Pampell's later for a soda, and you guys can come back here with me. Mom can go on and check out whatever leads she turns up, okay?"

Caleb and Aidan turned shining eyes and expectant faces toward Dylan. After all, was it so much to ask? "Okay," she said.

Caleb raised a triumphant fist. *"Yes!"*

Aidan clapped her hands.

"Come here, you rotten little rugrats," said Dylan. They all crowded around Matt's wheelchair in a huge suffocating family hug, while Dylan, thinking of lost little boys, squeezed shut her eyes and swallowed very hard in order to hold back the tears.

But no matter how hard she tried, that miserable, inevitable feeling of dread and foreboding would not stop creeping up and over her, like water in a sinkhole. She fought to keep from drowning in it as she clung to the warm bodies surrounding her.

EIGHT

"Stupid, clumsy, goblin-brained troll!" shouted Shadow, his voice reverberating throughout the Secret Caverns, his fury and frustration swelling into his throat. *"Blubbering, infernal coward!"*

Who could have imagined that a troll would refuse a ride on Moonlight?

A true mazemaster *would have planned for just such an eventuality in his strategy,* the Secret Caverns seemed to whisper. *A true* mazemaster *would never be surprised by anything the trolls did.*

Shadow grabbed an unlit torch and smashed it against the cave wall until the wood splintered. The vibrating *crack* felt good in his hands. He hurled away the torch.

By the goblins! Shadow had thought he'd *earned* the power of the *mazemaster*, but apparently, the Secret Caverns didn't think he had proved himself worthy yet!

Why, even the gift of the *mindslayer* had failed him!

He paced the tunnel in a swirl of purple velveteen, fists clenched.

There was only one thing to do. Shadow was going to have to *prove* that he was worthy of the power of the *mazemaster*. There would have to be no surprises next time.

Meanwhile, he would have to lose one hundred points for bungling the job.

Shadow winced. *One hundred points!*

Still, it was only fair.

He promised himself that if he brought back another troll from under the noses of the dragons, without incident, he would award himself *two* hundred points so that he could make up the difference.

A true *mazemaster* deserved no less.

Chris's Collectible Comics & Cards (We Buy, Sell & Trade) was announced undramatically by a simple black-and-white wooden sign. The display window was relatively small, so it was an easy shop to miss, but apparently well known to every comic book and baseball card afficionado in the area. Dylan was surprised at the amount of kids, parents (with wallets in hand), teens, young adults, and grown men who crowded into the store.

The place was crammed with boxes of individually sleeved comic books of all kinds—mostly featuring color-ful grotesque characters engaged in various types of life-or-death battle—and trading cards depicting everything from baseball, football, basketball, and soccer players to Marvel Comics characters and the Terminator. There were racks of bawdy posters displaying booby girls, and a large display of Dungeons & Dragons paraphernalia, including playing manuals for Dungeonmasters and players, miniatures, gamepacks, and maps.

"Cool!" Caleb cried and began darting in and out among the various boxes and displays like a busy bee in a spring meadow. Aidan headed straight for the Dungeons & Dragons area and stood transfixed next to a scrawny adolescent boy; and almost immediately engaged him in animated conversation about the merits of each particular miniature.

The clientele seemed to be almost exclusively male—in all shapes, sizes, and ages, (predominantly white, middle-class)—who spoke to one another in heated discussions about which card or comic was available and how much it might be worth one day.

It reminded Dylan of something a friend had said to her once: "Boys don't have toys anymore, you know. They have *collections*."

She wondered why it was so important to boys like Caleb that they have more G.I. Joes or more Battle Beasts or more Ninja Turtle characters than other boys. She decided that it wasn't too great of a jump from G.I. Joes to nuclear warheads.

The knowledgeable young man behind the counter was of indeterminate age. Even though Dylan felt certain he had to be in his twenties, he appeared to be foolishly young, perhaps even high school age. He was slight and thin of build—she guessed him to be no more than five eight or nine—bookworm pale, with plain brown eyes and short brown hair. He was wearing faded jeans and a camouflage fatigue jacket that she recognized as the distinctive Bushlan brand, which distinguished itself from regular cammies by depicting tiny individual twigs and leaves, rather than large splotches of color. It was virtually invisible in Hill Country brush. They were very popular at the moment. Though she was no trend follower, Dylan thought she wouldn't mind having a jacket like that herself.

There were a number of ways she could approach him, including pretending to be someone other than who she was and leading him into it, but she decided that in this case, there was no reason for deception. Customers took up a lot of his time, and he did a brisk business. She waited patiently at the end of the counter, and finally he worked his way over to her.

She smiled. "Hi. I'm Dylan Tandy, and—"

His eyes grew round. There was shadows under them, as if he didn't get much sleep at night, and pimples were scattered over his forehead. "You're that PI that's investigating that kid that got snatched!" he cried. Several people turned to stare. "I heard about that on TV last night."

Dylan glanced around uncomfortably and extended her hand to shake. His own hand was sweaty, and his handshake so limp she was afraid she might hurt him. He avoided making eye contact.

"I'm Chris Helmon," he said loudly.

"Yes, well, is there someplace where we could talk privately?" Dylan spoke quietly, hoping he would follow her example.

"I can't leave the counter." He shrugged apologetically. "I got a guy that's supposed to help me, but he didn't show up today." He gave a nervous little laugh.

She smiled again to put him at ease. "I understand Jeremy Scott collected baseball cards."

He nodded, glancing somewhere down and to the left of her. "I don't know most people's names that come in here, you know, unless, you know, they're already friends of mine, but I saw that kid's picture on the news last night. Yeah, he comes in here all the time. He can't afford the real expensive cards, but I think he spends most of his allowance." He laughed again.

"Chris, do you remember anything special about the last batch of cards that you sold Jeremy?"

He squinted over her head. "Not really. Tell the truth, it was pretty long ago."

"Was there anybody in here with him when he bought them? A friend, maybe?"

"Not that I remember. His mom, maybe. Yeah, I think she brought him that time."

She nodded, thinking. "I don't suppose anybody has tried to bring those cards back, say, to trade to you?"

He shook his head vehemently. "No. I'm pretty sure I'd remember that."

She passed a business card over the counter. "Chris, if anybody tries to bring those cards back, would you call me immediately? I mean anytime. It's very important."

He blinked at her. "You think somebody killed that kid for those cards? Because they weren't that valuable. I mean, it'll be twenty years before they're really worth anything."

Dylan said, "No, I'm not trying to imply anything. I'd just like to know if you see the cards. I'd like to know how whoever brings them back got hold of them in the first place, okay?"

He took the card. "Cool. Like spying."

"Mom? Could I have this, *please*?" Aidan stood suddenly by Dylan's side, holding out in the palm of her hand an exquisite miniature silver unicorn, dangling from a delicate chain necklace. Dylan was surprised to see such a dainty item in such a testosterone-driven place of business, but she could well imagine any little girl drooling over it.

"Aidan, I thought you were going to bring your own money from home."

"I did." Her daughter unfurled two wadded, damp dollar bills from her fist. Dylan picked up the necklace and checked the price. "You'd have a long way to go before you'd have enough for this little trinket," she said, knowing in her heart that she'd buy it in a minute for her sweet, happy child. Aidan so rarely asked for anything for herself.

"I'll do extra chores to earn the money. I'll pay you back, I promise!" cried her passionate daughter.

Dylan laughed and shook her head. "Conned again," she said, digging through her bag for her wallet. Still chuckling, she glanced up at Chris and froze.

He was staring at Aidan with a gaze so intense it made Dylan want to shield the child from it. She squeezed Aidan's shoulders protectively.

"Is this your daughter?" he asked.

Dylan wasn't sure she wanted to tell this strange young man anything at this point, but her guileless child nodded and said, "My name's Aidan. What's yours?"

"Aidan. Aidan." He rolled the name around on his tongue. "Very unusual name. Very pretty."

"Thank you," Aidan said.

"Uh, we'll take this, Chris," said Dylan, holding out the unicorn.

Tearing his gaze from Aidan's face, he glanced at the price, and said, "For a little girl as pretty as Aidan, I'll make a special deal," and took five dollars off the price.

Aidan jumped for joy. "Thank you, Chris! Now I won't have to do as many chores!"

He shook his head. "You telling me your mean old mom would make you work for such a pretty thing as this?" He winked at Dylan. She frowned.

Cops—even ex-cops—were always suspicious of something for nothing.

He rang up the purchase, wrapped it in tissue paper, placed it carefully in a small paper sack, and handed it to Aidan with a flourish. "You come back and see me any time," he said. "Who knows? I might have another special deal for you."

"A special deal?" Caleb had appeared. "What special deal?"

"Nothing," said Dylan tightly. "Chris has been too kind already. Let's go, guys."

With Caleb protesting loudly, Dylan herded the kids toward the door. She glanced back over her shoulder. Chris Helmon was still staring at Aidan, but he was no longer smiling. His eyes had a strange, haunted look to them.

A shiver crawled down Dylan's spine. Turning her back to Chris, she closed the door firmly behind her children.

NINE

Things had not gone well for Shadow. After he left the comic book store, he'd had no trouble finding another troll and convincing him to come along for a ride on Moonlight. But the stupid, cowering troll started blubbering before they even got to Shadowland. By the time they reached the emerald curtain, Shadow had to shove him inside the Secret Caverns.

"Where are we? I don't like this. I wanna go ho-o-o-me," wailed the troll.

"Be quiet!" cried Shadow. "These are the Secret Caverns, and your cowardly sniveling offends them." He dragged the troll by the arm to where he kept his lantern and clothing, which he quickly changed into.

"What are you doing? Take me home!" The slobbering beast yowled louder and louder. Why couldn't he show the Secret Caverns the proper respect? With a swirl of his purple cloak, Shadow said, "You have been chosen for the Shadow Game." Unfurling the scroll, he intoned, " 'The Shadow Game is simple for all to see; three rules must be followed accordingly . . .' "

The miserable creature howled through the entire reading.

"Silence!" shouted Shadow. "The rules shall only be given once in the hearing of trolls!"

The troll hunkered to the ground, hugged his knees, and wailed. His voice had a high keening edge to it that pierced the depths of Shadow's psyche and triggered a quivering rage hidden deep within. He felt it welling up inside, crowding into his throat, pressing against his brain. *"The Shadow Game will commence!"* he yelled, yanking the troll to his feet.

"I don't w-wanna p-play a game!" bawled the beast. "Mama! Mama!"

"You *will* play the Shadow Game!" Shadow thrust a torch in the troll's filthy little hand. He dropped it, sobbing ever louder, screeching for his mother like buzzards over road-kill.

"Take it!" hollered Shadow, forcing the torch into the troll's hand, where it shook so mightily he dropped it again.

"Your choice, you moronic blubbering filthy little coward! You may enter the maze in darkness!" He shoved the troll, who staggered forward a few steps and fell into a quavering, weeping heap. *"Get up!"* screamed Shadow. "Get up and play, you goblin-brained, dwarf-breathed, dragon-spawned piece of bat guano! *Get up!"* He kicked the troll savagely.

The monster covered his head and screamed, his voice rising to a pitch painful to the ear.

Fists clenched, chest heaving, Shadow stood over the beast, wincing at the noise. Didn't this dim-witted ogre-brain *know* that to be chosen and summoned to Shadowland was an *honor*? Didn't he realize that to play the Shadow Game was a *privilege*? Couldn't he see that being allowed to behold the enchantments of the Secret Caverns was to be touched with *magic*?

Grabbing the troll, he hauled him roughly to his feet again and pressed his own face close to its foul breath. Voice deadly quiet, he snarled, "You may choose your tunnel."

"NOOOOOO! I won't choose a tunnel! Mama! Maaaamaaaa!"

The shriek burrowed beneath Shadow's brain and touched something dark and secret beneath, something coiling and writhing, hiding beneath layers of everyday clutter like a hot red coal underneath gray powdery ash, something separate from him and yet a part of him, a living beast beyond his control.

Hands his own and yet not his lifted the screaming creature and hurled him into the wall of the cave, shocking the breath from him as he crumpled at Shadow's feet.

But it was too late for Shadow to hear the silence.

Again and again he slammed the loathsome creature into the cave wall until exhaustion finally overpowered the beast within and he stood, panting raggedly, staring unseeing at what he had done.

Damage control was the first item on Dylan's agenda after she turned over the kids to Matt. He'd gone home to see if he could pull some strings on the Dallas PD that might help make available to them a list of known sex offenders in the Kerr County area. It was Dylan's job to see if she could soothe whatever feathers the Scotts might have ruffled over at the Kerrville PD.

From the work she'd done during the past year, she'd gotten to know a couple of officers on the force fairly well and a few others by name and sight. Using the phone in the van, she called up a guy from the Criminal Investigations Division named Sergeant Dickerson and asked him to meet her at the Bluebonnet Café for a cup of coffee and a talk.

The café was a good place for people who liked to eat biscuits and gravy for breakfast and chicken-fried steak for dinner. It was quiet, and the deep banquets afforded some privacy. It was also neutral ground and less threatening than the police department itself might be following the Scott press conference.

Andy Dickerson was an ex-Marine and he looked it, with his jutting jaw, close-cropped crew cut, and steely eyes. He still did a full regimen of Marine Corps calisthenics every day and, at fifty, was hard as a rock and twice as strong. He had an unconscious habit of intimidating people, but Dylan knew him to be fair and an objective listener.

Still, when he came into the café, spotted her, and came

striding purposefully over, she felt a flew flutters of apprehension.

He started to speak, but she held up her hand. "Me first. Please believe me when I say I did not know anything about the Scotts' press conference. I never asked them to mention our agency publicly, and the last thing I would ever want them to do is put down the police, who're doing the best they can."

He never even blinked. She swallowed.

After a moment he said, "So, whatd'ya think, that we're a bunch of raging egos over there at the PD?"

"No! It's just—"

"Look, Tandy, all we care about is finding those kids. We don't give a shit who does it or how. You got something we could use, we'll gladly take it."

"And if you've got something *I* could use?"

"Well now," he drawled, "that depends. You go blurting everything out to the media, we're going to have a helluva time conducting a proper investigation."

"Andy! You know I wouldn't! I—" She stopped when he winked at her.

She chuckled and shook her head. "You just love to yank my chain, don't you?"

They grinned together and then both grew somber. Jeremy Scott and little Timmy Castillo were never far from their minds. "Forty-eight hours," said Andy. "Any time after that, the trail gets colder and colder."

"I know." She sighed. "I've been looking into the things Jeremy did forty-eight hours before he disappeared."

"Us, too."

She told him about Chris's Collectible Comics & Cards. He'd already checked it out. They discussed Campbell Scott's insistence that Jeremy would never leave the park with a stranger, would never ride on a motorcycle without his parents' permission, and didn't own a red Jurassic Park windbreaker.

Finally Dylan pulled the scroll out of her bag and carefully unfurled it on the Formica table.

Andy frowned. "What's this?"

"I found it in a big juniper tree, alongside a nature trail in Singing Winds Park the day after Jeremy disappeared."

He softly read aloud, " 'Trolls must always beware of the Shadow, for e'en in sunlight trouble may follow. . . .' " He glanced up. "What the hell's this got to do with the Scott boy?"

She shrugged. "Your guess is as good as mine."

He rolled the scroll back up and handed it to her. "Well, my guess is that it doesn't have a damn thing to do with him."

The Secret Caverns were not pleased.

Shadow had behaved dishonorably.

He had lost control of the beast within and had stolen the Secret Caverns' pleasure at beholding the troll as it traveled the labyrinth.

Which meant he had *still* not fully earned the power of the *mazemaster*.

To do so, Shadow knew that he would have to embark on a Heroic Quest. It was the only way to restore his honor and earn the power.

And he knew just how he would do it.

The *mindslayer* would defeat them all. The *mindslayer* would earn the power of the *mazemaster*. The enchanted Secret Caverns would be pleased. The beast within would be at rest, and Shadowland would be at peace again.

The Quest would be fulfilled, and Shadow would be the Hero, for all ages, and all time.

Kneeling down on one knee, Shadow bowed his head over the inert form of the stupid coward troll and accepted the challenge bestowed upon him by the Secret Caverns.

Then he lifted the limp form in his arms with the kerosene lamp and carried it deep into the bowels of the Secret Caverns for a befitting entombment.

TEN

With the disappearance of the third child, the winds of panic began sweeping through nervous central Texas communities like early winter rustling through restless treetops, heralding cold and death.

Panic brought rumors, whispering down jittery phone lines, murmuring over shopping carts, echoing across empty church pews. . . . A satanic cult was snatching children for sacrifice. It was an act of terrorism. The children were being sold to rich foreigners. There was a salivating psycho, just paroled from a crowded Texas prison system, bent on a sexually perverted bloodlust for little boys. . . .

The Associated Press picked up the story. It was a slow news week, and the media began converging on the peaceful, lovely little town of Kerrville in a bloodlust of their own. Tabloid-TV producers took up residence in one of the hotels.

Kerrville reeled from the assault. Residents wanted to shout to the world: "BUT WE'RE NOT LIKE THAT!"— while, at the same time, they grappled for the first time ever with real fear as they lay in their beds at night.

It was a loss of precious innocence. And—as everyone who had ever lost his or her virginity knew—it could never be regained.

A *Happening Now!* producer caught up to Dylan on her car phone as she was headed out to the state park by the river, where the last child, a seven-year-old boy named Eric Rathbone, had last been seen. The crime scene crew had already been out, but there was nothing to find. Sergeant Dickerson

70

had told her that officers were still questioning heartsick campers, trying to find out if they'd seen anything. Apparently, the family had driven up from San Antonio and rented one of the cabins on the water, something they frequently did throughout the summer. The kids and the father had all been tubing while the mother set out things for a barbecue. Eric had gotten out of the water and had walked over to the large central building to use the rest room. He never came back.

When the car phone rang, Dylan was lost in puzzling out the pattern that she felt had to connect all the lost boys. For three boys to vanish from the same small town within a two-week time span was too frighteningly obvious. The kidnapper had to be local, someone who knew the area— maybe even knew the children. Otherwise, why would they dare leave with him?

"Dylan Tandy," she said distractedly after the third ring. She was really in no mood to speak to anyone.

"Ms. Tandy? My name is Marilyn Seales. I'm a producer for the *Happening Now!* show."

Dylan slammed on the brakes. She'd almost run up on somebody's rear end. "Er, what can I do for you?"

"We understand you are investigating Jeremy Scott's disappearance for the Scott family."

"That's correct." All Dylan's ex-cop suspiciousness went on alert.

"We're going to be doing a remote from Kerrville, live, on Monday, Ms. Tandy. We'd like it very much if you'd consider appearing on our show. Our host specifically requested you."

Someone honked behind Dylan. She'd been sitting through a green light. "Why?" She pressed the accelerator.

"Because we believe a private investigator would have more leeway in discussing a case than a law enforcement officer."

"Uh-huh. You telling me you couldn't find a Kerrville cop who'd do it?"

"Well, Chief Reynolds is being very close-mouthed about this investigation."

"So you think you can get me to say things about the case that a cop wouldn't dare say."

"Well, not exa—"

"Let me ask you something—Ms. Seales, is it?"

"Yes."

"What do you possibly hope to accomplish with a program like this?"

"We think it will be an educational vehicle to help parents understand the issue, and to prevent it from happening to them."

"Bullshit." Dylan sped up to pass a rattletrap pickup ahead of her.

"I beg your pardon?"

"Look. You people are no worse than the gawkers who back up traffic in order to rubberneck a car wreck, looking for cheap thrills."

There was a pause. "I'm sorry you feel that way, but I have to disagree with you. A show such as ours could generate hundreds of tips that might help solve the crime."

"So what are you going to do? Huh? Parade the grieving parents before the nation? Make some melodramatic and unfounded conjectures about the fate of those boys? Or will you just hold off a little while until we have a mutilated body you can show off?"

"Ms. Tandy! I do not understand why you are being so hostile. If you stop to think about it, this would be excellent exposure for your business."

"Nothing you do is going to help us find those boys. If anybody knew anything, they would have come forward already. All you are going to do is trade on tragedy, and if you think I would sell my soul for a piece of the action, you are sadly mistaken."

The woman was stammering out a reply when Dylan hung up on her. Almost immediately she felt a twinge of regret. There were several reputable American programs, such as *America's Most Wanted* and *Unsolved Mysteries*, which had helped to solve many crimes and bring hundreds of wanted felons to justice. In fact, she knew in her heart that if either of those organizations had called, she'd have cooperated fully.

But this was different. It wasn't about solving a crime or even finding those children. It was about emotional pandering of the worst kind, and she would not lend her name or reputation in support of it.

Jeremy deserved better.

Shadow stood very still, took deep breaths, and entered into the state of *not-being*.

The danger of his position sent little thrills of excitement throughout his body. Yesterday he'd returned to the scene from where he'd taken his last troll, and the place was crawling with dragon-warriors. They were all poking around, looking for clues, but none of them, *none* of them, had found his secret message!

He'd had to be very crafty. The dragon-warriors were on the lookout for him. Well, they didn't *know* it was him, of course, but they were peering high and low, trying to find the individual who could be so incredibly smart as to steal trolls right out from under the very snouts of the dragons without a trace. Yesterday he'd used the state of *not-being* to blend in beautifully with other onlookers until a dragon-warrior came over and asked them all to leave.

Now he was using the state of *not-being* to disappear into the trees. Several devices enabled him to do this. One, the tree-shroud, covered his face. The other, his Eagle Eyes, allowed him to watch the dragon-warriors from a great distance. All they did, he noticed, was question dragons. Nobody even bothered to look for his secret message.

Perplexing. He'd checked the big juniper tree at the park sometime back, and somebody, sometime, had removed his last secret message. The dragon-warriors didn't seem to know anything about it. Yet, in Shadow's heart of hearts, he knew who *must* have found it: that would be his Worthy Opponent.

Shadow couldn't help but laugh out loud. This was going to be so much fun! That haughty Dragon Queen would strive in vain to defeat the *mindslayer*, and when all was said and done, he would be a *true mazemaster*!

As with Darth, he'd left the scroll in the same spot where he'd made away with his last troll. If the Dragon Queen was as shrewd as she thought she was, she'd find it. If not, then she was not a Worthy Opponent.

There were so many exciting developments unfolding in this game! It was turning out to be his greatest adventure of all! For he knew a secret about the Dragon Queen, a mighty secret of great power. Once she proved herself a worthy enemy, Shadow would use this secret to the greatest advantage.

But first, she had to prove herself worthy.

As Shadow contemplated this, he spotted her vehicle pull into the campgrounds.

The Dragon Queen!

His heart began hammering in his chest. Yes! *Now* the game could commence!

Focusing his Eagle Eyes, he watched her emerge from her vehicle and stride over to one of the dragon-warriors, her coppery hair shimmering in the sun. Shadow had never had a chance to study her as up-close as the Eagle Eyes allowed. She had long legs and was pretty behind those striking sunglasses. She seemed to spend a lot of time talking to the dragon-warrior, and Shadow grew increasingly impatient. Why wasn't she looking for the secret message?

Maybe she wasn't so worthy after all.

As she moved on to speak to a couple of dragons, he fought pangs of disappointment. What was he going to have to do, draw her a map?

He could understand why some *mazemasters* grew frustrated with gameplayers who lacked vision and imagination.

Brilliant mazes were often wasted on dullards who failed to appreciate them.

The Dragon Queen left the two dragons and wandered off on her own, over to the far cottage, the last one within the confines of the campsite. Dragons preferred it because trees and foliage crowded up next to it and muted road noises from the nearby highway and also afforded them a certain privacy.

Shadow's last troll had been staying there just before Shadow lured him to the Secret Caverns.

It's not there! he wanted to scream. *You're cold as ice.*

The troll's dragon protectors were still staying in the cottage, in futile hopes that he would return to them. Clearly, they didn't know who they were up against! The Dragon Queen put her arms around the female dragon. Shadow was getting bored. *Hurry up!*

After an interminable period of time, the Dragon Queen left the cottage and strolled over to the central latrine, her face screwed up in thought. Shadow almost leapt for joy. *You're getting warmer!*

The Dragon Queen circled the building, head bent to the ground. At one point she stopped and peered up into the branches of a juniper tree. Anticipation tingled all over Shadow's body. *You're getting hot!* He could hardly contain himself. Oh, he had *known* she'd be a Worthy Opponent! He'd known it all along!

At the cavernous doorway of the latrine, she hesitated. *You're burning up!* After a moment she disappeared into its cool, shadowy recesses.

Shadow trembled so hard he almost dropped his Eagle Eyes. With every fiber of his being he willed her to find the secret message. Up until now he hadn't been able to play the game at all. The trolls he'd captured were stupid, blubbering cowards. No challenge at all. Why, he could run them through the maze of the Secret Caverns easier than he could steal troll treasure!

Even the dragon-warriors were no match for his genius.

The magic box made no mention of the secret messages, and he'd seen no evidence that they knew anything about them. Riddles, right under their very snouts! (One thing was for certain: If they couldn't even find his carefully placed secret messages, then Shadow hardly need fear their finding Shadowland!)

But the Dragon Queen . . . she was different.

Shadow's mouth was dry and his hands sweaty. He licked his lips and tightened his grip on the Eagle Eyes, focusing sharply on the entrance to the latrine.

"You're so hot, you're about to burst into flames," he whispered. The Heroic Quest was about to begin!

Dylan spotted the ribboned scroll on a high ledge just inside the entrance to the park rest room. Her heart stopped.

While it was true that she'd been looking around—just in case—it had only been a vague hunch, really. She never seriously believed that she'd find another scroll.

Because that was just too scary to contemplate.

She had to stand on tiptoe to reach the scroll. Again, she handled it very carefully. The parchment was the same. Even the ribbon was identical.

Goose bumps swarmed over her body. She found herself holding her breath and let it out in a tight sigh. Slowly slipping the ribbon off the rolled-up paper, Dylan took the barest edges of the scroll into her fingertips and unfurled it.

> *If Dragons would search in vain for the trolls,*
> *The riddle to solve is hid in the scrolls.*
> *In creatures enchanted, in mazes and castles*
> *The Dragon Queen seeks, but the Shadow still*
> *baffles.*

A cold shudder worked its way down her spine. *"Oh, God, oh, God,"* she whispered. Her breath began coming out in short pants, and for a moment, she feared that she might hyperventilate. She leaned against the wall, took deep breaths, reread the scroll. Mechanically she closed the message and slipped the ribbon over it. She didn't have an evidence bag—PI's didn't collect evidence ordinarily, only information—so she placed it gingerly into her tote, next to the other scroll.

Then, as if in a dream, Dylan withdrew the other scroll and reread its cryptic message:

> *Trolls must always beware of the Shadow,*
> *For e'en in sunlight trouble may follow.*
> *The state of* not-being *will defeat*
> *   dragons bold*
> *And the* mindslayer *will triumph—*
> *   be it foretold!*

Replacing the first scroll into her bag, Dylan slid down to the cool concrete floor of the rest room and put her face in her hands. Her scalp felt tight and her chest seemed to be swelling up against her throat.

Dylan, like most cops, did not believe in coincidences.

As a homicide detective in a major metropolitan area, she'd investigated hundreds of murders through the years. Most were fairly cut-and-dried: passions run amok, urban warfare, even (the very hardest) child abuse. Then there were the sneaky murders: the poisonings, the arson-murders, the conspiracies. And there were the psychotic murders: seemingly random, haunting crimes which left behind devastating aftermaths. Sometimes every detective on the team knew who had committed a murder, but they could not make an arrest because they didn't have a "smoking gun." Other times an overzealous investigator stepped on some legal toes somewhere and a case was lost. And sometimes they never were able to find out just who had taken another individual's life. These were the hardest cases of all. Once she and a partner had conducted over three hundred interviews and never even turned up a hard suspect. Those were the cases she tended to take home, the cases that slid in between her and Matt in bed, the cases that intruded upon her dreams.

But this. This was like nothing Dylan had ever seen in all her years as a homicide detective. For she knew, now, what all the investigators had known deep inside; that they were not searching for a kidnapper. They were hunting a killer.

A killer whose mind dwelled in a world none of the investigators had ever known; a world filled with mysterious rhymes and deadly riddles; a world peopled with lost little boys . . . and a world stalked throughout by someone who called himself "the Shadow."

PART II   THE QUEST

Oh I was young and easy in the mercy
   of his means,
Time held me green and dying
Though I sang in my chains like the sea.

> —DYLAN THOMAS
> "Fern Hill"

. . . and anyway (goblins) don't care who
they catch, as long as it is done smart and
secret, and the prisoners are not able to defend
themselves.

> —J.R.R. TOLKIEN
> *The Hobbit*

ELEVEN

The Heroic Quest actually began before Shadow was ready.

The Dragon Queen's troll—the Dragon Princess—saw Shadow before he saw her. She came up behind him and said, "Well, *hi*!"

Shadow whirled around so sharply that he bit his tongue. She stood there, all freckles and grins. From around her neck, on a thin chain, gleamed the Magic Amulet. Shadow found himself staring at it as he struggled mightily to collect his thoughts and assume the power of the *mindslayer*. Oh, he was unprepared!

"I was at the card shop, you know? Comic books and stuff? The day I got my unicorn?" She touched the Magic Amulet gently.

"Yeah," he breathed.

"I didn't expect to see you at the library. You like to read?"

He nodded. This wasn't the way he had planned it! She had caught him unawares!

"Me, too. I read all the time. Daddy says I'm a book-worm." She giggled.

He tasted blood where he'd bitten his tongue.

"Did you ever feel like you've read all the books the library has that you really want to read, and then you don't know *what* you're going to do?"

"Sometimes." He swallowed. Where were his powers?

"Me, too. Mom says I ought to write some of my own, but I don't know. If I could just write them, that would be fun,

81

but in school we have to write them over and over to get them right, and I just *hate* that, don't you?"

He nodded.

"*Aidan!* C'mon, let's go." A dragon with wheels was calling to her.

"Coming, Daddy!" She glanced back at Shadow and dimpled. "I gotta go now. Maybe I'll see you around."

Shadow managed a crooked smile, and the Dragon Princess skipped away. While she was checking out her books, he slipped out the front door of the library, hurried down to Moonlight, yanked on his helmet, and drove quickly around the side of the building, where he puttered, waiting.

A moment later the Dragon Princess and the wheeled dragon emerged from the library. He had her books piled on his lap, and she shrieked with laughter as he reared up on his wheels while going down the ramp to their vehicle. Shadow watched as the dragon opened the passenger door, tossed the books in the back, and heaved his body onto the passenger seat. He disassembled the wheels, folded them, and stuffed them into the back seat. Then he pulled himself over to the driver's side of the vehicle, and the Dragon Princess got into the passenger side and closed the door. Shadow made a mental note of the fact that this vehicle was different from the one the Dragon Queen drove.

Shadow watched as they pulled into traffic. A moment later he followed.

On the magic box one time he'd seen how somebody could be followed. You had to stay back so that they wouldn't get suspicious. Besides, on Moonlight he could cut across grass if he had to.

Shadow was angry at himself for not being prepared. How could he have let her surprise him like that? He realized the danger of moving freely about in the land of the trolls. The longer he did so, the weaker his powers became.

It was not easy, following the dragon. He whipped in and out of traffic, and he made a couple of stops; once at a grocery store and once in front of a house where he honked the horn. A moment later the male troll—the Dragon Prince?—came out and climbed into the vehicle.

Shadow kept expecting the dragon to watch for him or to notice that he was following. But he seemed intent on his errands and busy with traffic. Apparently it never occurred to him that someone could be following him. This helped Shadow to relax somewhat, but when the dragon headed out toward the countryside, Shadow wasn't sure what to do.

For a while he was able to keep up, as the dragon breezed through a main thoroughfare with a fair amount of traffic. But eventually he turned off onto a narrow lane with no traffic. Shadow was forced to keep going. There was no way he could have followed at that point without being noticed. But he memorized the location.

For the first time Shadow felt a tremor of excitement. This was an unexpected boon, indeed! Why, *now* he could find out where the Dragon Queen lived!

It opened up all sorts of possibilities.

Dylan finally caught up to Sergeant Dickerson out at Singing Winds Park, where he was buttonholing people, trying to find out if anyone else had seen a little boy leave the park on the back of a dirt bike. In spite of the Scotts' doubts, it was the only lead they had that could give them any direction in which to start looking for a *modus operandi* in the kidnappings.

Dickerson read over the second scroll with growing dismay. "You found this in the rest room at the public park?"

She nodded.

"And you're sure it might be related."

"C'mon, Andy. It's just too big of a coincidence."

"Geez." He rubbed bloodshot eyes. "We'll give it to the FBI guys."

"Right."

"Next time you find one of these, leave it where it is,

okay? We'll need to take pictures of it and all. Otherwise all we got is your word."

Dylan felt a hot flush work its way down her neck. How in the name of all that is holy could she have possibly forgotten basic police procedure? With all her experience, *how*?

"Andy, I blew it. I am so sorry."

He shook his head in dismissal. "Forget about it. This case is making us all crazy. I put my pants on backwards this morning."

She grinned at the image and thanked him in her heart for being so kind. She deserved a butt-chewing, but he was extending a certain professional respect that she appreciated.

She wouldn't make the mistake again.

On the other hand she prayed there wouldn't *be* another time.

"What do you make of these rhymes?" asked Dickerson. "They don't mean anything to me."

"Well, the guy's obviously in some kind of sicko fantasy world."

He shook his head. "Most of these creeps are. But hell, Tandy, I've never seen anything like this. Maybe I'm just a small-town cop, but did you ever see anything like this in the Big City?"

"Never."

"What the hell's he talking about here? Geez. Dragons and trolls and enchanted creatures and what have you. It's crazy."

She nodded miserably. "I think that's the point, Andy."

"I don't even know what the hell a mindslayer is, do you?"

She shrugged.

He gave a heavy sigh. "Maybe the FBI guys'll have some idea. They can check it for prints with all their super-duper double-back-flip technology. Run it through their high-tech computers. Have a shrink examine it and the VICAP people—Violent Criminals Apprehension Program—and see if we can get some kind of behavioral profile on this guy."

She gave him a sideways glance under her lashes. He met the glance and quirked up one corner of his mouth. They were both thinking the same thing. "Then when all is said and done," he drawled, "we probably still won't know jackshit more than we do right now."

Dylan had reached the point where she needed some expert assistance, and she knew just where to get it.

It was almost lunchtime when she turned the van down the lane leading to her house. She thought back but couldn't remember when she'd last eaten lunch at home. Since the Scott case, she'd also missed supper with the family, and if school had been in session, she knew she wouldn't even have seen the kids at night when she got home late.

They were very fortunate that Matt could be there with the children, but that didn't keep her from missing them fiercely, feeling guilty as hell, and fighting down a little pang of jealousy now and then because he got to watch them grow up and she had to do it in spurts.

On the other hand, they both knew that Matt was every bit as capable as she to perform the physical tasks of private investigation; the surveillance, document research, tailing, and the like. But the truth was that she loved doing it. The truth was that she was barely able to perform simple word processing on a computer and didn't want to take the trouble to learn to do all the intricate maneuvers he did daily. And the truth was, she'd go nuts at home all day.

As she got out of the van, she heard the shouts and squeals of children at play out back. She wandered around the house and down the sloping grass to the creek. Ancient cypress trees lined the banks of the stream, their gnarled and whitened roots poking through the waterlike stairsteps. The little waterfall rushed over smooth round rocks, sudsing up and trapping leaves in the cold, clear water and forming a little pool, where waterbugs skittered over the surface and small fish bit at them from below. Birdsong filtered through the sun-dappled shade. A red-winged dragonfly hovered over the pool before flitting away. Gentle breezes ruffled the trees.

This was Dylan's hiding place, her solace, her refuge. As a little girl, she had hung from these same trees as Caleb and Aidan were doing now. No matter how fractured her thought processes when she was under stress, Dylan could always come here to sit and piece herself back together again.

Something she hadn't done in weeks.

She was learning that when you were self-employed and operated a home office, you were never really away from work. It dogged your heels at the supper table and nipped your ankles in front of the TV and yipped at you in bed. During the past year Dylan had worked more than at any time when on the police force, for a lot less money, and no security whatsoever.

More than once she'd wondered why they were doing it at all, and then she'd come to this place and know.

"Mom! Hey, Mom's home!"

"Mom! What are you doing home?"

The sheer delight in her children's voices washed over Dylan like a soothing balm. They clamered down from their respective trees and crowded around her, chattering over each other like monkeys, each demanding a bigger part of her than the other was getting.

"Hey!" She held up her hands in a time-out signal. "Gimme a break, here."

"Are you here to stay?" asked Aidan.

"Oh, I wish I could, honey. But no." At her daughter's crestfallen expression, she added, "But I will have lunch with you guys, and actually, to tell you the truth, I could use your help with this case."

For a brief moment they were stunned silent, then both started talking at once.

"Oh, *cool*! Can we go on surveillance with you? I always wanted to spy on people!" cried Caleb.

"You mean, we really get to help find Jeremy Scott and the other kids?" asked Aidan in an awed tone, her face creased with worry.

Both reactions were typical. To Caleb, it would be an adventure. Something fun. To Aidan, it would be serious stuff indeed. More sensitive than her brother, she had not forgotten that lost children were involved.

Dylan lowered herself to the banks of the creek, kicked off the running shoes she usually wore on the job, peeled off her socks, and plunged her hot, tired feet into the cold water. It felt delicious. From her tote bag she withdrew photocopies of the two messages. She patted the grass beside her. "Sit down here, and you guys be quiet for a minute."

For once they obeyed immediately.

"I think that whoever has taken those boys is leaving behind a message of some kind to us."

"What kind of message?" asked Caleb.

"Little poems. Here. This is the first one. I found it in the park where Jeremy was last seen." She handed copies to both children, who read silently.

Aidan finished first. Caleb said, "What's a *mindslayer*?"

Dylan handed them the second rhyme. "I found this at the state park where the last little boy disappeared." After they'd read it, she said, "These messages were rolled up like scrolls and tied with a ribbon."

"What color ribbon?" asked Aidan.

Dylan blinked. She'd hardly noticed. After a moment she said, "Purple."

Aidan nodded. She read the poems again.

"This sounds like Dragon Warriors," said Caleb.

"What's Dragon Warriors?" asked Dylan.

"It's a video game. It's got all these mazes and things you've got to get out of."

"Does it have a mindslayer in it?"

He shook his head. "But we could rent it at the video store, and I could show you how to play it."

Dylan nodded. "Good idea, Caleb."

"Mom?" Aidan was still studying the poems. "I think these are riddles."

"Riddles?"

"Yeah. Like, in *The Hobbit*, Bilbo Baggins—he's the hobbit—had to speak in a riddle in order to escape from Gollum."

"What's a Gollum?" asked Caleb.

"It's a monster who guarded a cave when the hobbit was trapped."

"Did it work?" asked Caleb.

"Not really. But Bilbo escaped anyway because the magic ring gave him power."

"What kind of power?"

"Well, in the beginning, it was just the power to remain invisible. As long as the hobbit wore the ring, he was invisible."

"In the beginning?" Dylan realized it had been a mistake not to have called on her experts sooner.

"I haven't read all the *Lord of the Rings* stories yet, but in *The Fellowship of the Ring*, they said that the magic ring gave power according to who possessed it."

"What does that mean?" Caleb skipped a stone across the little pool.

"It means that if you were good, you could use the ring for good powers. But the ring would kind of get to the guy who was wearing it after a while. I mean, the *power* got to them."

"Oh, I get it!" cried Caleb. "They couldn't handle the power. They got the big-head, right?"

"Well, what happened was . . ." Aidan, ever one for a dramatic moment, took a deep breath and said, "They would use their power for evil."

TWELVE

Shadow had been thinking about the game.

At first he'd been in total and complete control. The power had thrilled and enthralled him. Like a puppeteer, pulling the strings on a group of marionettes, he'd made trolls and dragons alike dance in time to his music.

But he had soon grown bored.

Like watching a sporting event in which the home team scores dozens of points against their opponents, thoroughly dominating the game and devastating the opposing team, the fun had gone out of it. Cheers soon grew hollow when there was no challenge to stimulate them.

So. He decided to give the Dragon Queen a very slight advantage.

He would send her a warning.

If the Dragon Queen were forewarned, she would be more vigilant. Which would make his role in the game that much more difficult.

Challenging.

Fun.

He took great care in deciding just how he was going to do it. Then, from the riverbed he withdrew one small, perfect, creamy-smooth rock. It hefted just so in his hand. It smelled of algae and felt cool when held against his cheek.

He almost hated to part with it.

After thoroughly drying the stone, Shadow dipped a small brush into a bottle of black paint and drew two vertical, parallel lines on the surface of the rock. Then he painted a crossbar connecting the lines. The crossbar slanted slightly, which made the insignia look somewhat like a lopsided letter *H*.

The next part was terribly risky, which made it all the more exciting. As soon as the paint was dry, Shadow put the rock deep into his pocket, mounted Moonlight, and traveled the route he'd seen the wheeled dragon take with the Dragon Princess.

At the country road that turned off the main highway, Shadow stopped for a moment. Inside him, his love for the game battled with his natural fear of getting caught.

If Shadow were caught by the dragons, they were sure to find the Secret Caverns. He would probably never be able to return to Shadowland again. Even if he did, he knew the Secret Caverns would never welcome him.

Was it worth the risk? He started to turn back.

And then he remembered: *Extra points for courage and valor.*

He headed down the road.

"So, who do you think the Shadow is?" Dylan slapped some mustard on whole wheat and dug around through the cold cuts laid out on the kitchen table.

"An old-time radio star?" Matt withdrew two canned Cokes, one Pepsi, and one Dr Pepper from the refrigerator and tossed them overhand to Caleb.

"You mean, a singer?" asked Aidan, opening her own package of turkey breast.

"No, no. They used to have these neat cliff-hanger shows on the radio—back before TV was invented—and you had to tune in each week to find out what happened. *The Shadow* was one of the best."

"Cool," said Caleb. "Do they still do that?"

"No, but you can buy cassettes with some of the old radio shows," said Dylan. "I'll look for some the next time we're in a bookstore." She opened a package of potato chips. "Anyway, I don't think this is supposed to be the same Shadow."

Aidan took a bite of her sandwich and chewed thoughtfully. "There was a Shadow in *The Fellowship of the Ring*," she said.

"Oh?" Dylan felt overwhelmed by her lack of knowledge of the fantasy world. "What kind of character was he?"

"He wasn't a character, exactly. He could change shapes and become, well, all kinds of trouble."

Her anxiety growing, Dylan nodded. If she could sit down and read all these books, it might help her understand the meaning of the notes (riddles?), but there was no way she could take that kind of time. She met her daughter's clear, intelligent eyes. Aidan gave her a pixie grin. "You really do need my help, don't you, Mom?"

Matt laughed. Caleb said, "I haven't read all those books and stuff that Aidan has, but I can tell you that there isn't a Shadow kind of character in Dragon Warriors."

Matt's smile faded. "You think this guy's playing some kind of weird real-life Nintendo game?"

Dylan shook her head. "I don't know what he's doing. I thought if we brainstormed long enough, we might come up with some kind of clue." She sighed. "We used to do that in Homicide all the time."

"You mean, *we're* being detectives now?" yelped Caleb.

"In a way, you are."

"Cool."

Dylan gave Matt a look across the table that said, If I hear that word one more time . . .

He winked at her. Suddenly she wished she could stay home the rest of the day. Sometimes it was awfully hard, being her own boss.

"Mom?" Aidan was still thinking. "If this guy is the Shadow, then 'trolls' must be kids."

They all looked at her.

"Then who are the dragons?" challenged Caleb. "You know so much."

"Well, who's going to search for the trolls?" Aidan looked from one to the other.

"Police."

"Volunteers."

"Parents."

They were quiet a moment. Then Dylan said slowly, "If dragons are police or parents or whatever—authority figures—then who is the Dragon Queen?"

"Somebody's mom," said Caleb.

"Jeremy's?" Dylan looked from her children to her husband.

Matt gave her an intense gaze and pursed his lips.

"I don't think so, Mom," said Aidan, "because there's more than one kid gone."

"Then whose?"

"Oh, God." As soon as Matt said it, he glanced away from them, struggling to compose his expression, Dylan could see, so as not to alarm the children.

But she could tell from their faces that it was too late. *"What?"*

"The press conference," he said. "The Campbells said they had hired you to find Jeremy."

Aidan's freckles stood stark against her whitening face. "Mom, the Dragon Queen . . . It's *you.*"

Shadow stood very still, took deep breaths, and entered into the state of *not-being*. His heart was pounding so hard he could feel the spasms in his rib cage.

His courage had surprised even him! The Secret Caverns would be so pleased!

Moonlight was well-disguised some distance away. Shadow lifted—very slowly—the Eagle Eyes and focused them on the Dragon Queen's vehicle. He hadn't expected to find it here. At first he was terrified to think of her being so close. But in the end it had made the game that much more exhilarating.

Moving swiftly, like cloud shadows across a meadow, he had crept up to her vehicle and placed the Warning Rock right on the driver's seat. He shivered now, just thinking about how close he was to her and how risky it had been to do such a thing right in front of the Dragon Queen's own abode! She could have come out any minute!

He would get a hundred points for this act of heroism. Maybe more.

Now, he waited.

This was a lovely place, filled with trees and wild things. It was quite easy for him to blend in with the surroundings. A hot breeze ruffled his clothing. Sweat trickled down his neck and into the collar of his shirt.

He wondered if she could somehow sense him near, and his heart jackhammered at the prospect.

Even if she didn't feel his presence, she would have to know it when she found the Warning Rock.

What then? Would she come searching?

The Eagle Eyes almost dropped from his sweating hands. Perhaps he should leave. Quickly. This was too dangerous. He didn't have the Secret Caverns to protect him here!

He started to move, but the front door opened and he froze, barely breathing. He was not so close that she could see him at first glance, but then again, she *was* the Dragon Queen. Who knew what special powers she had?

Her stride wasn't as determined as it had been the last time he'd seen her. She moved slowly, as if she were preoccupied with her thoughts.

Almost there. Cotton-mouthed, he waited, watching.

She reached the door of the vehicle. Opened it. Shadow trembled.

Tossing in her tote bag, she sat down and reached for the door.

Shadow held his breath. He couldn't bear it!

The Dragon Queen stopped, her hand in midair. Frowning, she reached beneath her, groped around a moment, and withdrew the Warning Rock.

Still as a breathless dawn, Shadow waited.

She stared at the rock a moment. Turned it over in her hand. Glanced toward the house. Shook her head.

And tossed it onto the grass.

In stunned disbelief Shadow did not move until long after the vehicle had backed out of the drive and headed down the country lane toward the road to town. Tight-chested, he stood, staring blindly toward where the rock had fallen.

So. This was how she heeded a warning.

From deep within the darkest places of his mind, rage stirred itself, uncoiled, and struck with a venom that poisoned Shadow's every thought. The heat spread throughout his body and dizzied him. Without heed for safety, Shadow erupted from his hiding place and sprinted toward the spot on the grass where the Warning Rock lay, lost and unheeded.

Choking back the bile that curdled in his throat, Shadow fell to his knees in the grass, groping furiously for the rock. His hand closed over it. Deafened and blinded to all but his own fury, Shadow grasped the rock, spun to his feet, and hurled it toward a front window, which broke with a sparkling tinkle of glass.

Then he sprang to his feet and, with the wind at his heels, vanished back into the trees whence he had come.

THIRTEEN

Chris's Collectible Comics & Cards was as crowded as before when Dylan paid a second visit. She'd intended to have a talk with Chris Helmon without the distraction of the kids around, but Chris wasn't there. She decided to look around the store.

Comic books by the hundreds lined the walls, hanging by sleeves in special racks. There were a number of characters she recognized and many she didn't: *Thor, The Avengers, Excaliber, The Punisher*. All depicted spine-tingling adventures with, she discovered to her surprise, complicated story lines, reasonably difficult vocabulary, and modern sophisticated themes, such as the environment or child abuse. But they still offered that same old cliff-hanging, bloodthirsty appeal that kept kids combing the aisles, looking for the latest issue.

Even if comic books made reading too easy, with stimulating color graphics on every page that regular books didn't have, Dylan decided that at least it *was* reading. For active boys like Caleb, who seldom took the time to sit down and read a book that wasn't assigned, comic books at least lured him to read *something*.

Dylan's mind was suddenly seized with that peculiar double image that detectives often "saw" in their heads while following leads on a particularly difficult case. She had been thinking about Caleb, but the image she saw in her mind was Jeremy Scott.

An active boy. A Little Leaguer and a tree-climber and a

skateboarder. Where did he like to come when he had a few dollars burning a hole in his pocket?

Chris's Collectible Comics & Cards.

Her heart did a quick double-thump. What if *this* were the connection? Three busy, active boys had all disappeared within a two-week time span, boys who knew better than to get into a car with a stranger.

But what if he wasn't a stranger? What if those kids had browsed this very store at one time or another before their disappearance?

Dylan gave furtive, suspicious glances at the other customers. As before, *they weren't all kids*. Young adult men also frequented the place, trading cards and swapping comics. Big boys who never quite grew up.

In order not to draw attention to herself, Dylan wandered the store, fingering merchandise, her brain tumbling in on itself like a spinning lottery cage. Jeremy had obviously been here before. She was going to have to do some checking to see about the other boys.

And what if she was right? What then? Suppose she told Sergeant Dickerson. What were they supposed to do, put a tail on every young adult male customer until one of them spoke to another kid?

She could picture it: A young man approaches a little boy in a park. They speak briefly. The boy follows the young man to a car and gets in with him. Four thousand cops descend on the scene, surround the car, drag out the driver, force him to assume the position, rescue the child . . . and then find out it's his kid brother.

She couldn't resist a smile over that one.

Dylan rounded a corner and found herself at a large Dungeons & Dragons display. Her attention focused on an assortment of miniatures, fantastical creatures of every imagining: a seven-headed hydra, orcs, elves, dragons, wererats, warlords and wizards, warriors of both sexes and all species, giants and skeletal fighters . . .

Her mind seized on a thought so bold as to sicken: *In*

creatures enchanted, in mazes and castles . . . the Dragon Queen seeks, but the Shadow still baffles.

Shadow paced the length of the Trove Room in long, angry strides, his purple cloak flaring behind him. *"How could she ignore the warning of the Shadow?"* he shouted, his voice bouncing back to him. "Does the Dragon Queen think her power is so great that she need not even heed notice of impending disaster?" Fury curdled his stomach and caused him to tremble.

He wanted to break something . . . or hurt someone.

He had given her—his Worthy Opponent—a gracious opportunity to surrender. After all, it was the decent thing for one to do when embarking on a Heroic Quest. One proved oneself more honorable than one's enemy. One gave the enemy every opportunity to understand the consequences of underestimating one's own great power to destroy.

After all, the purpose of a game of strategy was not bloodlust.

But she had been *foolish*! She'd taken a precious opportunity to either give up or, at the very least, fortify her boundaries and prepare for attack—a generous gesture of goodwill on Shadow's part—and she had thrown it out the window. *Out the window!* In front of Shadow's own eyes.

It was clear to Shadow that an opponent so stupid should be allowed *no* mercy. After all, she had done nothing to deserve it. If anything, she had deliberately provoked Shadow's wrath.

She would learn to be very, very sorry, because Shadow would never again give her such an opportunity.

Dylan studied the miniatures, scrutinizing them as if they held the very answers she sought in their tiny hands. They were quite small. Most of them were less than an inch in height. They were amazingly and skillfully crafted and beautifully hand-painted. Some were arranged in battle formations. Others occupied special displays. They were all laid out beneath a locked glass case.

Next to the miniatures was a stack of individual Dungeons & Dragons gamepacks. Each one depicted its own enchanted world full of danger and magic for the characters to occupy. Dylan thumbed through an accompanying book on the game and discovered that it was surprisingly complicated and intricate. Each character had an array of physical and emotional characteristics which determined its strength, stamina, intelligence, special skills, and magic; all of which was designated by the throw of dice, some of which had as many as ten sides. A complex chart kept track of these characteristics (as well as various weapons or armor) by a point system. Points could be lost or gained depending on the success or failure of the character who navigated the adventure and on the cosmic determination of the die. A gain in points meant moving up a detailed hierarchy, acquiring new powers and wisdom along the way. It all took place against the classic backdrop of good versus evil.

The entire thing was orchestrated by the exalted Dungeon Master, who set up the adventure, placed choices before the adventurers, and whose final word on the outcome was infallible.

Dylan took a slow breath, deep enough to fill her lungs, and let it out in a long sigh. Her stomach felt queasy. It was that paint-by-number kit all over again.

Once when Dylan was little, her grandmother had bought her a paint-by-number kit. Since oil paints were used, the idea was to use up all of one color in the designated spots on the canvas; clean the brush; then use up all of another color, until the painting was done.

When she'd first started painting, none of it made any sense. It was a collection of brown blobs, then blue blobs, then white blobs. It wasn't until the painting was about half done that it started to make any sense at all, but it never really looked complete until all the spots were filled in and Dylan had leaned the painting against the mantel and backed up across the room. The further away she got, the better the painting looked.

That clumsy little painting never ceased to flash into Dylan's mind whenever she reached a certain point in an investigation; the point where all those little multicolored blobs began to fit together.

In this case, the picture that was beginning to emerge was a portrait; the portrait of a killer.

It would take a few weeks for the FBI to confirm, but he was probably a young adult male, white, with an intense interest in Dungeons & Dragons, who befriended kids who came into this store, followed them, then later lured them into his car with—what? A comic book? Baseball cards? Dungeons & Dragons miniatures?

What he did with them after that was anybody's guess.

A bizarre sex ritual? It was hard to imagine him using young boys for anything else.

Then what?

Maybe he was another John Wayne Gacy, burying them all in his basement.

Dylan thought of Jeremy Scott, and her heart wept.

And now the killer was making some sort of macabre game out of the whole thing, and he had somehow chosen *her* to be his playing partner.

That made this investigation more deeply personal than Dylan had ever known. The fact that children were missing—and probably dead—was wrenching enough. But for her to be somehow intimately involved *with the killer* was almost overwhelming.

If it was a game, it was a deadly one.

With grim determination Dylan began loading her arms full of everything she could find related to the game of Dungeons & Dragons.

After all, if she was going to *win* this game, she'd better damn well know the rules.

• • •

Before embarking on any Quest, Shadow knew, the most important thing to do was stock up on provisions. He had to prepare for any eventuality. Not to do so could result in a perilous loss of points.

Into the Trove Room he lugged quantities of pork and beans, Beanie-Weenies, Vienna sausages, canned chicken, beef jerky, candy bars (the cave's natural coolness kept them from melting), and bottled water. He brought a sleeping bag and a sterno cooker and plenty of scrolls and writing supplies. Lantern oil and matches. Toilet paper and a small gardening spade. An air mattress for under the sleeping bag.

It wasn't easy. Moonlight could only handle so much of a load at a time. Some of the stuff Shadow carried in journey-pouches he'd stolen from the trolls.

Weapons were no problem. After all, he had the power of the *mindslayer*! He didn't *need* any weapons, because he seldom had to use brute force. All the same, he kept his dagger.

When his provisions and weapons were squared away, Shadow sat down and began figuring his points for everything that had happened so far. It took a lot of careful thought and backtracking. His score, when he'd finished, was disappointingly low. After all, he'd lost one troll in the Secret Caverns and had not been able to capture another. Then, there was that unpleasant incident when he had lost control. . . . He didn't like to dwell on that.

On the other hand he'd shown cunning and courage on more than one occasion, so the sheet was relatively balanced. But the Quest was only beginning! Just think how many points he'd be able to accumulate when it was fulfilled!

Once the Dragon Queen lay in shattered defeat, the Secret Caverns would know that Shadow had conquered not just the beasts without, but the beast within, and had proved himself superior. The Secret Caverns could rest peacefully beneath the sheltering trees. All would be well in the world of Shadowland.

And the power of the *mazemaster* would be his forever.

"You know anything about a little rock with an *H* painted on it?" Matt's voice sounded as though he were right next to her as Dylan pulled up at a traffic light and stopped.

"Yeah. It was in the seat of my car. I sat on it."

"Well, it got thrown through our living room window."

"What?"

"Pretty as you please. The kids and I spent the better part of the afternoon fixing it."

"Who did it? Caleb?"

"Nope. We were all still in the kitchen, cleaning up after lunch."

"Wait a minute." The light turned green, and a car behind Dylan honked her into noticing. "When did this happen?"

"Right after you left."

"But, Matt, there wasn't anybody around when I left."

"Apparently somebody was. What did you do with the rock, anyway?"

"I threw it out."

"Where?"

"In the grass. Right by the driveway."

There was a long silence as Dylan and Matt both processed that information. Dylan said, "It was thrown through the window after I left?"

"Not five minutes after."

"But that's crazy! There wasn't anybody there, and anyway, they couldn't see that rock from the road or even the driveway, unless they were looking for it."

"Or unless they saw you throw it out."

"That doesn't make any sense! Even if somebody were there—which they weren't—then why would they go pick up that rock and throw it through our window?"

"Dylan, it's not just your average everyday rock, you know. It's got an *H* painted on it. Did you ever stop to think what it was doing in the seat of your car in the first place?"

"I figured it belonged to one of the kids. You know how junky they can be."

"I asked. It doesn't. They never saw it before."

The cold finger of a shiver traced Dylan's spine. She reached over and turned down the van's air-conditioning.

"Hey, Red? You still there?"

"Yeah. I'm here."

"What do you make of it?"

Dylan pursed her lips, whipped into a parking lot, and pulled back out on the wide thoroughfare, heading back toward the direction of home. "Shit," she said.

"What?"

"I missed the goddamn message, that's what! Jesus, Matt! The guy knows where we live!"

"But how can he? Our business address is a post office box, and our home address is a rural route number. Hell, even I have trouble finding it sometimes."

"I'm coming home."

"No. Now, listen, you are busy in this investigation. Jeremy's parents need you to keep following leads. The kids and I are fine."

Dylan's fingers were so cold she could barely feel them on the steering wheel. She turned the air-conditioning off. "Matt! Don't you get it? He found me! It's part of the game! Oh, God, *he found my children!*"

FOURTEEN

Quiet had returned to the Secret Caverns.

In the golden glow of a lantern, sitting cross-legged on his neatly folded sleeping bag, Shadow was thinking. Perhaps there was more than one reason why the Dragon Queen would fail to heed his warning. Colossal stupidity, of course; that went without saying. Arrogance, maybe. But perhaps . . . just perhaps . . . she was ignorant as well as stupid. Maybe she was simply not comprehending just who it was she was dealing with.

In other words, it was possible she did not completely understand how dangerous Shadow really was.

Maybe she needed a little proof.

Shadow got up from the sleeping bag, crossed the Trove Room, and began sorting through his collection of journey-pouches. When he had found the one he was seeking, he emptied the pouch of its contents and carried it over to where he'd been sitting. For a long moment he stared at the journey-pouch.

Then he got out paper, quill, and inkpot and began to write.

When Dylan pulled up in front of her house, she could hear the kids playing at the creek again. She raced around back, shielded her eyes from the bald Texas sun, and picked them out through the trees, knee-high in the water, busily working on their dam. Matt was nowhere to be seen.

She whirled around, ran up the sloping back lawn, strode across the deck, slammed through the back door, crossed the

103

kitchen in about three strides, and flung open the door to their office with such force it banged against the wall.

From his position at the rolltop desk, Matt jumped and pivoted to face her.

"Why aren't you out there with those children?" she demanded. She could feel the heat, radiating off her fair complexion.

He gestured calmly toward the desk. "I had work to do."

"How could you leave them unsupervised? How could you?"

"I didn't realize they needed a chaperon for dam-building."

"He's out there, Matt! Don't you realize that?"

"Dylan, I want you to calm down. Come sit in my lap and we'll talk about it."

"I don't *want* to sit in your damn lap!"

He crossed his arms over his chest and regarded her.

"Don't you dare look at me like that! I'm not some hysterical female you've got to calm down out on the beat."

"I'm having a little bit of trouble taking *your* word for it that you're not hysterical. You should see yourself."

With her legs in a wide stance, her hands on her hips, still panting, she glared at him.

He stared calmly back.

After a moment she relented. With a long sigh she crossed the room and plopped down in his lap.

"Ouch!"

"You didn't feel that!"

"I should have."

She grinned in spite of herself.

"Think about it, Red. Some kid throws a rock through our window that has the letter *H* painted on it, and you come flying home in a panic that we're being stalked by a kid-killer."

"I might believe that if we still lived in the city. But I remind you that our home is now in the country. There aren't any kids nearby. If there were, Caleb and Aidan would be playing with *them* instead of trying to kill each other all day."

He didn't say anything, and she knew she'd gotten through to him.

"So, what do you think it means?"

"How the hell should I know?" she snapped. After a moment she said, "I'm sorry. This whole thing has just unnerved me."

"I know."

"He knows where we live!"

"Maybe. Come on, Red! You've been a detective long enough to know not to assume anything! You do not know for a fact that this Shadow guy threw that rock. And besides, if he wanted one of our kids, wouldn't he have approached one of *them*, instead of drawing all this attention to himself?"

She shrugged. "I guess so."

"Besides, these are cop's kids. They'd never get into somebody's car without permission from us. They know too much."

She rested her head on his shoulder and nodded reluctantly.

"Anyway, I take a break now and then. I go out on the deck and listen and watch for a while. Make sure everything's all right."

"Awww. And I thought you didn't care."

"I don't. I'm just scared of you."

She put her arms around his neck, and he squeezed her tight. But the cold fingers of terror which had gripped her stomach on the way home would not let go.

Restlessness pushed her from her husband's lap. She ran her fingers through his thick, curly hair. He caught her hand and kissed it. "I'm going to go look around," she said. He nodded and turned back to his work.

She searched the woodsy area around her house for almost two hours, looking for anything, anywhere—a footprint, a gum wrapper, *anything* that could provide a clue to the elusive Shadow.

But there was nothing.

Sweat drooled down her body and pooled in her bra. Always, Dylan dogged this feeling of *wasted time*, that no matter what she was doing, it was the wrong thing. At any moment the Shadow could strike again, and another precious child could be lost forever. Because she, Dylan Tandy, had wasted her time.

The fact that police, sheriff's deputies, Texas Rangers, and the FBI were also following fruitless leads did nothing to make Dylan feel better. After all, in this bizarre game of hide-and-seek, Shadow had picked Dylan to be It.

Exhaustion dragged at her. It was like no other fatigue she had ever known, this hopelessness. A high-pitched whistle drifted to her through the trees. Matt was calling her. Trudging through tangled brush, she headed for the house.

He was waiting on the high, wraparound porch. "You better head right over to the Scotts'," he said ominously. "I just got a call from Colleen Scott, and she was practically hysterical."

Dylan bypassed the ramp and took the steps up to the porch two at a time. "Did she say why?"

The lines around his mouth deepened. "All I could make out was something about a scroll."

Scotty had the door open before she'd even made it up the sidewalk. "What the hell's going on, Dylan?" he demanded.

She was beginning to get used to his abrasive manner and no longer let it bother her. The stress he must be under was unimaginable to her.

She stepped up to the front door and laid a calming hand on his tense arm. "Show me what you got," she said.

As they walked through the house, he talked. "Colleen went to get the mail. Our mailbox is out on the street, you know. Anyway, there was this piece of paper, all rolled up and tied with a purple ribbon. She thought maybe it was some kind of sympathy note or something—we've been getting a lot of really nice cards and letters from people all over the Hill Country—and she just pulled the ribbon off and read it right there by the mailbox."

He paused. "You wanna drink?" he asked. "Must be five o'clock somewhere in the world."

"Ice water would go down great, Scotty."

He shook his head and pressed a trembling hand to his eyes. "I don't think I can take this anymore, Dylan." His voice was so low she could barely hear him. "She expects me to be so strong, like he's not *my* kid, too! Like *my* heart hasn't been torn out—" Tears spilled over and he wiped them roughly away with the palms of his hands. "God help me."

She took one of his hands in both of hers and squeezed. "Listen, nobody expects anything of you. But I can tell you one thing: I don't know how you do it. I really don't. If I were in your shoes, they'd have to put me in a straitjacket."

He shook his head. "You gotta go on. You gotta keep hoping. Otherwise . . ." He gave a shaky sigh, then headed over to a liquor cabinet, where he poured himself a stiff drink. "I heard her scream," he said. He stared into space for a moment and took a big swallow.

Gently Dylan said, "Scotty? Can I see the scroll?"

He shook himself. "Sure. It's in there on the kitchen table." When he didn't move, Dylan went to fetch the scroll herself. There was no sign of Colleen. Dylan guessed she was lying down.

Before facing the scroll, Dylan took a glass out of the kitchen cabinet, filled it with water, and gulped it down. The scroll lurked there on the table like some sort of malevolent presence with an intelligence and evil of its own. When she unfurled it, her hands were trembling.

> *When Shadow gives warnings*
> *   that others don't heed,*
> *Perhaps a reminder is what they will need.*

To see that the mindslayer
   has won over all—
Check for the journey-pouch
   'neath the riverside wall.

Nausea clenched Dylan's stomach. The fact that she had been right about the message from Shadow brought her no comfort.

"It's from the kidnapper, isn't it?"

Dylan jumped. She hadn't heard Scotty come up behind her.

"Yes."

"Then maybe you better tell me what's going on."

She nodded. "All right. But first, I'm going to call Sergeant Dickerson. While we're waiting for him to get here, I'll explain to you what's been happening."

"Just tell me one thing." Scotty's eyes bored through hers. "Is my boy dead?"

Those eyes, red-rimmed, desperate, afraid to hope, caught Dylan's soul like steel shavings to a magnet. "Th-there's no evidence that Jeremy is dead, Scotty."

"But what do you *think*? That's all I want to know. Do you think he's dead?"

Of course that baby's dead! she thought. *His happy little life was snuffed out for no reason whatsoever by somebody who gives no value to human life, and who would destroy us all for his own amusement. He killed that sweet child, and so help me God, I won't quit until he pays for it!*

Those were Dylan's thoughts. She met Scotty's intense gaze and said, "Never, ever give up hope. As long as there's no body, then Jeremy could still be alive."

The tension seemed to go out of his body in a *whoosh*. Before he could read the lie, she turned away from him and reached for the phone.

"Geez, Tandy, does this make any more sense to you than it does to me?" Sergeant Dickerson scratched the back of his short-cropped head. They were seated at the Scotts' kitchen table. Dylan had put Scotty to work, making coffee. While it brewed, she sent him to check on his wife so she and Dickerson could talk.

"Some of it does. I brought this from home." She reached into her tote and withdrew the smooth, round rock with the letter *H* painted on it. While he turned it over in his hands, she told him about finding it on the seat of her car, tossing it onto the grass, and having it hurled through their living room window five minutes after she drove away.

"You think he was in the bushes, watching you?" Dickerson asked.

"Had to be."

He shivered involuntarily. "Lock your doors, Tandy."

She nodded and pursed her lips, fighting the urge to run straight home, collect the kids, and lock them up in safe little cages, out of harm's way.

"You know, we could put some men out around your house, hiding in the bushes, in case the guy comes back. What do you think?"

"I think it's a great idea. I know I'd feel a lot better."

"Be a great way to catch him, too."

She agreed, but knew in her heart it would never be that easy.

"Now. What do you make of this *H*?"

"Hell if I know, Andy. Nothing this guy does makes any sense to me."

He set the rock aside. "We'll worry about that later. What do you think a *journey-pouch* is?"

She shook her head.

"And what's he talking about here? What riverside wall? There isn't one that I know of."

Dylan rubbed her hands all over her face, forgetting that she was wearing mascara. "I don't think he speaks in literal terms. Like, the 'Dragon Queen.' We figure that's me. 'Trolls' must be his victims. So . . ." She sat bolt upright. *"Backpack!"*

He quirked an eyebrow at her.

"Jeremy's backpack was stolen a couple of weeks before he disappeared.

"The journey-pouch."

"Maybe." She was beginning to be excited, but in a sickening, mixed-emotion kind of way. If this Shadow guy had Jeremy's backpack, then he must have been stalking the child for weeks. And if he was displaying it now, then Jeremy almost had to be dead.

"Okay. We'll go with that for now. So where the hell is this riverside wall?"

"Maybe it's a street," said Scotty.

Dylan and Sergeant Dickerson exchanged glances. Neither had heard him approach. He must have been listening in.

"There's Riverside Drive, over on the south side of Kerrville. Right by the state park."

"But it doesn't have a wall," Dylan pointed out.

"All the same, let's go check it out," said Andy. They got to their feet. Campbell Scott stood in front of them, his arms crossed over his chest.

"I'm going with you," he said. "I don't give a damn what you find. Jeremy is my son. Don't give me any bullshit about police business, either. Jeremy is my son."

Dylan glanced at Andy. He nodded. She reached out and squeezed Scotty's tension-hardened arm. "Let's go," she said.

FIFTEEN

Shadow stood very still, took a deep breath, and entered into the state of *not-being*.

The sounds of small-town summer filtered down around him through the swaying boughs of the park trees . . . the satisfying *crack* of ball meeting bat, the distant growl of a lawn mower, the *fht-fht-fht* of sprinklers sending rainbow sprays of water over grass, the shrieks and laughter of children at play. They were familiar, comfortable sounds which provoked nostalgia in the adults who heard them, sending memories of happy, innocent days gone by to haunt them in a contented sort of way and make them long to return to a place that was forever gone.

But Shadow did not hear these sounds, for they were not of his world. The state of *not-being* wrapped him in a cottony silence and muffled all sounds save those which he permitted.

A she-dragon and a troll no higher than Shadow's waist entered his field of vision. The troll had stubby legs and a head almost too big for his neck. The dragon dawdled along, pulling the troll gently by the hand. She picked him up and settled him into the seat of a swing. Then, taking care not to let go of the swing's chains, she paused him high into the air and swooped him back down again to a gale of giggles.

"Woooooo!" she cried. "Woooooo! Mama's little boy is going so high!"

As if she'd hurled a spear into Shadow's heart, her laughter pealed swiftly across the grass and pierced him to the very core of his existence. He gasped.

"Wooooo! He's going so high, but Mama won't let him fall. Woooo!"

The troll squealed in delight.

Trembling overtook Shadow.

"Mama won't let her baby fall. No, siree. Mama won't let him fall. Mama loves her baby boy, forever and always."

The soft, gentle cries flew past the sparkling sprinkler rain, stabbed through the cottony haze that armored Shadow, and laid bare his soul with a pain so agonizing he was blinded by it. He staggered backward, groping with numbed hands as if there were someone there to catch him should he fall.

But there was no one.

It hurt as no physical wound ever could, and, like lifeblood rushing from the body of a dying man, the memories flooded out.

He cried out one word: *"Mama!"*

Then he turned and stumbled crazily away—as far away as he could get—from the world of lawn sprinklers, swings, and laughing children whose mothers loved them, forever and always.

Riverside Drive ran parallel to the section of the Guadalupe River that flowed along the northeastern edge of Kerrville State Park, from where Eric Rathbone had disappeared. Sergeant Dickerson drove Dylan and Scotty the entire length of the street and back again, but there was no wall.

"Must not be talking about Riverside Drive," commented Dickerson.

Dylan took her sunglasses off and leaned her head wearily against the car's passenger window. She caught a glimpse of herself in the side mirror. Smudged mascara ringed her eyes like a raccoon. *Shit,* she thought, *I look as bad as Scotty.* She put the sunglasses back on.

"It's like a nightmare," said Scotty quietly from the backseat. They had a little trouble hearing him, and Dickerson turned down the volume on his police radio. "You cannot believe that this is happening to you. It's like you're surrounded by this protective armor of unreality. You just know you're going to wake up and find out the whole thing was a terrible dream, and you'll go into your child's room and find him slee—" A sob took him over.

Dylan and Dickerson were quiet. They both knew there was nothing they could say, nothing they could do to end this man's nightmare.

After a moment Scotty said, "Colleen wants to start printing up flyers and things, you know, missing persons stuff. I know she's right, but I can hardly bring myself to do it. I keep thinking we'll find him, you know?"

Dylan turned sideways in her seat and looked at the man. He had aged ten years from the confident businessman she'd met only a scarce few days before. This was a situation in which he could not take charge, could not make things happen. The total loss of control, of the ability to protect his family from harm, had damaged him almost as much as the loss of his son. Whether they found Jeremy or not, whether the child was alive or dead, Campbell Scott's world would never be the same again.

She wondered if anyone's would.

She reached over the seat and clasped his hand, forcing herself to look into his despairing eyes. "We'll never stop looking, Scotty."

He nodded and stared blindly out the window.

Riverside Drive dead-ended at the Texas Lions' camp. Dickerson had made his second U-turn there and had followed the street where it wound around and crossed Highway 27 (where the highway was known as Memorial Boulevard), had made the big curve, and was following the parallel path of the river. They traveled north, the river only visible from the street in patches, until they had crossed Cartuck and Carmichael streets and closed in near the dam which divided the State Park part of the river from the rest of the city. People could be seen fishing off the dam and tubing in the dammed-off slow currents along the park's boundaries where Eric Rathbone had last played with his family.

Dylan sat bolt upright in her seat. "Wait a minute. Take a look at that dam. Wouldn't you say it resembles a wall? I mean, looking up from the river?"

Dickerson was skeptical. "That's stretching it a little, don't you think?"

"You got a better idea?" cried Scotty. "For God's sake, it's worth a try!"

Sergeant Dickerson glanced back at his passenger. "Sure, buddy. You're right. Let's take a look. Don't *touch* anything, though, you understand?"

Scotty nodded. He looked as though he were trying not to vomit.

Dylan wasn't so sure about this herself. What if they found his son's body? She could see the same doubts in Dickerson's eyes, but neither of them had the heart to refuse him. They'd want to be there if it were their kid. They just weren't sure if Scotty would be able to take it. *Hell*, she thought, *could we?*

A cold sweat broke out on Dylan's body. It was a relief to emerge from the air-conditioned car into the summer heat. Still, she shivered. Keeping Scotty near her side, Dylan began to search along one side of the dam's banks while Dickerson searched the other.

It didn't take long.

Dylan heard Scotty's gasp before she saw the backpack. She followed the direction of his gaze, and there it was, a bright red waterproof schoolbag, nestled in plain sight in the riverbank's greenery. It was the kind of bag that could be bought for less than ten dollars in any discount store in the country. Dylan had bought a few for her own kids. What clearly set this one apart were the clumsily drawn letters in black marker in one bottom corner: *J.C.S.*

Scotty whirled suddenly and threw up.

Dylan shouted for Dickerson and withdrew a pair of

plastic gloves from her tote bag, which she snapped on. Dickerson came scrambling up the other side of the dam and hurried over to the car, where he withdrew a camera from the trunk before jogging over and sliding down to join Dylan and Scotty.

"Is that it?" Dickerson asked the white-faced Scotty.

Scotty nodded. "Those are his initials," he whispered. "Jeremy Campbell Scott." His hands hung at his sides.

Dylan took a step forward, but Dickerson stopped her. "I think we better call the FBI," he said. "There may be footprints or something around here, and we could botch the whole thing. I'll get hold of my chief and the Ranger who's assisting."

Her skin crawled with frustration, but Dylan knew Dickerson was right. Many a case had been trampled to death by overeager cops. She thought of the Green River murders, in which failure to conduct a proper police search of the area where the first body had been found had perhaps cost investigators the chance to catch the killer and caused them to overlook three other bodies—one of which was left there after the failed search was called off.

"Let's stretch some crime scene ribbon around here," added Dickerson. "When they get here, don't let anybody over the ribbon unless I give the okay. I'll line up some uniforms on it as soon as we get situated."

Dylan nodded. "Right." It was like being a cop again, and she was comfortable with taking his orders. She turned to Scotty and said gently, "Why don't you sit down in the car? We'll let you know if we find anything."

Scotty gave her a bleak-eyed stare, then followed meekly behind Dickerson as he hurried toward the car.

That left Dylan one brief, blessed moment alone with the backpack. Taking care not to move one step forward or back from where she was, she crouched down and, with her pen, pulled back the bag's overflap for a quick glance inside.

Buried just within the top of the missing child's back-pack, tied neatly with a purple ribbon, was another scroll.

• • •

Shadowland.

He had to get to Shadowland.

As soon as he got to Shadowland, all would be well again. He would be Shadow, and the pain would go away. The Secret Caverns would protect him, just as they always had.

With fragments of memory streaming out behind him in shreds like long hair in the wind, he pushed Moonlight to the limits of speed, heedless of anything except escape.

He was shaken to the depths of his soul. The power of the *mindslayer* had fled, and the state of *not-being* had not guarded him.

No matter how fast he went, the memories still clung to him, and he pressed Moonlight ever harder to leave them behind.

Shadowland.

He had to get to Shadowland.

Moonlight hit a bump and sprang through the air, but he held to the course. Something inside him was screaming. It wanted to hurt him, but he wouldn't let it.

At least, he tried not to let it.

The pain!

It was a terrible, open, bleeding wound, and he wanted to scream he wanted to cry he wanted to *die* he wanted not to feel not to feel the pain the terrible terrible pain.

Moonlight hit the turnoff in a spray of gravel. They went into a slide and he fell to the side, where he was dragged through burning dust and rock and stickers and weeds, which ripped through his jeans and peeled layers of skin off his leg and arm.

He did not feel the pain. It was nothing compared to what shrieked inside him.

Panting, sweating, he stumbled to his feet and limped over to check on Moonlight, who looked as scraped and sore as he did but none the worse for wear. He remounted and continued at a breakneck speed until he reached the boulder, where he came to another splaying, pivoting stop.

Stashing Moonlight behind the boulder, he staggered up the hill. His leg was stiffening up, but he did not notice. Plunging down into the grotto, he raced just one step ahead of the demons that would consume him.

Shadowland.

The Secret Caverns beckoned.

Sobbing, he broke through the emerald curtain and limped down the cool dark tunnel to where he kept the lantern, which he lit with fumbling, shaking fingers.

The Secret Caverns cried with him. He could hear them.

His leg slowed him down somewhat, but it didn't take him long to reach the Trove Room. With a final, grateful cry, he unzipped the sleeping bag and crawled inside.

He felt the Secret Caverns surrounding and comforting him like a mother's womb. Shivering, he curled himself into the fetal position until the warmth came back to him.

Then he put his thumb in his mouth and fell into a deep sleep.

SIXTEEN

Within ten minutes of Sergeant Dickerson's call, the little state park dam near Riverside Drive was swarming with officers of every size, shape, color, and badge. Kerrville Chief of Police Kirk Reynolds headed the task force of police detectives and sheriff's deputies. He was a young, aggressive chief with extensive experience in law enforcement who brooked no nonsense from the media. His tall, lanky form and youthful appearance often caused others to underestimate him, but not for long. The task force was assisted by several Texas Rangers and a small army of FBI agents, commanded by Special Agent Rick Forrester from the San Antonio office.

Dylan had expected the FBI to take on an overbearing, somewhat snooty attitude toward the small-town cops, but she found that they were respectful and courteous. Chief Reynolds did not seem to resent their presence, but to welcome it, and he and Agent Forrester appeared to have a good working relationship.

Dickerson introduced Dylan to Agent Forrester. He was classic FBI, from his conservative dark suit to his unreadable expression. He had graying dark hair, cool blue eyes, and more lines and wrinkles than he deserved for a man barely fifty. His handshake was firm and hard. She returned it in kind.

"A PI, huh?" The look he gave her was one of pure skepticism. He might as well have said, "A psychic, huh?"

Dylan did not blink from beneath his sardonic gaze. "I make it a point not to interfere with the police investigation,

118

Agent Forrester," she said smoothly, "but I do have some information that I think you will need."

They were standing together on the top of the small concrete dam. Below, crime scene specialists picked their microscopic way around the innocent-looking little book-bag, while officers in all kinds of uniforms combed the banks of the river on either side of the dam, searching for either a body or any other kind of evidence. Police detectives questioned bewildered merrymakers who, just minutes before, had been frolicking in the water, minding their own business. Uniformed officers kept traffic, the curious, and the media at bay behind yellow crime scene ribbons.

Agent Forrester did not dismiss Dylan's suggestion, but neither did he jump for joy. "Okay," he said. "We'll talk in my office." He led the way over to his car, where she joined him in the front seat. Immediately she pulled copies of all the scrolls she'd received, the strange little rock, and a purple ribbon. In minute, police-report detail, she filled him in on everything that had happened to date. When she was finished, all traces of skepticism had vanished from Forrester's face.

"Why weren't we told about this sooner?" he demanded, his face accusing.

"I'm not sure. There must have been a mix-up between local authorities and your office."

He grunted. "Where are the original scrolls?" he asked.

"Sergeant Dickerson is having them checked for prints."

His brow crinkled. "Our guys will want to check them over."

She nodded. "When we first found the bag, I flipped up the overflap with my pen. There is another scroll inside."

"Excellent," he said. "That means it hasn't been handled. We'll use the lasers on it."

"I was hoping your team could do a behavioral profile as well."

"Right. I'll line up a specialist. It takes a little time, though. Might be ten or twelve days."

Dylan bit her lip. *More wasted time.*

"You have any ideas on this guy?" he asked.

"Yes. But you have to promise me one thing."

He pursed his lips. "Can't do it."

She sat back in her seat and folded her arms over her chest. They locked gazes. Finally he said, "I can't promise anything. Just tell me what you want."

"I don't want all you glory boys to take over this thing, yank it out of my hands and keep me in the dark. This guy has some sort of personal thing going with me. Only me. You remove my influence from the case, there's no telling what he might do."

Forrester considered that. After a moment he said, "You could be right. Why don't we use you?"

"You mean as a bait?"

"Sure. We'll have you go more public. Do some media appearances. See if you can draw him out."

"I'm ready when you are."

"Fair enough. Now. What's your angle on this guy?"

She said, "Have you ever heard of a little store called Chris's Collectible Comics and Cards?"

He hesitated. "I remember something about the Scott boy's backpack being stolen. . . . Didn't he have some baseball cards in it that he'd bought there?"

"Right."

"We checked it out. There didn't seem to be any connection."

"So you talked to the guy who runs it."

"Yeah. What was his name? Chris . . ."

"Hel—" Dylan sat straight up. "Oh, my God."

"What?"

"Helmon. The guy's name is Chris Helmon."

"So? We ran a check on him. Guy's clean as a whistle."

"Helmon." She fumbled around in her bag and withdrew the rock with trembling hands. "Don't you see? His name begins with the letter *H.*"

• • •

Burning pain awoke Shadow from his unnatural sleep. He no longer remembered what had driven him to it in the first place.

Gingerly he stretched his legs inside the warm embryonic bag. Blood from his abrasions had dried and stuck to the brushed flannel interior. Shadow had to pull himself loose in places, and it was very painful.

Still stupefied from his deep sleep, he sat up and examined his wounds in the dimming light of the lantern. He remembered the accident which had caused them, but he did not remember the reason for the accident beyond going too fast.

The clothing around the wounds was shredded and filthy with dirt and blood. The road had scraped him all along one side of his body. He worried about Moonlight. He would not be able to take care of them here. The Secret Caverns were not equipped for it.

With a heavy sigh Shadow realized that there was only one thing he could do: He would have to go home.

And once there, Shadow knew, all his magic and special powers would most surely abandon him, leaving him cold and alone, just like the soul leaves the dead.

The search for the body of a child along the banks and beneath the waters of the Guadalupe River near the state park had to be called off at dark. Draggers and divers had found nothing but promised to resume their search at dawn. Local volunteers who knew the lushly foliated area along the banks of the river assisted officers in their fruitless search for some evidence of Jeremy Scott, alive or dead—or of Timmy Castillo or Eric Rathbone or anybody else who happened to fall into the clutches of this strange new predator. They found no more evidence of the boys, alive or dead.

Jeremy Scott's bright red backpack was spirited away by the FBI and sent to the Washington, D.C., lab for extensive testing. No one would be allowed to view or touch the bag's contents until after they had been thoroughly examined. Agent Forrester promised to keep Dylan apprised.

Chief Reynolds sent officers to track down Chris Helmon and bring him in for questioning by himself and Agent Forrester. Although Chris's Collectible Comics & Cards had closed by the time Jeremy's bag had been found, Agent Forrester assigned agents to begin an undercover operation as customers in the store, and Helmon's house was put under surveillance.

By darkfall much of the investigation had been taken out of Dylan's hands, but she knew it was far from over. Sergeant Dickerson put three good men hiding around the perimeters of her house, to watch for any sign of the killer's return. She was grateful. She knew it was the only way she'd be able to sleep.

Finally there wasn't much else Dylan could do for the night but go home. She was glad that Agent Forrester had taken her seriously, but she couldn't shake this nagging feeling that they were all missing something.

Molasses dragged at her feet as she entered the front door. Matt was asleep on the couch, a pile of computer papers resting on his chest. Some had slipped off to the floor. Pandora was draped over his legs like a big furry afghan.

Dylan stroked the animal, who made little murmuring noises in her throat, and laid the back of her hand to her husband's cheek, who smiled slightly in his sleep. Though it was only ten P.M., the house was uncharacteristically quiet. Dylan found that Caleb had already gone to bed, which was not unusual on days in which he had played particularly hard. He'd be up early the next morning, she knew.

Aidan was reading in bed. Dylan leaned against the doorjamb and studied this child, so precious to her that it was frightening. She kept thinking about Scotty, the anguish in his voice, the gray, raw grief on his face. When she had time to slow down, to think about it, to face it . . . she was terrified.

"Hi, Mom!" Aidan cried suddenly, her whole body happy as a puppy's.

Dylan crossed to the bed and sat on the edge of it, drinking in her child's face, the wonder of it and the magic, this babe of her womb, so sweet and so dear.

"What's the matter?" Aidan's face crinkled with concern.

"Nothing." To hide the desperation in her own eyes, Dylan hugged the child. One day Jeremy went off to softball practice, and then he was gone. Eric Rathbone left his family for five minutes to visit the rest room. Timmy Castillo went out to play with his friends. All gone. Probably forever.

The gaping, aching holes they left behind could never be filled. Once a mother lost the child of her womb, a father a part of his soul, there would never be any way to replace the loss. Never.

How could anyone steal another's life before it had even come of age? Was life so very worthless to them?

"You're worried about Jeremy, aren't you?" asked her wise little girl.

Dylan dabbed at her eyes and nodded. She was almost unspeakably weary.

"I know you'll find him, Mom."

Dylan shrugged. What was the use of finding a body, except to give his parents something to bury? Anger and hatred for the killer burned within her, but she had nowhere to go with it, no way to *use* it, and so it charred little parts of *her*. Depression, Dylan had once heard, was anger turned inward. And yes, she was angry at herself, for every day that passed without finding Jeremy, for every other child who disappeared, Dylan felt like a personal failure.

She shook those cobwebby thoughts from her mind. "What are you reading?"

"The Fellowship of the Ring."

"I thought you already read that."

"Well, almost. I didn't quite finish it. It's very long, you know."

Dylan flipped through the book. Over five hundred pages. She'd never have had the patience to stick with such a tome when she was Aidan's age. "Sometimes you amaze me, kid."

Aidan smiled. "I keep thinking I'll find some clues that will help you with the scrolls."

"Well, I appreciate that very much. I know if there's anything in there, you'll find it. It would be a big help."

"Mom? Do you think that guy that took those kids threw that rock through our window?" Anxiety lined the child's forehead.

Dylan smoothed away the lines with her fingertips. "I don't know, honey. But I don't want you to be afraid. Right this minute there are officers outside, watching the house. They'll protect us."

"What if he sneaks past them? Could he come through my window and steal me?" Aidan's voice shook.

"No way. Those officers would grab him before he even got here. And if they didn't, I would come in here and shoot him."

Aidan's eyes rounded. "You would?"

"Absolutely. Nobody's gonna hurt my baby."

Dylan didn't know if she was setting a very good example for her child, talking about shooting intruders, but it seemed to relieve Aidan's anxiety, which was more important for the time being. "Don't stay up too late reading," she said, kissing Aidan's soft cheek. By the time Dylan reached the doorway, Aidan was back into her book.

Dylan's body begged her to put it to sleep. But she couldn't. Every moment was another moment of time wasted. Instead, she took a bracing shower, washed her hair, and scrubbed the smeared makeup off her face. Then, wrapped in her favorite comfy terry cloth bathrobe, she started a pot of strong coffee.

Matt still slept in the living room. She left him where he was, turning off all lights except for one dim lamp.

In the kitchen she rummaged around in the refrigerator

for a snack. There wasn't much to choose from. Irritation toward Matt flared up. Did he expect her to do everything? Couldn't he go by the grocery store and stock up once in a while? Dylan knew her irritability was caused by fatigue, but this had always been a sore point between them.

In the crisper she found some luscious Hill Country peaches, plums, and tomatoes she'd picked up a few days before at a roadside fruit stand. Perfect. She grabbed up a handful of all she could carry and piled them up on the table for a fruity pig-out.

Then she spread out all the books and materials she'd bought earlier at Chris's Collectible Comics & Cards on the subject of Dungeons & Dragons. Peach in hand, she took a juicy bite and began to read.

The game was incredibly intricate. Both the *Player's Handbook* and the *Dungeon Master's Guide* were crammed with details in small, fine print. With the Dungeon Master's assistance, each player created a character for himself within certain classes, species, races, ages, and abilities. Armor and weapons were assigned to beginning characters by the Dungeon Master; more were earned through battle or overcoming other challenges in the game. Magic was a special privilege reserved for the very few. Those blessed with certain spell-casting abilities often had fewer weapons.

Combat and battle melees, as well as enemies encountered, were orchestrated by the Dungeon Master through gamepack guidelines, the throw of the die, and choices made by the participants during the course of the game, such as which tunnel to take in a cave. Successful navigation of the adventure often resulted in discoveries of vast amounts of treasure.

There was a certain spiritual alignment that characters were expected to follow, based upon whether they were basically good or evil, and points to be lost or won at each turn of the adventure.

At one point Dylan raised her head and stared in amazement at the little pile of peach pits and plum seeds on the table before her. She refreshed her empty coffee mug and glanced at the clock: two A.M.

She felt as if she'd journeyed to another world. It was all so bewildering. All these dry details began to run together after a while. Grainy-eyed and dopey, Dylan was about to call it quits for the night when, flipping through the *Dungeon Master's Guidebook*, her glance fell to the particular class of character known as the "Thief."

Among the various "Thief Abilities," one fairly jumped off the page: the ability to *hide in shadows*.

Trembling, Dylan fumbled for the *Player's Handbook* and looked up the Thief's abilities for more detail. Apparently a thief was able to assume invisibility by blending into his surroundings, a skill he could develop through *dress and practice*.

So *that's* what "Shadow" (of course, now his name made sense) meant when he talked about *not-being*.

Dylan was on to something. She *knew* it. Excitedly, she began flipping madly through the books' pages, poring over them, certain that somewhere she would find a definition for *mindslayer*.

But that's where Caleb found his mother the next morning, slumped over an open book, sound asleep, her mouth open and drooling, her hand flung out palm up on the table, her nearby coffee cup resting empty on its side; dreaming futile, frustrating fragments that eluded her just as assuredly as did the cunning *mindslayer*.

SEVENTEEN

When Dylan opened her eyes, she was in her own bed, dressed in one of Matt's roomy T-shirts. Slanting lines of sunshine crept from behind the Levelor blinds and sneaked across the floor toward the bed. She'd been so deeply asleep just the moment before that it was hard to realize she was awake. She stared dreamily at the clock. Ten A.M.

Dylan rocketed from the bed and banged out of the room, still so dazed from sleep that she didn't stop for a robe. The rest of the house was quiet. Bare feet slipping on the polished floors, Dylan careened through the kitchen and made a clumsy entrance into the office, hands shaking from electrified spurts of adrenaline.

Matt was on the telephone.

Frustrated, Dylan rubbed her hands over her face and dragged her fingers through her hair. The deep sleep had left her heavy-limbed and stupid-headed. *Oh, God, she'd wasted so much time!*

Matt hung up the phone and turned to her with a smile. "Morning, sleepyhead. I hope you feel a little more rested today."

"How could you turn my alarm off and let me sleep this late?"

"You didn't turn the alarm on in the first place, remember? You fell asleep at the kitchen table. You were so out of it when Caleb found you, he thought you were sick."

"Well, why the hell didn't you throw me into a cold shower, Matt? For God's sake, look at the time!"

He glanced lazily at his watch. "Uh-huh. Ten after ten. If

127

you hurry, you can probably still put in a sixteen-hour day."

"What's that supposed to mean?" Dylan wanted to rip his head off and stuff it down his throat. Or something.

"Look at yourself. You're worn out. You can't keep pushing yourself like this or you won't be any good to Campbell Scott or anybody else. You need a clear head."

"I don't need you to tell me what I need." Dylan's anger sent waves of heat off her body. She was all emotion, too exhausted even to argue logically. "How can you expect me to sleep when that boy is still out there somewhere?"

Matt's expression was undergoing a subtle change. It started out cheerful, moved into patient, and was now beginning to set in a stony line she recognized all too well but was too angry to care. "Dylan, you're getting lost in this case. Your emotions are bogging you down. If you want to be clearheaded enough to outwit this Shadow guy, you can't keep running on empty. I can tell you, he's not losing any sleep."

"How the hell would you know whether he's losing sleep or not?"

Matt's voice level dropped a little—a sure sign that he was fighting his own temper. "This is a ridiculous conversation, and I refuse to have it with you. You slept a little late, you're pissed off at yourself, and you're taking it out on me. Fine. But you're not doing anybody any good like this."

"Oh, it's so easy for you to tell me whether I'm doing any good or not. You sit here all day in your nice clean office with your nice quiet computer and write up all your nice reports, while I'm out there running myself ragged chasing down leads. . . . Tell me, how many grieving mothers have *you* held in your arms lately?"

Matt gripped the arms of the wheelchair so tightly his knuckles whitened and little purple spots appeared on them. He said, "You want to trade places? I'd be glad to, anytime."

Dylan knew she'd gone too far, knew she should apologize, but some little demon seemed to have possessed her in her sleep. All the rage she'd been stuffing down deep inside her, all the frustration and grief and despair, seemed to have staged some sort of coup and taken over her emotions. The whole world had gone black, and compromise was no longer a part of it.

She turned and walked out.

All the Dungeons & Dragons paraphernalia was still strewn over the kitchen table. It mocked her. Though she'd searched practically until dawn, there was no *mindslayer* to be found that was a part of the Dungeons & Dragons game.

Her stomach churned. There was fresh coffee, but she poured herself a small glass of club soda instead to see if it would settle her stomach. Though she'd had a shower the night before, she took another one, hoping that would shake the dust from her brain. It did, somewhat, but all that rage still burned inside her.

Jeremy Scott was dead, and she'd given false hope to his father. Jeremy Scott was dead, and some nutcase creep thought it was some kind of sick game. Jeremy Scott was dead, and his killer had come right up to her house in broad daylight to make a fool of her. *Jeremy Scott was dead*, and at the rate they were going, they'd never even find a body for his parents to bury. JEREMY SCOTT WAS DEAD, and so was Eric Rathbone, and so was Timmy Castillo, and so might be some other child because she was too *stupid* to read clues that were right in front of her eyes.

She hated herself. She hated Matt. She hated the whole world.

When Dylan had gotten dressed, she strode back into the office without fanfare and said simply, "I've made a decision."

Matt turned and gave her his unreadable cop face. She hated it when he did that, and she knew that he knew that she hated it. She said, "I'm going to do this case *gratis*."

"Oh, *you* decided, did you? So what am I, a big blob of bread dough? Is my little teeny tiny contribution so very minuscule that *you* can decide we work for free?"

"No, I didn't mean it like that—"

"I don't give a good goddamn how you meant it, Dylan. I would just like to remind you that this business is a partnership, even though it's clear that I don't do anything but sit around on my butt all day in my nice clean office working at my nice quiet computer writing my nice little reports while you, and you alone, are out there in the cold cruel world busting your hump for all those poor grieving mothers."

"Wait. I—"

"You just can't come strolling in here and announce to your resident flunky that *you* have decided anything. And besides, I have no intention of doing all this work for free. In case you have forgotten—and it truly seems at times that you have—we have kids of our own to feed and support. We need this money. We've worked hard for it. Campbell Scott appreciates that. He doesn't want our charity."

"It's blood money, Matt."

"Oh, for Christ's sake!" He pivoted, yanked up a thick file, and hurled it across the room. Papers showered out and drifted to the floor slowly, as if to frustrate him further. "We're running a *business*, Dylan! We offer a service. People hire us to take advantage of our expertise, expertise which took years of experience to acquire. They trust us that we will do the best job possible for a fair fee. They don't expect anything more or anything less. You can't stop charging a client every time you feel sorry for him." Matt's voice grew progressively louder as he spoke. Just like his daughter, high spots of color appeared in his cheeks. "What the hell are you talking about, anyway? *Blood money?* For Christ's sake!"

"We're collecting money off the body of a dead child, Matt! Doesn't that bother you?"

"We are offering comfort and the strong arm of assistance to a grieving family, doing everything in our power to find their son—dead or alive—and to see to it that his kidnapper comes to justice. They feel better, knowing we are out there looking. If it were Caleb, I'd pay every dime we had if that's what it took to find him. I wouldn't think twice about it and neither would you."

"Mom? Are you okay?"

They both jumped. Caleb stood in the doorway. Tension layered the room like cigarette smoke in a bar. Their son glanced from one to the other, anxiety etched on his face. Dylan crossed the room and gave his solid young body a hug.

"I was worried about you this morning," he said. "I thought you were sick. I tried to wake you up and you just kept saying nonsense stuff."

"You mean I was talking jabberwocky? I'm sorry, honey. I'm just real, real tired, that's all." Dylan glanced over the top of Caleb's head at Matt.

The boy ducked his head and buried it under her chin, a gesture from his early childhood. He wanted to say something, but he didn't want her to see his face. "Mom? That bad guy who's been taking those kids, Shadow? He wants to hurt you, doesn't he? Because he knows you're looking for him. That's why he threw the rock through the window."

Dylan considered her answer. "Don't forget, sweetie, I'm not the only one looking for this man. There are dozens of police officers and sheriff's deputies and Texas Rangers and FBI agents searching for him day and night. Now, why would he want to hurt me?"

Face still hidden, Caleb shrugged. Dylan could feel the tightness in his shoulders and back. This case was taking its toll on the entire family. "The thing is, he's crazy, Mom. He doesn't need a reason, does he?"

Good point. Dylan gave a *help me* glance toward Matt. He said, "Hey, big guy. Your mom's one tough old broad. She can take care of herself. Tell you the truth, I shudder to think what she might do to the guy if she ever got her hands on him."

Caleb chuckled, and Dylan felt him relax slightly. "Do you think you'll ever find him?" he asked and raised his face to look into her eyes. He was getting so tall, and so very much like his father, with the boy's face beginning to take on the contours of the man. Perhaps that was why a mother's love for her son was always so fiercely proud.

She ruffled his blond hair. "I couldn't do anything without your dad's help," she said, glancing significantly toward Matt. "We're a team. We'll find this creep. It's just a matter of time."

A faint shadow of a smile worked its way over Matt's face, and Dylan knew the fight was over. But things were still unsettled between them. Somehow the atmosphere in her home had undergone a subtle change. Her children were anxious and insecure, worried about their mother and frightened for themselves. She was frustrated and exhausted all the time, angry at the world. Matt felt under siege and was busily constructing all his little mental defenses even as she watched.

Somehow, this "Thief" who called himself Shadow had invaded Dylan's own home and stolen its most precious asset—their feeling of safety. Just a couple of weeks before, they'd been happy and easy in this old country house by the stream, and now their own fear stalked behind them like a shadow.

Somehow, Dylan knew, things would never be quite the same again, and if her rage hadn't been there to add starch to her spine, the sadness would have swallowed her right up.

EIGHTEEN

Although Dylan was not allowed to participate in or even to observe the questioning of Chris Helmon, she was permitted to view the videotape of the interview afterward at the police department. Chief Reynolds and Special Agent Forrester, both seasoned officers, made Chris look even younger than usual. Reynolds towered over him while Forrester sat like a stern father across the table from him. Helmon's combat fatigue jacket looked too big for him, and though the interview took place late at night, his chin showed little beard. He was friendly and cooperative and seemed to have no idea that he was under suspicion himself.

The interview lasted three hours.

Chris admitted again that he had known Jeremy Scott from his store and, when shown pictures of the other two boys, said he thought he'd seen Timmy Castillo in the store a time or two, but insisted that he'd never seen Eric Rathbone, except in newspaper photographs.

When Agent Forrester handed him a photocopy of the first scroll Dylan had found, it felt as if her heart would leap from her chest. Obviously they weren't going to fool around with this kid. He read it, handed it back, and said, "What's this?"

His face was so innocent, his eyes so guileless, that Dylan felt goose bumps crawling all over her skin. She'd only met one true psychopath in her life, and she would never forget those eyes as long as she lived.

She and another detective had been questioning a suspect about a series of slasher murders of prostitutes in South

Dallas. All through the interview he had looked at them just the way Chris Helmon was looking at Forrester.

Until her partner stepped out of the office. He was gone maybe two minutes. The suspect was handcuffed and sitting across a table from her. She was armed. They did not speak. But ever so slowly he'd turned his head and given her the full force of his penetrating gaze.

It was the only time she'd ever been raped by a man's eyes.

The reaction Dylan had experienced to that stare was primeval; the classic fight-or-flight of sheer raw terror. A cold sweat broke out over her body as their eyes met across that table, and for the first time she knew the smell of fear. Her hands went numb and she felt rooted to the chair. If her partner had been one minute later in returning, she'd have bolted from the room to escape the guy.

Or shot him.

But the detective returned; the killer glanced away; and in the very next moment his eyes and face were sweetly empty as a small boy's. For a few brief, mad minutes, Dylan had wondered if she'd imagined the whole transaction, but after the interview she'd had to change blouses because hers was soaking wet.

It's not that Dylan had never been afraid during her adventurous days riding patrol in some of Dallas's rougher neighborhoods, but this was entirely different, for one major reason: The guy *appeared to present no threat*. After all, his hands were behind his back, handcuffed. There was a table between them. She was armed. They didn't even speak.

All the same, those two minutes alone with him in that closed room were the scariest of Dylan's life.

And now . . . it was happening all over again. Here was this, this . . . *boy* . . . with his friendly smile and easygoing manner, so guileless and innocent and convincing . . . and yet, Dylan *knew*, and the officers questioning him knew, that he was a cold-blooded murderer of children.

And he had been friendly to Aidan. It made her physically ill.

By the time Forrester had shown him another scroll, Dylan was trembling. Again, he claimed not to have any idea what it meant, though he seemed progressively interested.

Just like Ted Bundy.

"You got a lot of Dungeons and Dragons stuff in your store," remarked Chief Reynolds.

Helmon's face lit up. "Yeah, it's my passion. I hand-painted all those figures," he added proudly.

"You play?" asked Forrester.

"Yes, sir. I'm the Dungeon Master of a little group. We get together one night a week and play."

Dylan's stomach knotted. *Oh, God, why hadn't she guessed that? It was so damned obvious!*

"Ever play any real games?" Forrester prodded.

"You mean live-action games, with costumes and stuff? Where you act out the adventure?"

"Right."

"No, but I'd love to. They have conventions and things where they do that. I hope to be able to go sometime soon."

Forrester glanced at Reynolds. Dylan felt the significance of the glance through the TV screen. Both remained impassive, but she knew they were as excited as she was.

That's when the idea came to her. It was one of those bold plans that come to hunters when they're figuring out how best to stalk their prey.

She leaned forward, watching every nuance of Helmon's expression, pushing the Pause button now and then to jot down a quote or other notes.

When Forrester handed him the rock with the letter *H* painted on it, Helmon turned it over and over in his hand, scrutinizing it.

Dylan's extremities went cold.

"You know why anybody would throw a rock with the

letter *H* on it through Dylan Tandy's window?" asked Chief Reynolds.

For a moment Dylan thought Helmon wasn't going to answer the question. He seemed fascinated by the rock. Finally he shook his head and handed it back.

Wait. Dylan hit the Rewind button, then replayed the scene with the rock. Again. And again.

No doubt about it. When Helmon handed over the rock, *the ghost of a smile fluttered across his face.*

Dylan told no one at the police department about her plan. One good thing about not being a cop anymore was that she no longer had to go through channels to get permission for anything. Naturally she intended to discuss it with Matt, but she figured that there was less chance of something going wrong if as few people as possible knew about it. After all, she reasoned, her life would not be in danger; she would not need any backup. She would also not need a platoon of cops around to give her away.

Meanwhile, Chief Reynolds called a press conference. With Dylan standing just to the side and behind him, he made an announcement to the growing crowd of reporters and camera crews who had descended on the small town since the kidnappings began.

"This investigation has had the full cooperation and the integral involvement of the Tandy-Armstrong Investigations, Inc. of Kerrville. The kidnapper has contacted Dylan Tandy on several occasions, and we believe that the only way we are going to be able to reach him is through Ms. Tandy."

"Didn't you find Jeremy Scott's backpack?" interrupted a disembodied voice from somewhere behind the blinding lights.

"Yes. It has been sent to the FBI labs in Washington, D.C., for a full analysis."

"Was there any sign of the other boys?"

"No."

"How has the killer contacted Ms. Tandy?"

"I'll let her answer that."

Dylan stepped up to the clot of microphones and tried not to squint into the lights. She considered her words carefully. She'd already been briefed by Chief Reynolds and Agent Forrester on what things they did and did not want released to the media. They had to have several unknown facts to use in ferreting out all the false confessions such a public case seemed to attract.

"He calls himself Shadow," she said, "and he seems to be lost in some sort of fantasyland. He writes poems about it."

"What kind of fantasy?" shouted someone.

"That's what we're still trying to figure out," said Dylan guardedly.

"Can we see the poems?"

"Not yet. The FBI is still analyzing them."

"Have you got any fingerprints?"

"That's one of the things they're testing for."

"Is there any evidence that the missing boys are alive or dead?"

"There's no evidence one way or the other."

"Do you have a profile yet on the kidnapper?"

"We're still working on it."

"Have you got any suspects?"

"No one has been arrested yet."

"Do the families know that you've been contacted?"

"Yes. Officers have briefed all the families, and they are all willing to cooperate in any way they can."

"Why did the kidnapper contact you, Ms. Tandy, instead of the police or a reporter?"

"We don't know. My agency was hired by the family of Jeremy Scott to assist in the investigation. We don't know why the kidnapper chose to communicate with us."

"You have two kids of your own, don't you?"

"Yes."

"How are they taking it?"

"They're a couple of tough kids. They're doing all right."

"What did the poems say?"

"I'd rather not say at this time."

"Did the kidnapper contact any of the families?"

"Yes. The Scott family received one poem."

"What did it say?"

"As I stated before, I'd rather not say at this time. We don't want anything to compromise this investigation."

"You say he calls himself Shadow?"

"That's right."

"And he lives in a place he calls Shadowland?"

"Well, I said *fantasyland*. I don't know what he calls it."

Shadow jumped to his feet in front of the magic box. *They knew about Shadowland!*

He couldn't breathe. He couldn't breathe! He stumbled around until he could find a small paper sack, which he breathed into over and over until his heart stopped banging against his rib cage.

How could they know about Shadowland? *How?*

He hadn't said a word about it in any of the riddles. By the goblins, *did they know about the Secret Caverns, too?*

How could they know?

It was her. It had to be her. Of course, the Dragon Queen had special powers. She *knew*. And she had told everybody!

Shadow clutched his arms to his chest and rocked back and forth. What was he going to do? What was he going to do? *They knew about Shadowland!* Oh, no. Oh, *no*!

He rocked and whimpered. The Secret Caverns would be angry at him. He had to do something. He had to make it up to the Secret Caverns. He had to let them know that he could still be the *mazemaster*!

The Quest.

Yes. He would have to hurry now. The Magic Amulet would make a bountiful gift to the Secret Caverns, the most precious treasure of all!

And there was only one way to get the Magic Amulet.

Pacing the floor in front of the magic box, talking softly to himself, he began to plan.

By the time the afternoon papers went to press and the evening news was broadcast, one slip of a reporter's tongue had given a name to this nameless fear that had gripped the Hill Country for several weeks. Headlines read: SHADOWLAND KIDNAPPER STALKS HILL COUNTRY, KERRVILLE IS "SHADOWLAND" TO DERANGED KIDNAPPER, SHADOW COVERS KERRVILLE, and SHADOWLAND: FANTASY BECOMES GRIM REALITY TO KERRVILLE RESIDENTS.

The AP picked it up, and reporters from ABC, CBS, NBC, and CNN began making travel arrangements for Kerrville. Television docudrama producers and book publishers read the stories with relish, and soon there were so many phone calls to the Tandy-Armstrong Investigations, Inc. that Matt had to put on the answering machine to take all messages.

Kerrville residents were horrified. As if it weren't bad enough that someone had snatched three children in broad daylight from their beautiful, friendly, and quiet town; now the attention of the entire country was focused on them as if the whole town were filled with lunatics. City planners were deeply worried about the long-term effects on the tourist industry which supported the town; while at the same time, they were afraid to let their own children play outside in the front yard.

Townsfolk agonized: How could this happen in such an idyllic place? Theirs was a town anybody would love to grow up in, a town some people visited on vacation and never left again. It was a place to take your family to an outdoor play, or float down the river on inner tubes, or stand in a shady spot and capture on canvas. In a sense, Kerrville possessed some of the finer aspects of a life long-since vanished, a Mamie Eisenhower sort of existence where people were cocooned from the violence of their big-city neighbors in San Antonio, Austin, Houston, and Dallas—or Chicago or New York or Miami or LA.

Kerrville was supposed to be a place of sunshine—not a Shadowland.

But it wasn't just the townspeople of Kerrville who watched the evening news and worried. People all over the country who were watching soon realized that, if madness and murder could stalk a place like Kerrville, then everybody, everywhere was in danger.

And there were no safe places left for the children.

NINETEEN

After the press conference, Sergent Dickerson took Dylan aside. "Forrester faxed a copy of the latest scroll over to the chief. He wants to go over it with you and see if you have any idea what it might mean."

With a slight quivering of nerves, Dylan followed him into a room where Chief Reynolds sat with a Texas Ranger and three other detectives who were working on the case. She took her seat with the men.

Reynolds said, "Forrester has asked that I make no copies of the poem, because we don't want any chance that the media could get hold of it. If that happened, they'd have a field day and Lord only knows what it would do to this guy. I'm going to pass it around for y'all to look at, then we'll brainstorm ideas."

Dylan awaited her turn anxiously, and when she took the sheet of fax paper from the detective seated next to her, she couldn't hide a slight trembling in her hand. Sergeant Dickerson bent over and read along with her.

> *For secrets to unfold and clues to unriddle*
> *Perhaps the Dragon Queen should start in the*
> *   middle.*
> *After searching the Castle high and low,*
> *She might find a message from the Shadow.*

Dickerson took the sheet from her hand and passed it on. Dylan wished she could write it down.

141

When they had all seen the poem, Chief Reynolds asked for ideas. For a long moment no one spoke.

"Maybe the Castle is someplace like the courthouse," said Sergeant Fuentes, a shaggy-headed, mustached detective who normally did most of his work undercover in the seedier parts of town.

"Shit. That would take some nerve," said George Nachlinger, the big brawny blond Texas Ranger assigned to their district.

"Apparently lack of nerve isn't one of this guy's problems," commented Dickerson.

"Naw. He's got plenty of nerve when it comes to defenseless little boys," said Brent Hickman, a short, squat, balding detective who had recovered more stolen property than any other detective in the Criminal Investigations Department.

"Let's not get off the subject," said the chief. "Anybody have any other ideas?"

"Maybe the Castle is his own house," said Dylan with a shudder. She could see by the looks on the faces of the other officers that they felt the same way about it as she did. They couldn't search anybody's house without a warrant, and they couldn't obtain a warrant without solid probable cause. And so far, badly though they may want to search Chris Helmon's store and home, they had absolutely no evidence that would back a warrant. Nobody had been able to place him at the scenes of the boys' disappearances, or make any more connection between him and the missing boys than that a couple of them had been customers in his store. Nor could they drum up any other excuse to search. His background check had turned up no evidence of drug dealing or any other crime. All they could hope to do at this point was watch him like a hawk and pray he screwed up somewhere down the line.

"What do you suppose he means by 'in the middle'?" asked Fuentes.

"Who knows," said somebody gloomily.

"Let's go back over where each note was found," said the chief. "Dylan, tell us again."

In meticulous detail Dylan explained again about finding the first scroll in the boughs of a juniper tree in the park from where Jeremy Scott had disappeared; and finding the second scroll in the public rest room of the state park, where little Eric Rathbone had last been seen. The third scroll, they all knew, had been placed in the Scotts' mailbox. This fourth one had been found in Jeremy's backpack beside the state park dam, which had been alluded to in the third poem as the "riverside wall."

Something about laying it all out one-two-three triggered a small doubt which had been lying dormant in Dylan's mind since the investigation began. "Wait a minute, guys," she said. "Has anybody searched the construction site where the first boy—Timmy Castillo—disappeared? Could the kidnapper have left a scroll there?"

"We all covered it with a fine-tooth comb, looking for Timmy," said Nachlinger.

"Yeah. But you were looking for a *boy*, not a small rolled-up piece of paper."

"Still . . ."

"*Still*, you didn't find the first scroll when Jeremy disappeared, did you? Or the second?"

"Naw, we had to depend on a big-time PI to do that," said Hickman resentfully.

"That's not what I meant."

"Aw, settle down, Hickman," said Dickerson. "Tandy's got a good point. I'll go with her to check it out."

"I'll go with you," said Nachlinger.

"I'll call Forrester for some additional help," said the chief. "We got twenty-five FBI agents hanging around here, looking for something to do."

Everybody except Hickman chuckled.

"I still think the 'Castle' is the courthouse," said Fuentes.

"All right," agreed the chief, "take Detective Hickman and a few FBI people and look around. Any other ideas?"

The brainstorming went on for another hour, but although everybody in the room read the poem over at least three times, in the end nobody had a clue as to what it meant.

The search of the construction site from where the first child had vanished while playing with friends took up the entire afternoon and evening, with more than a dozen FBI agents, three Texas Rangers, Sergeant Dickerson, and Dylan. There was a sense of futility about the search from the beginning, because so much time had elapsed from when Timmy disappeared, and the site had changed dramatically with ongoing construction.

Over vehement protest, the workers were sent home. Then, using the baseline method of search, coordinates were stretched with string over every inch of the site, while officers and agents crawled on hand and knees or climbed up scaffolding, hunting every nook and cranny, every hole and puddle, for a little piece of paper rolled up and tied with a purple ribbon. They even searched earth-moving equipment and the insides of hundreds of pipes.

They found nothing.

By nine P.M. heat waves still baked the earth. The sun had dipped down behind the trees, but full dark would not come for another hour. Dylan pushed the hair out of her face with sweaty, grimy hands and picked out Sergeant Dickerson leaning against his car and smoking a cigarette. She hadn't even known he smoked and wondered if he was trying to quit. She walked up and slouched wearily against the car next to him.

"Maybe it got covered up with a load of dirt," she said.

"Or maybe he didn't get warmed up until the second kid."

"Or maybe—" Dylan straightened up and faced Dickerson. "You know, something has bothered me about this case from the beginning."

"The Castillo case? Or this whole Shadow thing?"

"Well, I feel as if the Castillo situation is entirely different from the last two. This Shadow guy likes attention too much. He's too proud of what he's done and how cute he's being with all these poems and stuff. He'd never have been able to stand still for over two weeks without contacting somebody, somewhere, with some kind of message. I've talked to the Castillos since you guys last interviewed them, and they still haven't received any kind of message from anybody remotely resembling the Shadow."

Dickerson took a long drag on his cigarette and squinted off to the west into an orange sky. "That may be true, but he just left that first scroll in a tree. You never went public with it, so he never knew you found it."

"Unless he went back to the tree and checked."

He tossed the cigarette down and watched it glow for a moment before crushing it with his shoe. "Okay. So how was he supposed to know *you* found it?"

"Maybe he didn't. I figure he heard about me from the Scotts' press conference right after they hired me and just picked me out as his opponent in this sick little game."

"But that still doesn't mean that he knew for sure that you got his messages."

"Well, I damn sure got the one with the letter *H* painted on it."

He frowned. "You thinking he's been following you?"

"God, I hope not. I'd hate to think that, as a PI, I'd be too blind and/or stupid not to realize when I'm being followed."

"But you think he's been watching you."

"I don't know about that, Andy, but I expect he may have been watching you guys go over the locations where the boys were taken. Maybe from off in the bushes somewhere with binoculars."

Dickerson patted his breast pocket as though looking for another cigarette, seemed to think better of it, and said, "They say serial killers often do that. They'll even help out in the search, you know, with all the volunteers." He shook his head. "Shit, that makes practically the whole town suspect."

"You've checked out all the known sex offenders in the area?"

"Yeah. We're keeping our eye on a few. None of them are smart enough to write poetry, though." His smile was fleeting. "Anyway. Back to the Castillo boy. What are you saying?"

"I'm saying that I think this Shadow guy may not be responsible for Timmy Castillo's disappearance."

Dickerson's Marine Corps jawline clenched. "C'mon, Tandy. We can't make an assumption like that this early in the game. Hell, maybe that first poem was about the Castillo kid *and* Jeremy Scott. It's not like the poem spells out anybody's name or anything."

Dylan was silent for a minute. She had never thought of that possibility. Still, until they had a firm suspect, most any scenario could fit . . . including the chance that they could be looking for *two* killers.

Matt's comment about putting in sixteen-hour days still rang in Dylan's ears when she pulled up in front of the house at ten-thirty. Back in her cop days she occasionally went out with the other detectives after their shift for a drink and a chance to clear all the blood and horror out of their minds before facing their families. But she wasn't one of the boys anymore. She realized, for the first time, how lonely Matt must have been through the years for that camaraderie. It wasn't that none of his old friends came around anymore; it was just that he was no longer a *part* of them. Just as she wasn't really a part of Chief Reynolds's team. She was included in the investigation, but she wasn't a *part* of them. She regretted, now, not being more sensitive to Matt in the past about things like that.

She regretted a lot of things.

As before, Caleb was already asleep and Aidan was reading in bed. Dylan had always despised the term *quality time,* but she had to face the fact that she had not only *not* taken any quality time with her kids recently, she hadn't spent *any* time with them at all.

Not to mention her husband. She found him propped up

in bed, reading the *Kerrville Daily Times*. She sat down on the edge of the bed beside him, and he laid down the paper. Dylan covered his hand with hers. "What I said this morning was unforgivable," she said. "I am so very sorry."

He nodded.

"I'm not trying to find any excuses or anything, but this case is making me crazy."

"You don't think I'm worried about it, too? That I'm not as heartsick about those boys as you are?"

"I know."

"Jesus, Dylan, I *worry* about you. This nut seems to have picked you out of the crowd for this macabre little game of his, and you are deliberately putting yourself into the position to provoke him further. There's no telling what he might do. Every time you walk out that door in the morning, I wonder if you'll make it back."

"But I was a cop all those years, Matt."

"Come on. You left patrol after I got shot. Homicide dicks pick through the droppings of the dead like vultures. They don't put themselves in the line of fire."

She grimaced. "I always thought you had a lot more respect for what I did than that."

"Aw, Red! I'm not trying to start a fight here. I'm trying to tell you how I feel."

"You never used to worry like this when I rode patrol," she pointed out.

"I was a cop then, too. I was out there with you, in a sense. This sitting at home waiting is torture."

She smiled faintly. "Now you know how police wives have felt for years."

"Yes, I do. And I have a helluva lot more respect for them now than I ever did before. They've got more courage than their husbands. Believe me, it's much easier to be out there doing it than sitting around worrying about someone who is."

She squeezed his hand. "I can take care of myself."

He shook his head.

"What?"

"The guy invaded our *home*, Dylan. You know Dickerson pulled those deputies off surveilling our house when the manpower was needed to search for the Rathbone boy. The kids are upset. If you were here more, you'd see the effect this whole thing is having on our household."

If you were here more. There was an accusation in the comment, but Dylan didn't take the bait. She felt bad enough about that as it was.

"I just have a hinky feeling about all this," he said, using the old cop's term about entering a situation that didn't feel "right" just before all hell broke loose.

Dylan stretched out on the bed beside her husband and put her head on his chest. He put his strong arms around her and held her so close she could hear the comforting *thu-thump* of his heart. *Hinky* was just the right word to express the way Dylan had felt all along, ever since Timmy Castillo had vanished.

It was a miserable, persistent, uneasy presence that gnawed at the underside of her skin with tiny sharp teeth of fear, warning her that, before it was all over, she would one day be eaten alive by it.

TWENTY

Winnie Freeman looked around for a doorbell to press and, finding none, banged on the door of an apartment located in a modest, run-down complex dominated by divorcées, single parents, college students, and lower middle-class families who all hoped to move into a home of their own someday. Marty had told her that they always played Dungeons & Dragons at his apartment on Saturday nights. This was her first time ever to play, and she wasn't sure what to expect. She tugged at her short, black, somewhat scraddledy hair with nervous fingers, pushed heavily framed glasses up her nose, and glanced around, her brown eyes taking in the little hibachi grills set out on the narrow balconies, the Big Wheels and tricycles, the modest compact cars and old clunkers filling the parking lot.

The Dungeon Master himself opened the door. He was dressed in camouflage fatigues and torn, faded blue jeans. He appeared to be very young, and he blinked at her from beneath a thatch of dull brown hair.

"Hi. I'm Winnie Freeman. Marty Davis invited me?"

"Oh, yeah. So you're the one I made up a character chart for. Come on in." She followed him into a small, cramped living room crowded with all the evidence of a bachelor's existence: piles of newspapers, a board-and-brick bookcase crammed with books every which way, an extravagant stereo system lining one wall, girlie posters, and junk food clutter.

She spotted Marty sprawled in a recliner and lifted her hand in greeting.

Marty Davis was obese. The T-shirt he wore barely stretched across his ponderous belly. There was a large pimple on his nose that had come to a head, and he had a five o'clock shadow. There was a giant bag of potato chips on the floor beside his chair, along with a two-liter bottle of Coke that he seemed to be drinking by himself. "Ah. Our new fighter arrives," he said, without getting up. "Let me introduce you around. You know our Dungeon Master, Chris Helmon?"

"I don't think so." She extended her hand, and he took it in a limp, weak handshake.

A scrawny girl with a tight skullcap of thin brown hair gave her a nervous smile. "That's Peggy," he said, then pointed to a big, baby-faced young man with cherub cheeks and thick downy red hair. "That's Greg."

The group ranged in age from late teens to early twenties. Chris was the oldest, though he looked as young as Greg. Winnie took a seat on the couch beside Peggy. Greg sat across the room in a straight-backed kitchen chair. Chris settled himself cross-legged in the middle of the floor.

Winnie noticed a colored-ink drawing in Peggy's lap, and she bent over to see. It depicted a gorgeous voluptuous blond warrior woman holding perched on her arm a magnificent hawk. The woman emanated power and strength. "It's my character, Empatha," said Peggy in a soft, shy voice. "She possesses various psionic powers, including animal telepathy."

"Wanna see my guy?" asked Marty. He handed a similar drawing over to Peggy, who passed it to Winnie. "He's a Paladin," he added. Winnie gazed in wonder at the drawing of a muscle-bound, sword-carrying, lance-toting, handsome fighter standing next to a huge, powerful, armored black stallion. "His name is Thor, after the ancient Norse god of thunder, and this is his warhorse, Lightning. Thor has the power to affect the undead as well as devils and demons, and his sword is a magic Holy Sword."

"My character's a cleric named Windwalker," said Greg.

He held up a tiny cloaked miniature holding what looked like a tall stick in his hand. Greg touched the stick. "It's his quarterstaff," he explained. "My cleric is also a fighter, and he uses the staff as a weapon."

"Who's your character?" asked Peggy.

"She's just a fighter," said Winnie. "I didn't know I was supposed to give her a name." They all stared at her. "I guess I could call her . . . uh . . . Rowena. Rowena was a heroine of ancient British legends." They nodded approvingly. "It's my real name," Winnie added softly, but only Peggy seemed to hear.

The Dungeon Master reached into his jeans pocket and withdrew a miniature of a lovely maiden warrior, clad in a silver form-fitting suit of mail, her long chestnut hair flowing out behind her. Clasped in one hand was a graceful bow. A quiver of arrows rested on her back. He handed it to Winnie. "Here is your character, Rowena," he said. "You may keep her if you wish."

"Oh!" she cried. "She's beautiful. I'd love to keep her. Thank you." She examined the miniature. Every single detail had been lovingly rendered with brushes that must have been no more than a hair's-breadth wide.

"Now. Are we ready?" he asked.

Peggy got up from the couch and fetched a box of matches, which she used to light candles placed all over the room. Then she turned out the lights and rejoined Winnie on the couch. Immediately the room and small gathering there took on a spooky, otherworldly aspect.

"Let's take a moment of silence to get into character," intoned the Dungeon Master.

Winnie glanced around. Everyone was staring at one candle or the other. Some fondled their miniatures. She held Rowena up and studied her in the mellow aura of the candle glow.

"This adventure takes place in the kingdom of Magna. Someone has stolen the Magic Amulet from the palace and brought eternal night to the kingdom. Until the Magic

Amulet is found, the kingdom will never know sunshine again. King Saxon has assembled your group to find the amulet. He has a personal interest in this amulet, for as soon as it disappeared, his daughter, Princess Aurelia, became very ill. If the Magic Amulet is not found soon, Princess Aurelia will die. The king has offered a magnificent reward to you, if you return the Magic Amulet to Magna. What say you?"

"Your Majesty," said Thor in a deep throaty tone, "it will be our honor to do your bidding. We pledge our lives to the task."

"Very well," said the king. "You will each have ten pieces of gold for the journey." He turned to Rowena. "For many years I have been plagued by my arch enemy, the Crimson Dragon." He reached out his hand. A servant scurried forward, bowed low before the king, and placed a golden arrow in his outstretched hand. King Saxon said, "My archers and magic-users have toiled for years, perfecting this arrow. It is a killing arrow. All you need is one hit in the eye of the dragon, and he will be instantly slain." He gave the arrow to Rowena. "If, as I suspect, the Crimson Dragon is behind this foul deed, then I charge you with his death."

Rowena knelt before the king and said, "My liege, I am honored. I will not fail."

The king nodded sadly. "I bid thee well."

The Dungeon Master spoke: "Empatha has already received telepathic messages from the palace hounds that a bandit group of orcs have spirited away the Magic Amulet and headed into the Forest of Gloom. Even moonlight does not penetrate this dark and hellish wood. Your group, led by Thor, enters the forest. Rowena brings up the rear.

"Empatha receives messages from forest animals along the path that the orcs have headed for Cloud Mountain, where they intend to hide the Amulet in a cave.

"Suddenly the Paladin, Thor, stiffens and announces to the group that he detects great evil awaiting them ahead. Do you wish to go forth or turn back?"

"Thor never retreats from danger, but he is willing to consult with his cleric. Windwalker, what say you?"

"We are a strong group of warriors and should be able to face any danger."

"Empatha is willing."

"Rowena is ready."

"Okay. As you continue on the path, you see a small group of heavily armed goblins. What do you choose to do about it?"

"Fight," said Thor.

The others nodded.

"Okay. Thor, you reach the goblins first and draw your lance and hurl it. Did you hit him?"

Thor tossed the die, counted numbers, and said, "Yes."

"Do you wish to go up and see if he's dead?"

"Not yet. We must tend to the others."

"Rowena, you draw and fire two arrows in quick succession. Throw the die to see if your arrows reached their mark."

Rowena threw the die, and Empatha counted the numbers for her, since she was inexperienced in the complexities of ten and twenty-sided dice.

The Dungeon Master said, "You have killed two goblins. Well done. A fourth goblin draws a dagger and attacks Windwalker. Windwalker, do you choose to cast a spell on the goblin?"

"Not necessary. I strike a blow to the goblin with my quarterstaff." He tossed the die. "He is mortally wounded."

"Okay. Thor, you pull out a dagger of your own and go to it in lethal hand-to-hand combat. Throw the die."

Thor did so. "You kill the goblin," said the Dungeon Master, "but you are given two hit points, and are wounded. What do you wish to do?"

"Two hit-points isn't that bad of a wound. All Thor needs is a good night's rest to be restored."

"All right. The fierceness of your group's fighting has broken the morale of the goblins, and they have run away.

Now, do you choose to check the first goblin to see if he is dead?"

"Yes."

"Okay. You approach the goblin, and he is indeed dead. Inside a pouch hanging at his belt is a map. Empatha learns from an owl in a tree that the map leads to the cave where the orcs have hidden the Magic Amulet. Do you wish to continue?"

Everyone shouted yes. Rowena was proud that she had killed two goblins in quick succession. She couldn't wait to get to the cave and find the Magic Amulet.

The adventurers, weary now from their long trek, traveled until they left the forest. They stayed the night at an inn, doubling up two per room in order to save their gold. A thief tried to con Rowena out of her journey-pouch, but she outsmarted him. The others were pleased that a newcomer could be so clever. They commended her, and she felt as if she were being accepted as part of the group.

The next morning they set out for Cloud Mountain, where the orcs had hidden with the Amulet. Cloud Mountain had once been a beautiful place, they were told, but ever since the evil Dragon took up residence there, all the trees had died and the grass turned to straw. Deadly lightning flashed continually over it from roiling dark clouds.

The party chose not to enter the cave by the main opening in the mountain, but to climb the mountain halfway to where there was a hidden entrance discerned by the cleric. Unfortunately, they underestimated the difficulty of the climb and were tired by the time they reached the small opening.

Thor had to leave Lightning behind. He drew a protective shield around the warhorse with his Holy Sword.

Once inside, the party found themselves in what they thought was a little hollowed-out room, but when they tried to walk to the end of the room, they found the wall was much farther away than it looked. Too late they realized they'd entered a space distortion trap, which rendered their map null and void and cost them valuable points.

When they attempted to return the way they had come, they fell down a long chute trap, which deposited them right in the middle of a room crowded with orcs. Screaming orcs began attacking them from all levels. They stood their ground, but the fight was bloody. Empatha was badly wounded and Rowena had to carry her. Finally the remaining orcs retreated into a dark recess of the cave. The cleric used his power of *windwalking* and became a mist, traveling ahead of the others to scout their destination unseen.

With great excitement he reported that he had seen a massive red dragon in a lair just ahead. However, the dragon's lair was just the other side of a pit crawling with deadly vipers. In order for them to cross the pit, Windwalker cast a spell on the vipers, who joined themselves, head to tail, to form a rope ladder of sorts which they used to cross the pit.

The hideous Dragon awaited them, huge and stinking, slimy and foul. The Magic Amulet dangled from a chain around his neck. As soon as he saw them, he belched a great stream of fire which singed their hair and made their weapons too hot to handle.

Empatha was far too weak to fight. Thor charged the Dragon but was driven back by the sulphurous flames. Windwalker attempted to cast a freezing spell on the Dragon, but the Dragon had drawn a Ring of Spell-Turning around himself, which threw the spell back onto the caster. Windwalker was immediately frozen in position.

Thor was given the choice to use his lance or draw his Holy Sword, which would give double damage on impact, since his alignment was Lawful Good and he was facing an opponent from the Chaotic Evil alignment. He chose to use the Holy Sword. He began thrusting and parrying with the Dragon in an attempt to distract it so that Rowena could draw her magic killer arrow. The Dragon was a powerful and terrible opponent. For each thrust of the Sword, he slashed at Thor with his mighty razor claws. After each round with the sword, he would belch fire.

Rowena strove mightily to get into position to draw her arrow, but the Dragon seemed to have eyes in the back of its head, because he used his tremendous tail to sweep across the cave floor and knock her down every time she tried.

Finally Thor was badly wounded and rendered virtually no threat to the Dragon. Rowena, alone, faced the glowing bloodred eye of the beast. She had never felt such terror, but Rowena wanted the Magic Amulet more than she desired to live, and so she drew her bow and affixed the arrow.

The Dragon breathed out a great wall of fire, but in the last second Rowena fired her arrow and threw her body up against the tunnel wall. The flames singed her brows.

The arrow struck the Dragon in its glaring evil eye. With a mighty scream he rose to a great height, then fell with a crash so great it caused an earthquake which could be felt all the way to Magna.

The freezing spell was instantly revoked. Windwalker used his healing power to return Empatha to health. Rowena climbed atop the putrid beast and extricated the Magic Amulet from his claws.

There was so much treasure hidden in the cave that they could take only those precious gemstones that they could carry in their journey-pouches.

Outside, Cloud Mountain had returned to its original splendor. The sky was a clear, clean blue, with cottony clouds adorning the mountain peaks. All the trees had bloomed, and the wildflowers were so profuse the air was perfumed. Lightning was grazing peacefully in a patch of clover.

When the band arrived back in Magna, the sun shone from the sky and all the villagers cheered. Rowena returned the Magic Amulet to the king, who placed it around his dying daughter's neck. Aurelia was instantly healed. King Saxon presented a treasure chest of gold to each of the heroes.

As a reward for her courage and valor, Rowena was elevated by the Dungeon Master two entire skill levels and given a magic arrow that could be used to find the lost. There was a great celebration at the palace. Festive candles lit the ballroom.

Suddenly Empatha rose and began blowing out the candles. A great light flooded the room. Rowena blinked and looked around her. There she was, back in Marty's apartment, staring at a skinny girl named Peggy.

Rowena/Winnie rose awkwardly to her feet, embarrassed to be so confused by the sudden intrusion of reality. Shaking hands with the Dungeon Master and calling a hasty good-bye to Marty, Winnie Freeman hurried out the door, clutching her little miniature close.

Still lost in the enchanted world of Cloud Mountain, she had trouble finding her way home, but by the time she'd parked in front of her house, she was emerging from the spell that had been cast over her by the Dungeon Master. She entered the front door and crossed dreamily into her bedroom, where she stood gazing at herself in the mirror.

Then, she underwent her third transformation of the day. First, she took off the thick glasses. Reaching up, she tugged at the short black hair until it had fallen off in her hand. Next, she bent over and removed a couple of brown contact lenses from her eyes.

Rubbing her fingers vigorously over her taut scalp, she shook out her rich auburn hair, turned to her husband, and grinned.

"I think I'm beginning to figure this Shadow guy out," said Dylan.

Matt answered, "Tell me about it."

TWENTY-ONE

"The Dungeon Master is like a small god," she said, pulling a brush through the snags in her hair. Matt watched her from his favorite spot on the chaise longue, the afghan tossed over his withered legs. Pandora strutted into the room and leapt onto the afghan, where she got comfy and settled in. "He orchestrates the entire adventure. The characters get to make choices, but he decides which choices they'll have to choose from. The only real chance in the game is left up to the throw of the die."

"Sounds a little like real life." Matt stroked Pandora, who preened beneath his hand.

"Oh, no. The thing is, it's very seductive to enter into this fantasy world; almost intoxicating." Dylan sprawled on the bed and propped her chin up on her hands. "In this magical world you get to be all the things you aren't in real life. In fact, you can be anything you want. You can be a spell-caster or a warrior, telepathic or all-wise. You can be beautiful or you can be horribly deformed. You can be evil or you can be good—it's all up to you."

"Not like real life, in which we can't choose whether we want to be born in a ghetto or not."

"Exactly."

"But in real life you can choose to leave that ghetto if you want."

"True. But it isn't easy. You must have great courage and persistence and ambition to overcome the handicaps you were born with—or stricken down with." Dylan smiled gently.

Matt returned the smile.

"If you lack courage; if you are lazy or weak or frightened in real life, you might choose to *escape* your existence rather than fight your way out of it."

"Through drugs or alcohol."

"Exactly. Or through fantasy." She flopped over on her back.

"Okay," said Matt. So the guy hates his life. Maybe he was abused as a kid or whatever. He wants to escape the reality of his existence, only he can't do it as a form of innocent entertainment of the imagination, which is what the game was intended to provide. Instead, he gets addicted to it."

"And the more his addiction to his fantasy—and his fantasy character—grows, the less tolerable his real life becomes."

"And the more he immerses himself in his fantasy."

"Until the fantasy becomes reality."

"And the reality becomes fantasy."

Dylan rolled onto her side and felt something dig into her thigh. She reached into her jeans pocket and withdrew the miniature. *Rowena.*

Yes. She was definitely coming closer to understanding the workings of Shadow's mind.

"One interesting thing about Helmon I noticed is that, as Dungeon Master, he tends to play fast and loose with the rules of the game."

"How so?"

"I'm no expert, but from what I read in the manuals, it seemed to me that he was making up rules as he went along."

"Do you think that's significant?"

"It could be. The way I see it, in the real-life game he's playing with the so-called Dragon Queen . . . he gets to make up *all* the rules. In fact, Marty told me that he gets into power plays with the other players sometimes. A couple of the players got fed up and left. Dickerson's checking on everyone who was a regular. Most of them are just kids, though, barely older than Jeremy Campbell. I'm much more concerned with these grown men in little boys' clothing. A Chris Helmon type—hell, maybe even Marty—could have not only a very persuasive come-on, but the strength and maturity to carry out a complicated kidnapping without getting caught by practically every law enforcement branch in the state *and* the FBI."

Matt considered this for a moment, then said, "So why would this Shadow guy snatch these kids? Is he a pervert, too, as well as a control freak?"

"I don't know for sure," she said. "Chris Helmon has no record of child molesting."

"That doesn't mean he never did it. It just means it was never reported."

"True. But maybe . . . just maybe . . . he was getting bored with his little Saturday night adventures. Maybe he wanted something really daring and exciting. Something that would make this whole town a sort of magic kingdom for him to maneuver."

"And the dragons—"

"—are his adversaries."

Matt nodded slowly. "But how could he bring himself to harm children?"

"They're not children to him, remember? They're trolls. According to Dungeons & Dragons literature, trolls are monsters."

"That would be funny if it wasn't sick."

"I know."

"So what about this *mindslayer* stuff?"

Dylan sighed. "I'm not sure, but I'd say he's making this stuff up as he goes along. See, the real-true Dungeons and Dragons game is highly structured and restrictive. You can only do exactly what the game decrees your character can do. And there's no *mindslayer* in the game."

"I see. This way he's not limited by anything but his imagination. He's playing a game of his own invention."

"Well, so far anyway. I'd like to put some real limitations on this guy before long. So far he's controlled everything—just the way a Dungeon Master would. But he can't control me."

"Let's hope not, anyway." Matt's voice sounded tired. Dylan got up and went over to rub his shoulders for a while. "You're exhausted, babe," she said. "I'm still jazzed tonight, though. Why don't you go on to bed. I'm going to get myself a snack."

He yawned widely. "Good idea. Hey—you did great tonight. I knew you would, but I have to say I'm very relieved to have you back."

"Me, too," she answered. "You don't know just how far away I've been."

"Mom?"

Dylan jumped, spilling a little milk on the front of her T-shirt. "Don't creep up on me like that, Aidan!" she snapped, brushing at the shirt with the palm of her hand. She'd been completely distracted by the night's events and never heard her daughter come in.

"I'm sorry."

Dylan held out her arm. Aidan came over to the table, where Dylan stood, rooting through the cookie jar and drinking milk, and snuggled into her mother's side. "No, *I'm* sorry, sweetie," Dylan said. "I had a long day and I shouldn't take it out on you."

"It's all right," said Aidan, her gentle forgiver. After a moment she said, "Mom, I was wondering . . . why do Caleb and me have two last names?"

"You mean, Tandy-Armstrong, instead of just Armstrong?"

"Yeah. When we lived in Dallas, I knew a few kids with two last names, but out here, me and Caleb are the only ones. Some of the kids think it's weird."

"Weird, huh?"

"Yeah. And I was wondering if maybe we could just use the Armstrong part from now on."

It never failed to amaze Dylan, the power of kids to yank adults out of the misty fog of their own problems into the glaring light of a child's world. She cupped the palm of her hand under her daughter's chin and looked into the mirror of her own green eyes. "What brought this on?"

Aidan shrugged.

"Aidan. We've lived out here a year. Why are you just now bringing this up?"

Her daughter glanced away. "I was afraid it would make you mad." She hesitated. "Sometimes they ask me if I was born at the Radio Shack. You know. Like a Tandy computer."

Dylan regarded her child for a moment. "Come here," she said. Aidan followed her into the den. "Over there on the bookshelf—the third shelf from the bottom, to the right, you will find a book called *Winesburg, Ohio,* by a man named Sherwood Anderson. Bring it to me."

Aidan did as she was told. They sat down on the couch and Dylan flipped through the well-thumbed book to a page with the corner turned down. "See here," she pointed. "This story is called 'Tandy.'" Aidan nodded seriously.

Dylan said, "When I was in high school, we read this story, and it made such a deep impression on me that I vowed from then on that I would never change my name, not even when I got married, and that my kids would always carry the Tandy name." She glanced at her child's beloved face. It was completely focused on what she was saying.

"It's about a drunken stranger who comes upon a little girl, seated on her daddy's knee. He drops down before her and takes her arms in his big hands. He says . . ." Dylan searched for the underlined part and began to read, " 'They think it's easy to be a woman, to be loved, but I know better,' he declared. Again he turned to the child. 'I understand,' he cried. 'Perhaps of all men I alone understand.' "

Dylan glanced at Aidan's rapt face and continued. " 'I know about her . . .' he said softly. 'I know about her struggles and her defeats. It is because of her defeats that she is to me the lovely one. Out of her defeats has been born a new quality in woman. I have a name for it. I call it Tandy. . . . It is the quality of being strong to be loved.' "

She paused.

"Go on," said Aidan.

"The stranger tells the girl, 'Be Tandy, little one . . . Dare to be strong and courageous. That is the road. Venture anything. Be brave enough to dare to be loved. Be something more than man or woman. Be Tandy.' "

Dylan closed the book. Her daughter's soft lips were parted. "What happened to the little girl?" she asked.

"She wouldn't let her family call her by her real name anymore. She insisted they call her Tandy."

Aidan nodded. "Me, too," she said firmly. "This is really cool. Can I take the book to my room?"

"Certainly." Dylan hugged her daughter.

Aidan jumped up and headed for the doorway, where she paused and looked back at her mother. "One more thing. I know I was named Aidan because it means 'little fire,' because I had red hair and Daddy said I was a real spitfire. . . ."

"Right."

"So why were you named Dylan? Was it that folksinger from a long time ago?"

Dylan laughed. "No, Bob Dylan's not *that* old."

The little girl grinned.

"I thought I'd told you before."

Aidan shook her head.

"Okay. When I was born, I had the umbilical cord wrapped around my neck and I nearly died. My mother said that all through it, she kept thinking of the lines of a poem from a man named Dylan Thomas that went, 'Do not go gentle into that good night. Rage, rage against the dying of the light.' She said I fought so hard to live that she decided then and there to name me Dylan."

" 'Do not go gentle into that good night,' " repeated Aidan softly. "What does that mean, Mom?"

"It means that someone very dear to the poet was going to die, and he was begging this loved one to fight it; not to die and leave them."

Her daughter gave her a long, thoughtful look. "I like that," she said.

"Me, too, sweetie."

"Mom, tomorrow is Sunday. Do you think you could take me to the library?"

Naturally Dylan had a thousand things to do on the Scott case, but this, she knew, was every bit as important. "Sure, honey," she said.

Aidan gave Dylan a pixie smile, blew her a kiss, and vanished.

Aidan Tandy-Armstrong wandered the aisles of the library, breathing in the scent of books and furniture polish that she loved so well. Already her arms were so full she could hardly hold all the books.

Gosh, Mom was getting so paranoid. She was so afraid some big bad kidnapper was going to jump out of the bushes and snatch Aidan or Caleb that she hardly ever had them out of her sight. But she had some reports to drop off at Jeremy Scott's parents' house, and Aidan really did not want to go because she knew they would be really sad and everything. So she convinced her mom to leave her at the library, but Aidan had to promise over and over and over that she would not go outside.

It made her kind of afraid but kind of excited, too. In a way it was just like the adventure that Lucy went on in the wardrobe in her favorite book, *The Lion, the Witch, and the Wardrobe*. She never knew what was going to happen next.

Aidan felt a presence behind her and turned around. "Well, hi!" she cried. It was that guy from the comic book store. She'd seen him in the library several times, and they'd talked about *The Fellowship of the Ring*. He liked it, too.

"I see you're still wearing your unicorn necklace," he said.

She touched it. "I wear it all the time."

"Listen, Aidan, the reason I'm here is, I saw your mom."

"You did? Where?"

"She was in that park over there where that kid disappeared."

"Jeremy?"

"Right. Anyway, they found another scroll."

"They did? Really?" This *was* exciting!

"Yeah. Your mom didn't understand anything about the poem."

"I know. She asked us to help her with the others."

"Well, that's the reason I'm here. She asked if I would come and get you and take you out to the park so that you could help her with the scrolls."

Aidan hesitated. "Why didn't she come and get me herself?"

"She wanted to, but she's all tied up with the police."

Aidan wasn't sure what to do. She'd promised her mother that she wouldn't go outside. On the other hand, it's not like this guy was some kind of stranger or something. And Aidan really, really wanted to help her mother with the scrolls. She had read the others over and over, trying to understand what they meant.

She wanted so badly to help her mother with this case. It would be something they could share, something they could do together. And if Aidan could help her mother figure out what to do, then she would find Jeremy and everybody would be happy again, and Mom would get to be home more.

She was thrilled that her mother had sent for her. Mom wanted to be with her, too! Her mother really needed her help. It made her feel very important and grown-up.

"Okay," she said. "Let me check out my books first."

"I'll be waiting outside for you," he said.

Aidan checked out her books as quickly as possible and hurried outside. The guy was nowhere around. Oh, no! He'd left without her! What would her mother think?

"I'm around here," he called.

The Butt-Holdsworth Memorial Library of Kerrville was a fascinating building because it was completely round. Aidan walked around the building about halfway, and there was that guy, standing next to a dirt bike, holding up a couple of black helmets.

Aidan stopped. "I can't ride on a dirt bike!"

"I already asked your mom. She said it would be all right as long as you wore a helmet and we didn't go too fast."

Aidan chewed on her lip. Boy, her mom must be really busy to agree to this. And she must really need Aidan's help. "But where would I put my books?"

"Right back here," he said. "In this bookbag."

She still wasn't too sure about all this.

"I saw the scroll," he said.

"You *did*?"

"Yeah. It said something about a lion and a witch—"

"The Lion, the Witch, and the Wardrobe?"

"That's it. I don't remember what the poem said exactly, but your mom said it was your favorite book, and you would probably be the perfect person to guess the message."

Aidan smiled happily. *She was going to get to help her mom.*

And ride on a dirt bike! Caleb would be so jealous! For *once* she'd get to do something first, instead of big brother. This was so great!

She reached for the helmet.

"Here's a jacket, too," he said. "It'll help protect you from the wind."

It was shiny black leather with studs and snaps all over it. Aidan felt as if she'd stepped right through that wardrobe. She shrugged on the jacket and pulled the helmet on over her thick strawberry hair. Her heart felt like a little bunny rabbit, running all over her chest.

"Ready?" he said. "Okay. Put your arms around my waist . . . that's right. And remember to lean *into* the turns."

In spite of the hot leather jacket, Aidan felt goose bumps break out all over. He started the bike, and she wanted to faint from excitement.

At first the ride was like nothing Aidan had ever known, an exhilaration beyond belief, a freedom so exquisite it brought tears to her eyes. All sound was muffled through the thick helmet and the rush of the wind. Everything was like a blur.

Then she kind of got used to it. She looked around and noticed something. "You missed the turnoff to the park," she said loudly. When he didn't answer, she hollered, *"You missed the turnoff to the park!"*

Then, "Hey! *You're going the wrong way!"*

Could he not hear her with that big helmet? Was he lost? She pounded on his back, but he ignored her.

They got on one of the big highways leading out of the town, and the dirt bike started to go real fast.

Aidan pulled her head back and *cracked* it, as hard as she could, against his helmet.

He took hold of her small wrist and began to twist, slowly and steadily, until it wouldn't go any further, but still he twisted.

Aidan screamed. She tried to pull her wrist free, and he gave it such a wrench that she sucked in all her breath in a rush and nearly fell off.

The dirt bike went faster. Everything familiar to Aidan began to slip farther and farther away. Tears blurred her vision. She didn't try to fight him anymore. He loosened his clawlike grip on her wrist but still held it in a clench.

After what seemed like forever, the dirt bike began to slow. Aidan thought about jumping off, but he was holding her so tight she knew she'd never make it. They turned a corner onto a caliche road, hitting the gravel a little too fast. The bike nearly went over, but the guy controlled it, then picked up more speed.

Aidan looked around her with alarm. They were in completely unrecognizable country, remote and rugged. There were no houses around. Where was he *going*? Her mom would be so worried.

The dirt bike took another turn or two. Aidan was so totally lost by this time that it made no difference to her where they went. Suddenly he slowed the bike to a stop.

Aidan climbed off with shaky legs. He yanked her helmet off her head and stashed the dirt bike behind a huge rock. Then he grabbed her again by the wrist and began dragging her up a steep incline, through brush and trees. It all happened so fast that there was little time to think about being scared.

At the top they both stopped for breath. Down below was a beautiful place, not like anyplace Aidan had ever seen. Like a fairyland. The guy plunged down into it, dragging Aidan behind him, and headed resolutely for this lovely green area that was like a curtain of weeping willow tree boughs. He parted the hanging branches and shoved Aidan inside.

Heart pounding, panting dry-mouthed, she gazed around her in disbelief.

They were in a cave.

Slowly she turned and looked up into the face of the guy from the comic book store, only somehow he wasn't the same guy, somehow he was different, his eyes were weird. . . . With a great, uncontrollable shudder, Aidan Tandy-Armstrong looked into the face of her captor, and then . . . she *knew*.

PART III THE MAZEMASTER

"If there really is a door in this house that leads
to some other world . . . I should not be at all
surprised to find that that other world had a
separate time of its own; so that however long
you stayed there, it would never take up any of
our time."
  —C.S. Lewis
    The Lion, the Witch, and the Wardrobe

This quest may be attempted by the weak with
as much hope as the strong. Yet such is oft the
course of deeds that move the wheels of the
world: small hands do them because they
must, while the eyes of the great are elsewhere.
  —J.R.R. Tolkien
    The Fellowship of the Ring

TWENTY-TWO

At first, few people in the state of Texas—save a few bored meteorologists—paid much attention to the tropical depression that formed out in the Bay of Campeche, a couple of hundred miles east of the Mexican city of Veracruz. It was a clumsy storm, slow to move and confused in its manner, as if it couldn't decide quite what to do with itself. Finally it began a lethargic northern journey through the Gulf of Mexico, gaining weight and momentum with each slow mile. Eventually it sprawled in concentric circles all across the western half of the Gulf, was moved to the status of "hurricane," and given the name of Alma, because it was the first such storm of the season.

At first the entire country sat up and watched Alma with much trepidation. Warnings were sent out all across the Mexican and Texas coasts. But Alma wasn't very ambitious. She spent out most of her power at sea before finally setting a course for the Laguna Madre of the Mexican state of Tamaulipas. Though her winds were still strong enough to do a great deal of damage to area marinas and poorly constructed coastal houses, Alma seemed content mostly to dump prodigious amounts of water on land.

She might have given out altogether when she hit the formidable Sierra Madre Mountain ranges of northern Mexico had she not met up with a squatting low pressure area that had moved in across Baja and the Gulf of California and settled in just where Alma was losing most of her strength. It was an energizing love affair for both of them.

171

The marriage of the two storm fronts sent them on a rolicking honeymoon, bound for Texas, where a great high pressure dome spraddled like a disapproving dowager, baking the state under endless dry hot summer winds. A collision course was inevitable, and a mighty celestial battle broke out in the skies over the central Texas Hill Country, deluging the river area with summer rains that some had not seen in a lifetime.

And all the old-timers said, "A flood's been long over-due."

Halfway through going over a report with the Scotts, Dylan was assaulted with a wave of anxiety such as she'd never known. At first she tried to shake it off. Heavy cloud cover and a drop in the barometric pressure had brought on a sinus headache, and she thought that perhaps her sudden queasiness was attributable to that.

Then there was the stress that always accompanied a visit to the Scotts, and the gloomy house. The afternoon was surprisingly murky, and the Scotts had let the house grow shadowy and close as if they didn't care whether they never saw light again. Dylan kept wanting to jump up and go around, turning on lights, but she tried not to let it bother her as she bent closer to Matt's perfectly typed report.

Her anxiety grew, became unreasonable, and finally cut her off midsentence.

"I'm sorry," she told the bewildered couple. "But I've got to go."

When they asked why, she heard herself saying, "I'm worried about my daughter."

It was as if her subconscious had given voice to the nameless dread within, and suddenly Dylan couldn't get out of the house fast enough. The closer she got to the library, the faster she drove.

She kept telling herself that she was being foolish and paranoid. Aidan was perfectly safe and perfectly all right, reading books in a library on a cloudy summer day. That's what she kept telling herself.

But by the time she pulled up to the library in a screech of brakes and a jarring conk against the curb, Dylan was no longer telling herself anything. She was running, bursting through the door, racing up and down aisles, fighting panic.

At first she whispered Aidan's name, and then she shouted it. When the librarian asked what was the matter, she stepped on her tongue and almost blubbered, describing her little girl.

"Oh, yes," the lady said, "I remember Aidan. Such a sweet, delightful child. I look forward to seeing her every week."

"Is she here? I can't find her anywhere." Trembling set in and Dylan clenched his fists at her side.

"She already left. About twenty minutes ago, I think."

"No," Dylan said. "She wouldn't leave without me."

The woman searched out the book cards from the books Aidan had checked out, and her assistant repeated that yes, Aidan had left and that no, she did not leave with anyone.

"She couldn't!" said Dylan. "She *promised* me."

They didn't know what to say.

Dylan dashed out the front door and ran all around the circular building, shouting Aidan's name.

Over and over she said to herself, "This can't be happening."

From the van phone, she called Matt, listened in wild frustration to the message from the machine, then said, "Matt! Are you there? Pick up. It's me."

No, of course he's not there, she thought. *He came to get Aidan for some reason. Maybe she wasn't feeling well.*

"Hi. What'cha need?"

"Matt! Do you have Aidan?"

"Why would I have her? Isn't she with you?"

"Oh, God. Oh, God."

"Dylan. What the hell is it?"

"She's gone. I left her at the library while I took your reports to the Scotts, and she left before I got back."

"What?"

"Oh, God. Oh, God." Violent shudders overtook Dylan.

"You left her *alone*? For Christ's sake, Dylan!"

"She *promised* me she wouldn't leave!"

"She's a nine-year-old kid!"

"But she *promised*!" The last word was a wail of self-recrimination, guilt, and terror. Dylan began to sob.

"All right. All right. This isn't doing us any good. Have you looked everywhere?"

"Yes."

"Did you try Hastings?"

"Hastings?"

"You know, the bookstore—it's right around the corner from the library, and Aidan loves to browse in there. It's open Sundays. I'll bet she got bored waiting on you and walked down to Hastings."

Relief flooded over Dylan. Of course. That had to be it. "I'll go check right now," she said.

"If she's not there, call me right away," said Matt, "and I'll be there as fast as I can."

"Okay."

Burning rubber the short distance to the bookstore, Dylan sprang from the van and raced into the large building. At first she tried to search the mazelike store alone but soon recruited help from the employees.

There was no sign of Aidan.

Desperately Dylan flashed her wallet photo of her child, but although some of the employees remembered Aidan, none of them had seen her that day.

By the time she redialed her home number, her hands were shaking so badly she couldn't even hit the numbers and almost had to ask for operator assistance.

Matt answered on the first ring.

"She's not there, Matt! Oh, dear God, she's not there!"

"Stay there. I'll be right over. Call Sergeant Dickerson."

But Sergeant Dickerson wasn't there. They said he was on a stakeout. Dylan explained to the officer in charge what had happened, and they promised immediate assistance.

But although the police department was only a block away, Dylan wasn't willing to wait.

Dylan knew where her daughter was, and she was going to get her.

Chris Helmon's house was located in a modest, well-kept neighborhood of white frame houses, trees, and kids. Fat raindrops splatted on the windshield as Dylan hit the street in front of his house so hard, her right front tire skidded up onto the curb. Leaving the van where it was, she killed the ignition, sprang out, and sprinted for the front door, heedless of the huge droplets striking her unprotected head and shoulders.

"Open the door!" she screamed, pounding with her fists.

Helmon opened the door and blinked at her.

She shoved him aside and raged into his house. "Where is she?" she demanded.

"Where is who?"

Dylan ran past him down the hall, flinging open doors as she went. "Aidan!" she yelled.

"What's going on?" He was right behind her.

"You son of a bitch!" she screamed, hurling her body onto his. They fell to the floor.

"He-elp!" hollered Helmon, bringing up his hands to protect his face.

She pummeled him. *"Where did you put my little girl, you bastard!"*

He cringed and cried out.

Dylan was no longer Dylan. She was a fierce she-lion, seeing blood and hearing nothing, thinking only of her young. Off in the outermost perimeters of her mind, she was only dimly aware of a pounding at the front door, of Chris hollering for help, of people surging down the hall, of harsh hands yanking her back in a choke hold, of Chris coughing and sputtering and whimpering, of herself, fighting and scratching and screaming until the choke hold meant business and her knees buckled and her vision blackened.

She was dragged backward, all the way to the living room, out of sight of Chris. Only then did her hearing return. Only then did she realize it was Sergeant Dickerson holding her back, yelling in her ear, *"Tandy! We've been watching him all day! He never left the house!"*

Sight, sound, and feeling returned to her numbed consciousness in a loud rush. Over Dickerson's voice she could hear ragged sobbing.

It was her own.

He let go of her neck but pulled her down to the couch, where he sat next to her, his arm gripped firmly around her shoulders.

"He got her!" she blubbered. "He got her!"

"No." Dickerson put both arms around her then. "Tandy, listen to me. It's not Helmon. We've been watching him day and night. He never left the house."

She pushed away from him. "He had to! You just missed him or something! He snuck out the back door or something! He's got my baby, *I know it!*"

The sergeant's eyes held all the sadness his job had ever known, all the poverty and filth, all the death and heartache. It was all there for her to read, and then she knew.

"No." She shook her head. "No."

His eyes filled with tears.

"She's not lost," Dylan said. "She's not. I can find her. I can. I c-can f-fi . . ." Her hands and feet went numb and her lips began to tingle. "Baby. My b-b-ba . . ."

Other officers had gathered in the room and were staring down at her with that same sadness that she'd seen in Andy's eyes.

Dylan knew what that look meant. She'd seen it in ambulance driver's eyes when they loaded up a child whom they knew would never make it to the hospital.

"This isn't ha-ha-hap-p-en . . ." Her tongue was thick in her mouth.

"Get her some water," someone said.

Waving away helping hands, she got to her feet. "I'm all right," she assured them. "I'm all right."

On unsteady legs she wavered over to a large mirror that hung on one wall of the living room. It was in a cheap gilded frame, like something one would buy at a "Starving Artists" sale. Dylan stared into the mirror.

Her face was the white of death, streaked with black rivulets of mascara. Her green eyes, blackened with dilated pupils, stared at her in stark, wild terror.

Aidan's eyes.

With one swift movement Dylan pulled back her head and smashed it, full force, into the mirror, shattering the image into brittle shards of forgetfulness.

TWENTY-THREE

For a long moment, as Aidan stared into the peculiar eyes of her captor, her mind raced with surprising clarity.

This was the Shadow. He lived in a fantasy world. He stole children and wrote poems to her mother about them.

Probably he brought them here, to this cave.

No wonder nobody had found them yet.

Which meant . . . they might never find her, either.

Aidan trembled. She was very, very frightened. Her thoughts began to get all jumbled up, and she didn't know what to do.

Be something more than man or woman. Be Tandy.

Aidan sucked in her breath. The thought had pierced through all that confusion like a dagger. And suddenly she knew what she must do if there was any chance at all to stay alive.

Immediately Aidan dropped to her knees and bowed her head. "My Lord," she said. "You are the great Shadow. I await your bidding."

Shadow gasped. "What?"

"You are the *mindslayer*, O great one. I am but a lowly . . . um . . . t-troll."

Aidan didn't dare look up. She was shaking so hard she was afraid she might fall over.

He didn't say anything. Aidan felt cold all inside. After an interminable moment she said, "I am honored you have chosen me."

"You should be," he said then, "for you are the Dragon Princess."

Aidan bit her lip. *Dragon Queen. Dragon Princess.* It was starting to make sense, in a fantastical kind of way. Her knees were hurting on the cold hard floor of the cave. She was afraid to look up into the eyes of this guy. She shivered.

"Get up," he commanded. "I will show you the Treasure Trove room."

Aidan scrambled to her feet. He prodded her blindly down a tunnel of the cave until he came to a lamp, which he lit. Gripping her arm tightly with one hand, he continued down the tunnel. She did not resist. *Be Tandy.*

Eventually they entered a large cave room. Shadow lifted the lamp, showing off a big pile of children's things: backpacks and toys and jackets and lunchboxes.

Aidan's breath stuck in her throat. For a moment she was afraid she might faint. Had he killed all these children?

Fighting a powerful urge to run, Aidan forced herself to face facts: Three children were missing—not enough to own all this stuff.

But where were the three children?

She let her eyes roam around the cave and spotted several passageways branching off. Maybe he had hidden them someplace.

"Well?" he demanded. "What do you think?"

She thought quickly. "I think the Shadow must be very great to have stolen all this treasure from trolls without the dragons knowing how to find it." She glanced at him from beneath her lashes.

He beamed. "Exactly!"

Her stomach churned.

He gestured grandly toward the floor of the cave. "Sit."

She collapsed cross-legged and tried very hard not to wring her hands. *Be strong and courageous. Be something more than man or woman. Be Tandy.* She took deep breaths.

Shadow turned and started to remove his clothes.

Aidan's heart began a wild pounding. In health class they had talked about what to do if someone started to touch your private parts. But nobody mentioned anything about being stuck in a cave at the time. Now she was too terrified to move. *Mama,* she thought. *Oh, Mama, help me please.*

To her surprise—and great relief—he made no effort to touch her but only dressed quickly in a medieval-looking costume with a swirling purple cloak that might have looked really cool if she hadn't been so frightened.

Finally he stood over her. "The Dragon Princess has been brought to the Secret Caverns in order to make a gift to them of the Magic Amulet." In the lamplight his eyes gleamed.

"The Magic Amulet?" Aidan's mind went blank. She was almost too scared to think.

He gestured toward her throat.

With sickening realization, Aidan closed her hand over her little silver unicorn she'd worn constantly since her mother had bought it for her. Her eyes filled with tears. "Not my unicorn," she said.

"Silence!" His voice echoed.

Aidan jumped, squeezing shut her eyes to keep from sobbing. *Be Tandy.* She clutched the unicorn. Her mother had bought it for her.

"Give it to me."

She was trying so hard to be brave. She wanted so badly to be smart. She thought if she could just be brave and smart she might find those kids for her mother. But the unicorn was her only connection to home. If he took it . . .

"I said *give it to me*!" Clasping his hand over hers, he yanked until the chain broke, then twisted her wrist cruelly until she cried out and the unicorn fell to the cave floor.

He pounced on it, hoisted it high. "Behold the Magic Amulet!" he cried.

Tears streamed down Aidan's face, but she did not make a sound.

He threw back his head and laughed.

She felt very sick and swallowed hard to keep from throwing up. She thought of her mother and father and brother, and it was all she could do not to fling herself to the floor in wild sobs. Worst of all, she had *promised* her mom she would not go outside. She could just imagine how frantic her mom must be, hunting for her at the library.

Oh, Mom . . . I'm so sorry. . . . A shuddering sigh escaped her. She clasped her arms close to her body and glanced around the room, taking note of the camping supplies and food.

No wonder they hadn't been able to find him.

Aidan was intelligent and mature enough for her age to realize the unlikelihood that she would be rescued. She'd watched her parents and a whole host of law enforcement agents search in vain for the other missing children. She'd seen how bewildered they had all been by the scrolls. And she'd heard a man tell her father once that there were dozens of unexplored caves sprinkled all over the Hill Country.

Part of her wanted to lie down and die, right there, and get it over with. But another part of her remembered her father. They said he had died once, after he got shot, but he had fought to live, and he battled little problems and big obstacles every day of his life and he never quit. She remembered, too, what her mother said about the name Tandy, and about not going gentle into that good night. She thought of her mother, and how fiercely she knew her mom would search; how she would never give up.

Aidan thought of all these things. She looked up at her captor, and she could see that he was crazy. She knew from his poems and from the things he said that, when he was living in the Secret Caverns, he wasn't like he had been the day she'd met him in front of the Dungeon & Dragons display at Chris's Collectible Comics & Cards. Funny . . . he'd shown her the unicorn necklace in the first place.

Aidan realized that she had entered into another world, a world she knew a little something about because of all her reading about dragons and mazes and enchantments and unicorns. She knew that if she was going to survive at all, she would have to do it on *Shadow's* terms, in *his* world.

From out of the mysterious folds of his cloak, Shadow

withdrew another scroll. Aidan's chest constricted with dread.

He began to read: " 'The Shadow Game is simple for all to see; Three rules must be followed accordingly . . .' "

Still trembling, her stomach still quivering, Aidan listened carefully to the rules of the "game."

He was going to give her a torch and chase her through the cave!

She could hardly breathe! This was so scary! What if she got lost?

Then again, what if she found a way to escape?

For the first time she felt a small twinge of hope.

She had to take care of something, though. She had to buy herself as much time as possible.

"You will have ten turns of the glass," he was saying with that strange gleam to his eye, "as a head start. Then, I will follow."

"Shadow? I have a question."

"Speak."

"If you catch me, can we start the game over? We could go down a different tunnel or something."

His eyebrows shot up. "You mean, you *want* to play?"

"Oh, yes," she said. "I feel like Lucy in *The Lion, the Witch, and the Wardrobe*. I always wanted to go on an adventure like this! My brother will be so jealous." She clapped numbed hands together.

He gave her an incredulous stare. "I have indeed found my Worthy Opponent." A smile cracked his face. "This is so cool! I can't wait to begin," he said, dropping for a brief moment his "Shadow" persona.

Aidan tried to swallow over the cold lump of fear in her throat, but couldn't. "Me, neither," she said.

Dylan's unconsciousness was merciless; it only lasted a few seconds and it spared her no pain.

Sergeant Dickerson and Sergeant Fuentes both had hold of her before she could hit the floor. She awoke quickly to the sight of blood and somebody crying, "Get an ambulance!"

"No ambulance!" she yelled, struggling to get free. "I want to see my husband and my son." She fought and scratched, blinking blood from her vision.

"Goddammit, Dylan, am I gonna have to cuff you?" Dickerson had her arm locked in a painful grip. "My God, woman—if Helmon had had a gun, he'd have been within his rights to blow your head off, and if you don't settle down, I'll shoot you myself!"

She gave him a wild look but stopped struggling.

"Er, I have some first-aid supplies in the bathroom," said a shy voice. They all looked toward the hallway, where a diminutive Helmon stood, still protected by a phalanx of officers.

"Sir, do you wish to press charges against Ms. Tandy?" asked a young officer Dylan did not know.

Helmon shook his head. "No. I'd just like for her to pay for the mirror, that's all. It was my mom's favorite."

Dylan shrugged. A droplet of blood fell to the front of her blouse. Thunder rumbled across the roof and rattled at the windowpanes. Against her will, she shivered.

"The bathroom's down here," said Helmon, leading the way.

Dickerson half dragged Dylan down the hall and into the bathroom, where he shut the door and dumped her unceremoniously on the toilet seat. Rummaging through the medicine chest, he said, "You're no damn good to your little girl like this, Tandy." He placed an antibiotic salve, several Band-Aids, and a small pair of scissors on the edge of the sink. He wet a washcloth, wiped it over her face roughly, then tilted her head back and pressed the cloth to her forehead. "You need stitches."

"I'm not going to the hospital," she said numbly. She closed her eyes so that she wouldn't have to look into his face. No matter how gruff he pretended to be, he could not hide that sadness from his eyes.

He lifted the cloth, checked, and pressed it back again. "Open your eyes. I gotta see your pupils."

She obeyed reluctantly.

"Okay. They're not uneven. You dizzy? Nauseated?"

She shook her head.

"Be still." He checked the cloth. "I don't guess you've got a concussion. You're still oozing some, though. I'm going to make you some butterfly stitches out of these Band-Aids. Hold this rag."

She did as she was told. None of this was happening. It was all a nightmare. She would wake up.

Just like Campbell Scott.

Dylan shuddered.

Andy finished fashioning his little butterfly stitches, then applied them gently to her forehead. She wanted to cry. She wanted to scream.

He cupped her chin in his hard palm and gave her a penetrating gaze. "You can do this, Tandy."

"You think?" Her voice sounded very small and pitiful.

"I *know*."

She sighed.

"We'll find her."

But she didn't believe him.

Someone else drove the van back to the police department, where Matt and Caleb awaited Dylan. She rode silently with Andy Dickerson. At one point she glanced over at him. It looked as though a cat had clawed his arms to shreds. "Did I do that?"

"Don't worry about it."

"I'm so sorry, Andy."

He shrugged. "You didn't know what you were doing."

It felt as though an ice pick had been stabbed through her skull. She pressed cold fingers to her eyes. "Maybe we should check the library again."

He shook his head. "She's not there, Tandy. I've already had some uniforms check it out."

"It's my fault. I never should have left her alone."

"Don't blame yourself. It'll just make you crazy. You gotta stay strong, for her."

A great yawning pit opened at Dylan's feet, and she knew she was going to fall in. "She's gone," she whispered. "She's just gone."

We'll never find her, she thought. *Just like we didn't find the others. I've lost her.*

The pit was not in front of her, after all, it was *inside* of her, a powerful, horrible emptiness, a void from where all the sunshine she had ever known had simply vanished.

Dylan stared blindly at the rain which cascaded in sheets down the passenger window of the car, like a flood of tears.

The whole sky wept for her Aidan, her precious little one, and Dylan knew that, for her, the sun would never shine again.

TWENTY-FOUR

The torch in Aidan's hand was heavy, but she knew that without it, she would be eclipsed in total, inky blackness. She didn't know what was more terrifying—wandering through an unexplored cave or facing Shadow. In spite of the fact that she only had ten turns of the hourglass as a head start, she sensed that to run in blind panic could get her killed.

What Aidan's parents did not know was that she often crouched in the hallway, eavesdropping, whenever they had their old friends over from the police department. She loved listening to all the war stories about their days on the streets. Without realizing it, she'd picked up a few survival skills from those stories. She knew without having to be told that the most important thing she could do was to force herself to think clearly.

The tunnel she was taking suddenly branched into two tunnels. Which should she take? How would she be able to find her way back?

Think.

When she stood still long enough to let her swirling fears settle, the first thing Aidan thought of was "Hänsel and Gretel." According to the old fairy tale, Hänsel and Gretel left pieces of bread in a trail behind them, to keep from getting lost in the forest.

But she didn't have any bread.

Besides, if she dropped things behind her, wouldn't that lead Shadow straight to her?

For a moment she stood, chewing her bottom lip. She

looked around. The torch's glow only extended in a small circle around her. Holding it aloft, she turned slowly around, her eyes sweeping the tunnel. Strewing the cave floor were smooth rocks which resembled the chalky caliche rock used to pave many rural roads in the area.

Chalky.

Aidan hefted a rock in her hand, crouched, and scratched it along the lower portion of the wall.

It left a slight mark.

Elated, she made another mark at the fork of the tunnel, near the floor of the cave—not readily visible to one not searching for it—then made a quick decision to take the tunnel on the left. Ducking into the cool black interior, she crouched again and made another small mark near the mouth of the tunnel.

Wait.

What was that? Had she heard a sound? Aidan peered behind her. She could see nothing. Still, her time had to be up by now. Hurrying along, her breath vaporizing in the cave's chill air, she scurried down the tunnel, clutching the quavering torch in one hand and her marking rock in the other, and trying very hard not to cry.

When the other children disappeared, Dylan had been galvanized to action. Law enforcement sprang to the ready, and parents, she noticed, believed fiercely that their children would be found.

But that was three—no, make it four—missing kids ago. Dylan, more than anyone, knew the hopelessness of the situation. In fact, from the beginning, she was convinced that Aidan was dead.

With that conviction her entire system seemed to shut down, as if her mind, body, indeed, her very soul, had gone numb.

At Sergeant Dickerson's insistence, Matt and Caleb took Dylan home. It was the longest, and worst, car ride of their marriage.

At first nobody spoke. Then Matt said, very quietly, "How could you leave her alone? After everything that's happened, how could you have left her unprotected for even one minute?"

"I didn't think anybody would drag her out of the library, and she promised me not to go outside."

"So you presumed that she did not know the kidnapper and couldn't be fooled into going willingly?"

Dylan put her hand over her eyes. Her head was screaming in pain. She wanted to scream with it. "I thought Aidan, of all children, could be trusted not to fall for anything like that."

"But that's just it!" Matt shouted. "She's a *child*! She can't be expected to reason like an adult!"

Dylan began to sob.

"Dad," said Caleb shyly from the backseat. "It's not Mom's fault. She told Aidan to stay there and Aidan didn't do it."

"Anytime there's a chain of command, the one in charge is always responsible," snapped Matt.

Dylan felt the squeeze of a young hand on her shoulder. She reached up and clutched at it. She could not seem to stop sobbing. It was as if every tear she'd ever held back at any scene of death in years and years of homicide work was flooding from her, and she feared being swept away by it.

"Don't you know I blame myself?" she cried. "Don't you think I've realized what I've done?" Weeping raggedly, she looked at her husband and was chilled to her soul. His face was grim and set and unforgiving.

She wanted to die.

"Mom, you're bleeding!"

Dylan reached up and touched the makeshift stitches made by Dickerson. They had soaked through. Blood oozed down her forehead. Matt dug around in his pocket, produced a handkerchief, and handed it to her without sympathy. "Pretty stupid thing to do," he remarked coldly.

"Dad! Don't be so hard on her!" Caleb's voice broke.

Matt ignored him.

Outside Matt's car, rain gushed from the heavens as if the clouds had split wide open. Though the wipers were working full speed, they couldn't keep up with it. Water splashed up from the wheels like the wake of a boat.

Dylan blotted bright red blood from her head and dabbed mascara-blackened tears from her face. Just like the rain, they kept coming. Her head was pierced through with pain and her heart with grief. Losing Aidan was unspeakable enough, but she had never seen her husband like this.

It was as if all the love he had ever had for her had been shut out of his mind.

When he pulled up into their drive, Dylan bolted from the car before he'd even come to a stop. Stinging cold rain smacked her face like a whiplash.

Soaked, still crying, she stumbled through the front door, ran for the refuge of her bedroom, slammed the door, flung herself across the bed, stuffed a pillow in her mouth, and started screaming.

She screamed and screamed until her voice went hoarse. Then she cried some more.

Dimly she heard the doorbell ring. And ring again. And again.

The house was filling up with people. She didn't know who they were and she didn't care.

It was growing dark. Dylan curled her body into the fetal position and lay there, dead and empty and heavy and sore. The sobs had quieted, but the tears still came, flooding her eyes like the rains outside.

The bedroom door opened.

Dylan raised her head, hopeful that it might be Matt.

To her surprise, she saw the silhouette of Colleen Scott framed in the doorway. Colleen stepped into the room and shut the door.

Then this other mother whose child had been snatched from her did a rare and beautiful thing.

Without saying a word, she stretched out on the bed beside Dylan and reached for her hand.

They lay together in the darkening room, two grieving mothers, clinging to each other. Gradually the strength from one began to flow into the other, until Dylan's tortured soul was comforted, and her tears could finally come to a stop.

Aidan cracked her head sharply against a low-hanging stalactite and gasped to keep from crying out. She looked around. To the right was another tunnel. Memorizing the big stalactite to use as a landmark, she made her little scratch along the floor and turned into the tunnel.

Her face was instantly enshrouded in a huge spiderweb. A loud cry escaped her. Pawing frantically at her face, shivering uncontrollably, she danced out of the cobweb's sticky embrace and stood, brushing at herself to make sure there weren't any spiders on her. Her hair prickled at her scalp, and she shook it furiously. Her skin crawled.

Heart pounding, she held the torch out in front of her like a weapon, watching to make sure no great big spiders jumped down on her or anything, like what happened to that guy in the movie *Arachnophobia.*

Aidan was so busy looking up for spiders that she didn't see the object in front of her; tripped over it, and staggered wildly, clutching the torch to keep from dropping it. When she had regained her balance, she turned and held out the torch.

It was a sleeping boy.

Aidan just barely stopped herself from crying out, both in fear and excitement. She'd found one of the missing boys!

"Hey," she whispered. "Wake up." She nudged him with her toe. He didn't move. She didn't see how he could sleep so soundly on that hard cave floor, especially as cold as it was.

Aidan crouched over the child. After stuffing her marking rock in her pocket, she shook him.

Bringing the torch down low for a closer look, she

wondered if she would recognize his face from her mother's photographs, or if she would remember his name.

The torchlight flickered and jumped, illuminating the thin legs, the flowered jams, the windbreaker . . . and the blood.

Blood—blackened with time—capped his head and masked his face. Blood pooled beneath him on the hard, cold cave floor. Blood encrusted the eyelashes on eyes that stared up at her in horror.

High, piercing screams bounced and echoed off the cave walls like the cry of a banshee, chasing the child who ran in stark terror deep into the bowels of the labyrinth.

TWENTY-FIVE

Shadow came up short, listening with full concentration. He was certain he'd heard something. When no sounds penetrated the velvety darkness outside the glow of his torch, he continued on down the winding tunnel.

There it was!

Yes. This time he was certain he'd heard . . . *screams!* Shadow's heart began to pound. The Dragon Princess!

But from which way were the screams coming? At first they seemed to reverberate from every direction. Shadow continued on down the tunnel for a few yards, then stopped. The screams were growing fainter.

Oh, the Secret Caverns were teasing him!

He turned around and went back the way he had come for twenty feet or so. The screams seemed to be coming from the wall.

Another tunnel. *Yes!* She must have taken another tunnel.

Eagerly now, Shadow hurried back to the opening of the tunnel he had chosen. The screams had stopped, but Shadow wasn't worried. He was pretty sure which way the Dragon Princess had gone.

Turning to the right, he continued on for some way, until a huge stalactite loomed ahead. There were two ways Shadow could go: He could go on straight ahead, or he could take the smaller tunnel, which branched off to the right of the stalactite.

The thought of proceeding down that particular tunnel made Shadow very uncomfortable. His chest tightened and he hesitated for a very long time. Finally he hoisted his torch high and peered down the smaller tunnel.

The ragged edges of a large spider web drifted from the air currents stirred by his body and the flames of the torch. Shadow pursed his lips. He could no longer ignore the fact that the Dragon Princess had come this way.

She had seen.

Dry-mouthed, Shadow swallowed. This was a complication to the game that he'd forgotten all about.

What if the Dragon Princess found the other troll, and then what if she escaped, and then what if she ran and told the dragons, and they all descended on the Secret Caverns?

Setting his mouth in a grim line, Shadow set off down the tunnel, stepping carefully over the inert form of the troll at his feet. He was just going to have to make sure that the Dragon Princess did not escape.

Not ever.

Dylan slept a little, and when she awoke, Colleen Scott was gone. The clock beside the bed read eight P.M. Quiet murmurings from the other parts of the house told her that people were still there.

Dragging herself and her pounding head out of bed, she weaved through the murky bedroom to the bathroom. Flipping on the overhead light, she was staggered at the sight of herself. Dried blood and smeared makeup made her face look as though she'd been beaten. Her reddened eyes were nearly swollen shut from crying.

Dylan swallowed three aspirin and crawled into as hot a shower as she could tolerate and stood, wretched and washed-out, as the water pounded her shoulders and head. It was as if her insides had been hollowed out and there was nothing left to feel. Certainly there were no more tears left anywhere in her.

Her little girl was everywhere around her, within her and without, beside and above. All she could see or think was Aidan.

She remembered something Naomi Judd, the famous country singer, had said when ill health forced her to retire from music and send her daughter, Wynona, on alone: "We complete each other."

Without Aidan, Dylan was incomplete, unfinished. The loss of her daughter was this great gaping wound that kept oozing her lifeblood just as surely as did the injury to her forehead. How could she live through one day without that child's presence in this world, much less a whole lifetime?

She scrubbed herself. Scrubbed and scrubbed until her skin burned pink, as if she wanted to erase herself forever. After all, Matt was right. Because of her, Aidan was gone . . . and who knew what terrible things had happened to her?

Stumbling from the shower, she rubbed her body until it hurt and wrapped a big terry cloth robe around herself, not bothering to dry her hair. She had to see if—by some miracle—there was any news.

Padding from her bedroom on bare feet, past the utility room, into the breakfast nook, Dylan gazed around her in wonder.

An efficient group of women had prepared a meal, served it, and was in the process of cleaning up. She recognized some of them as her country neighbors, and some she'd met briefly during their year in Kerrville. Another woman entered the kitchen, heading for the utility room with a heaping basket of laundry. Through the dining room, Dylan could see a knot of men gathered around Matt. Some were detectives she recognized; others were the husbands of the women in the kitchen.

If Dylan hadn't been all cried out, her eyes would have filled with tears. She'd been unprepared for the generous spirit of small-town country folk to draw near to a neighbor in trouble.

A woman who lived down the road, named Nora, spotted Dylan and came over. She was all country, plump and bespeckled. "How you doin', sugar?" she asked, wrapping Dylan in a warm embrace.

Dylan gave herself up to the motherly comfort of the hug. Her throat constricted. "Thank you for coming," she said. Thinking of Matt, she added, "I don't know what I'd have done without you."

The other women gathered close by but did not suffocate. One of them pressed her into a chair. "I know you're not hungry," she said, "but I'm going to fix you a bowl of chicken soup. You got to keep your strength up."

"I don't know if I can eat," choked Dylan.

The woman, gray and grandmotherly, sat down next to Dylan and put a warm hand on her arm. "Honey, when the Marine sergeant came to tell me my boy wasn't coming back from Vietnam, I wanted to die, too. But I had to think about his little brothers and sisters, just the way you got to think about young Caleb. He needs you, too. After all, it's his sister, don't forget."

Dylan's cheeks flamed. She'd forgotten all about poor Caleb. She nodded and squeezed the woman's hand. Someone handed her a glass of iced tea, and she drank thirstily. Nora said, "I'm gonna round up some bandages and see what I can do with that nasty bump on your head."

Dylan nodded and glanced around. There was no sign of the Scotts. Colleen had simply come to her like an angel in the dark. She wanted to thank the woman—whose own pain of loss was still so raw—but did not know how. She ducked her head.

"Mom?" Caleb suddenly stood at her side. "Are you all right?"

Dylan clasped her son tightly to her breast. "I'm okay," she said. "How about you?"

"I'm scared," he whispered.

She nodded. "Me, too, sweetie."

"Dad's just upset," he offered. "He didn't mean to hurt your feelings."

Dylan wasn't too sure about that, but she didn't say

anything. After a moment they pulled apart. Dylan said,
"Have you eaten?"

"Yeah. All these people have been real nice."

She touched his pinched cheek with her knuckle. "I know."

"Mom?" He glanced around furtively. "Can I sleep with
you and Dad tonight?"

She stared at her big-footed, clumsy-handed son, and her
heart ached for him. At twelve he must really be frightened
to make such a request of his mother. Or maybe he just felt
the need to be close to them. His room—and Aidan's—
were all the way on the other side of the house.

She managed a weak smile. "Sure, honey. We've got
plenty of room."

His relief was palpable. He nodded and rejoined the men
in the den; still just a little boy, after all.

Dylan sat back and watched people bustle about, caring
for her family, offering what they could to help, even if it
was just a strong back or a sympathetic gaze. Nora showed
up and tenderly ministered to Dylan's cuts, her fingertips
sure and warm. The older lady brought soup, hot and
bracing. Somebody refilled her tea glass. In the background,
quiet country gossip drifted softly across the room like a
morning mist.

Dylan had believed that, once she left the police force,
she would never again feel that sense of fraternity and unity
she'd always felt with her fellow officers.

But she had underestimated the simple empowerment of
the sisterhood of country women in times of crises. Horrors
could rain down upon them as surely as the thundershowers
that pounded on the roof, and they would still find a way to
prepare a bowl of soup, fix a glass of tea, and stretch out in
the darkness to reach for another's hand.

She breathed in the beauty-shop, floury, perfumy scent of
them, and was strengthened.

Aidan stumbled to a halt, her heart banging against her rib
cage and throbbing in her throat, breath heaving in spasms.

Even when she squeezed her eyes shut, she could still see the boy. He was little, maybe a couple of years younger than she, and there was all that blood. . . .

It had not occurred to Aidan that Shadow had been killing the children he brought to the cave. She just figured he had them hidden someplace. She was going to find them, she'd thought, and they would all escape. Her mom and dad and all the moms and dads would be so proud.

But that little boy was *dead*! Just plain dead.

She shuddered to think what Shadow had done to him. Poor boy. Poor, poor boy. She wondered if he had cried for his mother, the way she wanted to cry now.

Aidan took deep gulps of air and looked around her. She'd run in such a panic that she had not made her little marks. There was no way of telling where she was or how she could get back.

She would not think about the little boy. She *could* not think about him. If she did, she would start running again and get even more lost. She would shut him completely out of her mind.

But she couldn't shut out the fear. It possessed her body and haunted her thoughts. Even now her hands shook so hard it was all she could do not to drop the torch.

What should she do? Should she try to retrace her steps until she came to the last mark?

Only she wouldn't come to the last mark. She would come to—she wouldn't think about it. *Couldn't* think about it.

And what if Shadow was right behind her? Was he planning to do the same thing to her that he'd done to that poor kid?

Icy needles of terror prickled over Aidan's body.

For a long moment she couldn't budge. Fear had cast her in a mold. It whispered to her, "Just quit. Huddle here in a hole and maybe he won't find you. Just curl up here and go to sleep. Maybe you'll never wake up. It would be so much easier than this."

And then another voice came to her from deep within her mind. It was her mother's voice, saying, *"Be something more than man or woman. Be strong and courageous. Be Tandy."*

And *"Do not go gentle into that good night."*

Aidan's chin trembled. She whispered, "I'll be Tandy, Mama. You'll see. I'll be Tandy. I won't go gentle."

Fumbling in the pocket of the leather jacket she still wore (and was increasingly grateful for), Aidan withdrew her marking rock, stopped, and made her mark on the floor.

Then she lifted the trembling torch high and headed on down the tunnel, toward the black unknown.

TWENTY-SIX

"Mom? Help me! Please find me! I'm lost! Mom?"

Dylan could hear her daughter's cries, but it was impossible to tell from which direction they came, because they had a hollow, echoing ring to them. She was searching through an incredible house, filled with long hallways and dark passageways and more doors than she could count. Every time she opened one door, she'd find herself in another hall, and none of them led to Aidan.

Aidan's calls grew more urgent. Dylan began to panic. She started to run. Flinging back one door, she'd run almost smack into another, and open that one to find yet one more long hallway.

"Aidan!" she cried.

"Mom! I'm here! Help me!"

Her daughter's voice was all around her, echoing louder and louder, reverberating through the walls of the house like a pulsebeat, but no matter how hard Dylan ran or how many doors she opened, she came no closer to finding Aidan.

Sobs choked her, and in the end it was her own weeping that woke Dylan.

She sat up, soaked through with night sweats, her own cries strangling in her throat. Caleb sprawled beside her, still sound asleep. Apparently, her sobs had only been loud in her own tortured dreams.

But it had been so *real*. Aidan's voice had been as clear as if she had cried out from the next room!

Trembling, Dylan got out of bed, stooping to pull the covers up gently around her son's tousled head. There was no sign of Matt. She wondered if he intended to sleep on the couch from now on. Heavy-hearted, she padded over to the window and peeked through one of the blinds. Rain still poured down relentlessly.

She felt cold, miserable, and terribly alone.

She'd been no better than any of the other parents who simply took it for granted that their rosy-cheeked lives would dance along forever while they were busy with other concerns. After all, she'd felt pretty self-righteous over all the time the Jeremy Scott case had taken, but the truth of the matter was that although she'd gotten more emotionally involved in the Scott case than the others, she was still a workaholic, scheduling time in to spend with her children when it was convenient for her.

Now there was no time left.

Most parents came to that harsh realization after the kids were grown. Others had the truth thrust upon them in much quicker, crueler ways, like when their kids got into trouble with drugs, alcohol, or teenage pregnancy.

Or when they woke up deep in the night to find the child gone forever.

Caleb stirred in his sleep. At that moment Dylan knew that if it weren't for her remaining child, she might very well have taken her own life. The guilt and pain—and the look in her husband's eyes—were almost too much to bear.

Rain pummeled the roof.

Wrapping her old robe around her shivering body, Dylan wandered through the dark house to the den. She wanted to be near Matt, even if just to watch him sleep. The isolation from him was killing her.

A sound—like a cough—came from Aidan's room. A glow from around the corner of the den meant there was a light on. Dylan's heart leapt. She hurried across the den and around the corner.

Aidan's door was open. Matt sat alone in the middle of the room, gripping in his hands a piece of construction paper. Crayoned on the paper in Aidan's handwriting were the words: *Be strong and courageous. Be something more than man or woman. Be Tandy.*

His shoulders jerked as great masculine sobs were wrenched from him.

Without hesitation Dylan hurried to his wheelchair, crouched in front of him, and pulled his head into her breast, where she held him and he clung to her, deep into the long, rainy night.

Aidan had not progressed very far down the new tunnel when she realized, to her horror, that her torch was dimming. The flames, which had shot out so high and so strong when the torch was first lit, were now paltry and fading.

It had never occurred to her that her torch would simply give out. She shook it a little and blew on it, but nothing seemed to help. The fire was going out.

Soon she would be plunged into absolute darkness.

She didn't want to cry. Really, she didn't. But she couldn't help it! What was she going to do now? Without a light she would be totally, horribly lost! She wouldn't even be able to see her marks!

She looked behind her with dread. Back that other way lay the unthinkable thing . . . and beyond that, the Shadow.

Aidan couldn't stop little whimpering sounds from coming out. She could either sit right down, in total, complete darkness and wait for somebody to find her (yeah, *right*); or she could go back the way she had come and hope that her torch would last long enough to help her find her way.

But what if Shadow caught her? He had *said* he'd want to play again, but Aidan didn't think she could believe him. He'd already lied to her in order to make her come with him to the Secret Caverns. Who knew what all he was lying about?

And then, just down the tunnel . . . She wouldn't think about that.

Aidan shifted her weight from one foot to the other in a misery of indecision. The torch dimmed a little more, and the suffocating black darkness of the cave crept a little closer, like a living thing, bent on choking her.

She turned and headed back the way she had come. Sometimes the torch was so dim she had to drop to her knees in order to search for her little marks. At times she couldn't make them out at all.

Her mouth was dry and her hands shook. She was cold and very, very frightened. This was like being trapped in a big, black maze that went on endlessly.

She began whispering to herself. "Maybe Shadow got lost, too. Maybe I'm going down a different passageway than he is, only I can find my way because of the marks, and I'll get to the Trove Room first, and then I can escape! I could steal his motorcycle and ride home, and bring Mom and Dad back here and show them everything. Yeah. Maybe I can do that. I can do that. I can do that."

A tiny beacon of light suddenly appeared straight ahead. "Maybe it's the Trove Room!" cried Aidan, and she began to run toward the light, holding up the torch with both hands, because her arms had gotten so tired.

No.

It couldn't be the Trove Room, because she hadn't come to . . . that thing she didn't want to think about.

Aidan stumbled to a stop, her heard pounding like a pinball machine. The light grew larger as it neared her.

Frantically she looked behind her. Should she run? Could she hide?

Frozen, she chewed her bottom lip. *Do* something! Be Tandy!

The light steadily approached.

Aidan thought she might faint. Her stomach felt like a lump of cold oatmeal. She could hear footsteps now.

She was certain he'd seen her, too.

The light filled the tunnel; the footsteps echoed off the cave walls.

At the last moment Aidan dropped to her knees, holding out her torch in a gesture of supplication.

The footsteps stopped. Head bowed, Aidan said, "The *mindslayer* has truly won this game. The Dragon Princess surrenders." She glanced up. "Maybe our next game will present more of a challenge to the *mindslayer*."

Then, heart in her throat, she waited for his response.

Dawn was a barely discernible pearlness to the wet darkness outside as Dylan sat drinking strong black coffee in the breakfast nook, staring at her own battle-weary reflection in the bay window. Rain drizzles on the window superimposed tears on a face that had no more tears left to cry. The sky, however, continued weeping through a heavy fog, and pregnant clouds promised more storms before it was all over.

Dylan was thinking about her daughter, and about the crayoned message Matt had found in her room: *Be strong and courageous. . . . Be Tandy.* She could see it in her mind's eye as clearly as if her child had spoken the words right in her ear.

Would Aidan be any less? How could Dylan give up on her little girl, assuming she was dead when there was no such evidence? For one thing, Aidan wasn't like the other victims; she was much closer to the case than the other children ever imagined. It stood to reason that with her wit and brains and guts, she may very well have bought herself some time.

Hope is a thing intangible, but when it floods the darkened soul with light, it becomes a thing the desperate can grasp as surely as a loved one's hand.

"Oh, Aidan, my sweet child," whispered Dylan to the ghost-image of herself in the crying windowpane, "I'll be Tandy. And I'll find you, I swear it. I won't give up on you."

Through the faint glow of his own faltering torch, Shadow stared at the Dragon Princess. Once again she had proved herself Worthy, had even subjected herself to the *mindslayer*, which was as it should be.

"Arise," he said, "and we will return to the Trove Room. I feel certain the Secret Caverns have another adventure in store for us."

The Dragon Princess got to her feet. By their fading torchlight it was impossible to read her expression. Was she in awe of the *mindslayer*? Frightened? Or treacherous?

Until Shadow found out for sure, he was going to have to keep his guard up. Shifting his torch to his left hand, he took hold of her arm and guided her down the tunnel. As they walked, he felt her stiffen slightly. He glanced down at her, but her face was inscrutable.

They almost fell over the troll.

The Dragon Princess gasped and yanked back, out of Shadow's grip. He grabbed for her arm and grasped it tightly. Whispering fiercely in her ear, he said, "This is the fate of all trolls who defy the *mindslayer*."

She was shaking. They stepped over the troll and ducked beneath the tattered spiderweb. At the mouth of the tunnel Shadow hesitated. Which way was the Trove Room? He couldn't remember! For a long moment he stood, looking up and down the tunnel, running his tongue over his lips.

The Dragon Princess's torch flickered. Suddenly it fell to the ground. She dived for it, jerking free of Shadow's grasp, and managed to catch it just inches from the floor of the cave. It almost went out. She crouched there, panting. Shadow peered at her. She seemed to be looking for something. But before he could say anything about it, she scrambled to her feet.

Finally he said, "This way." He took her arm again and headed toward the right.

She resisted. "Why don't we try this way, instead?" she asked. "The big stalactite was in my face when I first came this way."

He nodded, impressed. So it was. He remembered that. "Okay. We go to the left."

The Dragon Princess's torch suddenly sputtered and went out, plunging them into a mere candleglow of light from his own. They both began to hurry. With panic dogging their heels, they were just about to break into a run when they spotted the orange-amber glow up ahead of the Trove Room.

Shadow was so grateful to see it he almost laughed aloud, but he didn't want the Dragon Princess to know he'd been frightened. After all, he was the *mindslayer*! A few more successful adventures like this, and he'd be the *mazemaster*!

Back in the Trove Room he took a long drink of water and allowed the Dragon Princess to take one as well. He extinguished their torches and lit fresh ones. Time had lost all meaning to Shadow. This was the most intensely happy he'd ever been in his life. He could stay right here, playing games in the Secret Caverns with the Dragon Princess forever and ever.

He gazed at her. By lampglow she was quite pretty, really, with that cloud of strawberry hair and those green eyes. She had shown herself to be brave and resourceful. In fact, he thought that she had rather enjoyed the game. Maybe she was as happy as he was, and he wouldn't have to worry that she'd try to escape, after all.

In fact . . . the more he thought about it . . . the more he began to realize that he wouldn't have to think of the Dragon Princess as an *opponent*, really, but more as an *ally*. Why, they could explore the Secret Caverns *together*! For his *true* opponent, after all, was really the Dragon Queen, anyway! And she would *never* find them here!

Excited now, Shadow dug around in his supplies and produced several sticks of beef jerky, which he shared with the Dragon Princess as a sort of peace offering. This was going to be great!

It called for a celebration. Somewhere in all this junk, Shadow knew, he had some sodas. He bent over and began pawing through journey-pouches and supply bags. Now, where were they? *There.* He would toast her, and they would embark on an adventure together, and it would be *so cool*!

Soda can in hand, Shadow whirled around. The smile on his face froze.

The Dragon Princess was gone.

TWENTY-SEVEN

Almost immediately Aidan realized she'd picked the wrong tunnel. In her haste to escape from Shadow, she'd meant to take the tunnel that led out of the Secret Caverns and maybe hide from him in the trees and brush. Instead, she'd been so afraid he'd catch her before she got away that she ran down the wrong tunnel.

She might never have had the nerve to run at all, if she hadn't found that flashlight, sticking up out of a backpack. A flashlight would be much easier to handle and control than a torch. She'd just finished slipping it down into the roomy pocket of the black leather jacket when Shadow turned away from her to hunt for something.

Then she had to go and run the wrong way!

Aidan could tell she was in the wrong tunnel because it kept getting narrower and narrower, until she had to drop to her knees and crawl. She knew the tunnel leading out of the Secret Caverns did not do this. Who knew *where* she was going now!

She could just hear Caleb saying, "*Duh,* Aidan. Way to go."

It was too late to turn back, though. He had to be coming after her.

The tunnel closed around her, growing tighter. She slipped to her stomach and pulled herself along by her arms. There was barely enough room for her. The flashlight was easier to hold than the torch, but the light wasn't as strong. This was worse than the spiderweb! What if it all caved down on her head?

207

An acrid odor assailed her nostrils and she sneezed. It smelled like a birdcage that hadn't been changed in a long, long time. She started breathing through her mouth—a trick she'd learned from cleaning Pandora's litter box.

The narrow tunnel began to slide downward, like the water slides at Wet N' Wild. Aidan gripped her flashlight, and in the next moment her body popped out and tumbled into a large room with a slick floor.

Almost immediately the air was filled with swirling black creatures that flapped across Aidan's face and caught in her hair. She screamed, swinging the flashlight in an arc in front of her. A high-pitched squealing resounded all around her.

Still screaming, Aidan began to run. The slick walls of the cave and the screeching creatures seemed to close in around her. She hit the other side and began frantically feeling her way around it, flashlight extended, jerking spasmodically to keep the demonic things away from her.

Eventually she found her way to a hole of sorts, set in the wall about waist high. Laying the flashlight ahead of her in the hole, she hoisted herself up into it, crawled through another narrow tunnel, and emerged into a room that echoed everywhere with the luscious sounds of falling water.

Heart hammering, still panting, Aidan shone her flashlight up and all around—as far as the beam would extend. It was a magnificent room, hollowed out as if by the hand of God. A waterfall spilled forth from high in the ceiling and coated the far wall in a stairstep pattern, before blending with an underground stream below.

"Oh, my gosh!" she cried. "This is *beautiful*!"

For one brief moment she forgot all terror, all horror, all anxiety, and just gave herself up to the delight before her.

Just out of the beam of her flashlight, something moved.

Aidan's breath caught in her throat. The flashlight beam began to jitter. Slowly she moved it across the room.

Whatever she had seen, it was *big*.

Could it be a monster? Some sort of phantom creature that only existed underground?

After all, she still didn't know what all those awful things were that attacked her in the other room.

Maybe it was a wild animal, trapped in here like she was. Maybe it was watching her, right now. Eyes saucered, Aidan peered all around the room, searching for two red points of light. She swallowed. "Who . . . who's there?" Her voice was tiny and weak.

She cleared her throat and said (more loudly this time), "I'm not going to hurt you. And . . . I hope you're not going to hurt me."

A noise. She jumped, jerking the flashlight beam toward the sound. The light hit something, bounced back, hit it again—it was trying to get away—

"Wait!" Aidan cried. She'd seen what it was, and it was no monster. "Don't run away! Let me help you!" She scrambled along over moist boulders and rock indentations, clutching her flashlight like a beacon. It slipped from her grip and fell, dousing the light.

Aidan froze. The dark was so thick she could almost touch it. She held her hand up close enough that her breath grazed it, but she could not see the hand. Slowly, fighting panic, she crouched and began running her hands over the slick rock floor of the cave.

A low whimpering sound came to her.

Her hand closed over the flashlight. She banged it on the floor. Once. Twice.

The light came on. Shaking with relief, she pointed it toward the whimpering sound.

"I know you," she said softly. "You're Jeremy Scott."

TWENTY-EIGHT

People from town as well as country neighbors crowded the white limestone house, all offering help in some way. Because Aidan had vanished from the library downtown, rather than a park outdoors, as the other children had, the police had chosen not to search the area with the hundreds of volunteers who had scoured the countryside looking for the other victims. But people wanted to do what they could. Even if they didn't know Dylan or Matt, they'd been following the agency's work with the ongoing cases through the newspaper and news conferences. It made her and her husband more personal to them. Besides, this was a crisis that had struck, not just individual families, but the whole town, and the whole town hunkered down together to get through it.

This was Dylan and Matt's first real acquaintance with small-town ways, and they were very moved. People they'd never seen before straightened the house and cooked meals and kept Caleb occupied. One woman took Aidan's dirty clothes home with her, washed them, and put them away in the child's room, so that Dylan or Matt wouldn't have to cope with the tragic little chore. Someone else went to fetch Dylan's dry cleaning. A neighbor phoned Dylan's mother.

Dylan wanted to thank them all, but for the time being she had more important things on her mind. With rain spattering the windows and gushing down corner eave gutters, she paced her gloomy bedroom, thinking.

She had trusted Aidan to be sensible enough, and knowledgeable enough about the Shadow, to do exactly as she was told and stay in the library. But Matt was right. Dylan had completely underestimated the sinister cleverness of her nemesis. Somehow, he had managed to lure her daughter away from the library, in spite of everything she knew about the dangers.

Aidan *had* to know him.

This thought was one of the most torturing. Aidan would never have left the library with someone she did not know. Of that, Dylan was certain. Who then? *Who? WHO?*

Dylan had been so cocksure of Chris Helmon's guilt. He had the knowledge of Dungeons & Dragons and other fantasy games. He had even befriended Aidan.

But Sergeant Dickerson was certain it wasn't him.

In spite of her better judgment, Dylan had to consider the possibility that Dickerson was right.

Possibilities. There were so many! Helmon could be working with an accomplice—perhaps even a woman. Most children trusted women implicitly as caretakers.

Peggy? Could Helmon be playing some macabre fantasy game with the shy, soft-voiced woman who fantasized an identity for herself that could communicate with the animals? Or children?

Dylan sagged against the cool, moist windowpane, resting her hot, achy head against it and closing her burning eyes. Grief and fear threatened to overwhelm her again, and she swallowed, fighting it.

"Dylan."

She hadn't heard the bedroom door open. Matt's powerful arms grasped her around the waist and pulled her tenderly back, into his lap.

The tears she hadn't wanted spilled over and trekked down her cheeks. "I lost our baby, and you'll never forgive me, never!" she whispered.

He stroked her hair. "It's me who should be forgiven," he murmured. "I was angry and I blamed you. We can't let this come between us. Our little girl deserves better."

Relief made her weak. Wrapping her arms around her

husband, Dylan nodded, struggling to regain control, not trusting herself to speak.

He held her tightly against him. "We gotta stay together," he said. "It's the only way we'll beat this thing."

"*Ahem.* Excuse me, Matt."

They both jumped and looked toward the door. An elderly man whose name escaped Dylan stood sheepishly, reluctant to intrude on their suffering. "There's somebody here who says he has to talk to you both. He says for sure he has to see you, Dylan."

"We can't see anybody right now," said Matt.

"It's all right," Dylan said. "I think I know who it is. I called him earlier."

"Who?"

Chris Helmon pushed into the bedroom.

Aidan shone the beam of the flashlight into the boy's face. He cried out in pain and covered his eyes. "Oh, I'm sorry," she said. "I guess you're used to the dark, aren't you?" She moved the beam down a bit and stepped closer to him. He scrambled away.

"Jeremy? I won't hurt you. I'm Aidan Tandy-Armstrong. Do you know who my mom is?" She took another step toward him. He shrank back but didn't run away. "My mom's name is Dylan Tandy. She's a detective—you know, a PI? Like Magnum. Your mom and dad hired her to find you. Everybody in the whole town's been looking for you." She noticed he was wearing several windbreakers, which he clutched close about him. "Your parents are going to be so excited that you're okay." She took a step closer. "Can't you talk?"

He didn't answer. She moved closer. "We do have this one problem, though. I got here the same way you did. I rode on a motorcycle with this weird guy, and he's been chasing me through the cave. Now you and me have got to figure out a way to escape from him."

She stopped just in front of him. "You've been in here a

long time. I don't know how you did it. You must be real brave and smart. I'm real glad I found you, because you can help me figure out how to get out of here. It'll be an adventure, huh? Like that movie *The Goonies*?"

Aidan reached out and patted the boy's trembling shoulder. He flinched. She patted it again. "It's okay," she said softly. "It's gonna be okay." She chewed her lip. "Gosh, Jeremy, I don't know what to do. I'm just a kid. I mean, maybe you're crazy now or something, I don't know. But we have to help each other. Don't you want to go home?"

Slowly she raised the outerglow of the flashlight to the periphery of the boy's face. It was filthy, and his eyes were really spooky. Like there was nothing there. She wished she knew what to do!

Leaving her hand resting gently on his thin shoulder blade, Aidan flashed the light around the cave room. In a corner near the waterfall was a small natural indentation in the rocks. Several backpacks showed up in the light. She smiled. "I know how you did it! You snuck back through that small tunnel and stole some things from the Treasure Trove room. Food and stuff. You *are* smart. How in the world did you do it? Don't you have a light or anything?"

When he didn't answer, she took his arm lightly and led him over toward the little makeshift campsite. There was a burned-out torch, but nothing else. "Gosh, Jeremy, you did all this like a blind person? *Wow*." She patted him again. "I'd say you're really Tandy."

Still, he said nothing.

"I guess you're not used to having anybody to talk to, huh? That's okay. My daddy says I talk enough for three people. Tandy, see, that's a *good* thing. It means you're brave and strong. It's part of my last name," she added proudly.

One thing bothered her. "Jeremy? I don't understand. If you could feel your way through that scary room with all those creatures in it, and down that narrow tunnel into the Trove Room, and back again, they why didn't you just go down that tunnel that leads out of the cave? Why didn't you escape?"

Pondering the unanswerable, she sat down, reached up, and pulled him down next to her like some huge gawky puppet. "I think I'll try an experiment," she said. She turned off the flashlight. Instantly they were shrouded in total blackness.

Jeremy cried out and started whimpering loudly. She groped for him in the dark and held on tight. "It's okay," she said. "I've got the light right here, see?" She flicked it back on. "I just wanted to see something. I guess it's so dark you couldn't *find* the right tunnel, huh?"

She let go of him and they sat close. "But wait a minute. Why didn't you steal a lantern or something? He's got a bunch of them in there." For a long moment she sat thinking, then said, "I guess you didn't want to go too far past the tunnel, in case Shadow came back, or maybe you were afraid of getting lost. So you could only reach stuff he stole from tr—kids. Besides, in the dark, you probably didn't know he had all that camping stuff in there. Yeah. I'll bet that's it."

This presented her with a fresh set of worries. She put her head in her hands. "I don't know how long the batteries in this flashlight will last." Aidan yawned. All this heavy thinking was tiring her out—not to mention all the running she'd done in the cave.

A sound came to her. First a whisper, then a rustle. She put her hand on Jeremy's arm. "What's that?" The rustling grew louder. Suddenly the air was filled with it.

Aidan beamed the flashlight all over the great room. A flood of tiny creatures rushed from the next room, across the ceiling of the cave, and over the waterfall. She screamed.

Cold fingers gripped her arm. She looked toward Jeremy, careful not to shine the light into his eyes. He was pointing to something high over the source of the waterfall. She shone the beam in that direction.

The creatures were disappearing into that place. Aidan

was terrified, but she could see that Jeremy was not. She forced herself to study what was happening as best she could with a single flashlight.

Finally it dawned on her. *"Bats!"* she cried. She strained to see where they were going, but the flashlight was pitifully dim. A hand closed over hers as she gripped the flashlight and pressed against it. At first she didn't understand. Then, she turned off the light.

The powerful rustling noise eased, abated, and finally stopped. Only then did Aidan discern, high above their heads, something she had not noticed before.

A small, weak shaft of light filtered high across the cave ceiling over the stream, coming from the small hole that seemed to be the source of the waterfall. The same opening the bats had used to make their escape.

TWENTY-NINE

"I can help you," said Helmon with a lopsided grin, his youthful voice cracking. "Like, with the rock."

The older gentleman left discreetly. Helmon came deeper into the bedroom. Dylan got to her feet, and Matt pivoted his chair. "What rock?" said Matt.

"You know. The one that got thrown through your window."

"I figured if anybody could help us make sense of the messages, Chris could," said Dylan. Secretly she was still very suspicious of the guy, but what choice did she have?

Matt, lowering his voice, ignored Helmon and pointed out to Dylan that the poems and other information were supposed to be kept confidential. "Dickerson'll hit the ceiling," he added.

Dylan shrugged. "It's not Dickerson's little girl, is it?" She turned to Helmon. "Tell us what you know about the rock."

He shrugged. "I know it's not the letter *H*."

Dylan crossed over to the dresser, where her bag lay, and dug through it. For a moment she couldn't find the rock. In frustration she flung things out onto the floor until it turned up in the palm of her hand. She held it out to Chris. "What are you talking about? You can see right here. Somebody painted the letter *H* onto it." Her eyes narrowed. "I figured it might stand for the name *Helmon*."

He laughed then. It was a genuine laugh. Dylan and Matt exchanged glances. "Naw," said Helmon. "It *looks* like a lopsided letter *H*, but it's not. It's a rune."

"A *what*?"

"A rune. You know. An ancient Viking symbol. Tolkien's work was full of runes."

"What exactly is a rune?" asked Matt.

Helmon reached for the smooth, round stone in Dylan's hand. His touch was gentle and warm. Still, she recoiled from it. "A rune is an ancient symbol," he said, "a message, if you will. Each symbol has a different meaning. Usually the runes are arranged in groups of three, but even a single rune can hold a powerful message concerning the direction your life is about to take." He held up the stone. "This *H*, as you call it, is actually the runic symbol *Hagalaz*, meaning disruption at its most elemental, or of events going completely out of your control. It is a warning that you may sustain a terrific loss in the near future."

"Oh, my God." Dylan plunked down on the edge of the bed. "Matt—he threw that stone through our window *before* Aidan disappeared. Could he have been . . . ?"

"Warning you," said Helmon. "Letting you know you were about to lose something dear to you."

"And if we had understood that warning—"

"You might never have left your daughter alone."

"No." She shook her head. "This is too hard to believe." She looked up at him. "How can I trust you? How do I know you aren't making all this up?"

He grinned. "I figured you might say something like that, especially after you whupped my butt the other day, so I brought this." From the pocket of his fatigue jacket he withdrew a small book entitled *The Book of Runes*. Opening the inside cover, he handed the book to Dylan and pointed to the nineteenth runic symbol. There it was, exactly as it had been painted on the rock.

"You wanna know something really spooky?" he asked. Without waiting for an answer, he said, "This same rune can often warn of an impending *natural* disaster, like hail or a flood."

Outside, the sky growled with thunder, as if to underscore

his quiet statement. In spite of herself Dylan shivered. "Wait a minute." She looked up from the book. "The police showed you this rock and asked you about the letter *H*. Why didn't you tell them that it was a rune?"

He shrugged. "They didn't ask."

She wanted to hit him right in his complacent face, but she was too amazed by the information he'd given her. She looked over at Matt and read the same bewilderment in his expression.

"Why did you come?" she asked.

He grinned. "You called me."

She shook her head. "You must know I thought you had taken Aidan."

"I figured that out soon enough when my whole house filled up with cops about three seconds after you started beating the shit out of me. Apparently everybody thought it was me."

"It could still be, you know," she said stubbornly. "You could be trying to throw us off right now."

"I could, I could. But then, how could you be thrown off any more than you already were?"

Dammit. He was starting to make sense.

"Anyway, from what you told me on the phone, I could tell right away this guy was a D and D freak. Had to be."

"But there is no *mindslayer* in Dungeons and Dragons," Dylan insisted.

"I didn't say he was a *good* game player, did I? Just that he must have some kind of fascination with it, right? Plus, for some strange reason he thinks kids are monsters."

"What?" said Dylan. "Oh, the trolls."

"Right. I figure this whole thing is some elaborate game plan he's got going."

"Do you think those kids are dead?" asked Matt bluntly. Up until then, he'd been listening with quiet seriousness.

Dylan twisted her hands together. She didn't want to hear the answer. All the same, she looked at the young man plaintively. *Please, God,* she thought.

"I don't really know. I've thought about that. Could be he's got 'em all holed up in some big old house somewhere, playing this game with him."

Her heart leapt within her. *So there was a chance.*

"What about the scrolls?" asked Matt.

"Okay." He shifted his weight.

"Sit down, please," said Dylan, indicating the chaise.

He plopped down and leaned forward. "Okay. Like the rune. It was a warning, right? So he's also sending you riddles."

"That's what Aidan said!" cried Dylan.

"Like in fantasy literature," said Matt.

"Right. If you figure out the riddle, you live. If you don't . . ."

Dylan stared at the floor. A wave of dizziness assaulted her. Vaguely she wondered when she'd eaten last. A day? Two?

Struggling not to lose her train of thought, she looked at this plain young man with a boy's body and face. She remembered well the richness of his imagination when he had led her and "Rowena" on a great adventure on behalf of King Saxon. Maybe he was dreaming all this up, putting his own wild interpretation on the situation.

But what other interpretation was there?

If Shadow was indeed lost in a fantasy world, then who better to help find him than a fellow lover of fantasy?

Then again, what if this *was* Shadow, and he worked with an accomplice, and even now was playing mind games with her? Her head, still sore from the mirror incident, was starting to throb, and she rubbed it absently.

After all, what alternative did she have? *Madness?*

She looked over at Matt. He sensed her gaze and returned it, and in the steadiness of his blue eyes had her answer.

"Okay, Chris," she said, getting up to retrieve her bag. "Let's go over those poems, one by one."

Treacherous, lying, deceitful she-troll!

Shadow's rage knew no bounds. He had been about to

trust her, and she had *betrayed* him! He should have known she was nothing but a miserable piece of bat guano all along! With a scream of rage and frustration, he smashed his torch against the cave wall, sending a lick of fire leaping into the Treasure Trove. A jacket went up in flames.

Wild now, he yanked up a bottle of water and doused the small fire, sending choking smoke through the ventless room. This was *her* fault! *All her fault!*

Chest heaving, he wondered which way she could have gone. Dashing down the tunnel to the opening of the Secret Caverns, he shoved aside the vines and peered out into pouring rain. A stream now funneled through the center of the grotto where none had existed before. He glanced at it in surprise, but he had other, more important things on his mind.

Searching around the cavern entrance, Shadow could make out no tracks leaving the cave.

That meant she could have gone only one way.

Suitable punishment, he thought, and then, *I'm not ready for her to die.*

It wouldn't be fair. He wasn't through with her yet.

Perhaps the Secret Caverns realized this and had spared her life. Shadow hurried back down the tunnel, fetched a lantern, and followed the narrower passageway until he could go no farther, and then he listened.

The Caverns did not whisper to him, as they had done before, and he heard no screams.

He was so excited he almost forgot himself. But then he remembered. The whole object was to gain enough points to become *mazemaster.*

Think, he told himself.

He did not know where the narrow tunnel led. Perhaps it led to an escape route. Perhaps it led round about and back to the Trove Room. Or perhaps it dead-ended, and she would have no choice but to return the very way she had come.

That was the first eventuality for which Shadow had to prepare. He did not want any more surprises.

Scrambling backward to a turnaround space, Shadow hurried back to the Trove Room, thinking furiously. It was time he quit trusting to chance. It was time he took control.

It was time Her Highness ran into a few little obstacles in her journey. And this time the *mindslayer* would be prepared.

"Jeremy!" cried Aidan. "There's a way out! The bats just left the cave through that opening up there. Oh, *wow*!"

Leaping to her feet, Aidan scrambled over to the stairsteps of the waterfall, which were like huge blocks cut out of the rock. She tried to stay out of the water as much as she could, but the surface was slick as glass and the spray as drenching as a shower. Soon she was wet, and the cave's natural coolness chilled her to the bone.

The flashlight protruded awkwardly out of her pocket as she climbed, offering too little light. She managed to make it up three of the big "steps" before reaching one that was too high for her hands to grab on to. Squinting into the mist, she strained her neck back to see over her head, but the tiny opening was still much too high for her to reach this way.

With a shivering sigh she worked her careful way down and rejoined Jeremy.

"I guess you already tried that, huh?" she said, curling icy wet fingers together in a futile attempt to warm them. "Kinda stupid of me to get all wet like that. G-gosh, it's c-cold."

Jeremy turned away from her and began groping wordlessly through the backpacks in his little corner. After a moment he pulled out a worn sweater and wrapped it around her shoulders. It was about two sizes too small, but she clung to it. "Thanks," she told him, and yawned. "Listen, I know there's gotta be a way out of here *somehow*. My dad's always saying—he can't walk, you see? He has to go around all the time in a wheelchair because he got shot one time. Anyway, he's always saying that if you can't do something one way, you keep trying until you find another way to do it. He's really cool. He climbs mountains and stuff. Really!"

She stretched the sweater until it covered her nose and cheeks. "So I figure we gotta find some other way. Maybe on the other side of the stream there's a better way to climb. Or maybe there's another tunnel. Or something. You can help, Jeremy. You been here all this time and stuff. I mean, you could do it blindfolded." She giggled. "I made a little joke. Get it? You could do it *blindfolded*."

A strange, scratchy sound emerged from Jeremy. A choking sound. Alarmed, she swung the flashlight beam into his face. He cried out from the light, but not before she had seen the grin.

Jeremy Scott, little lost and blinded spelunker . . . had been *laughing*.

Aidan's young heart filled with hope. After all, Dad always said that if you could laugh, you could survive anything. Now all they had to do was figure out how to outsmart that Shadow guy. Caleb always liked to quote Arnold Schwarzenegger in *Terminator 2*: "No problemo."

They could do it. No problemo.

Except that, right now, Aidan felt so very tired. "Jeremy? Don't be afraid, okay? I gotta turn out the flashlight for now, okay? I thought we might sleep for a little while, and when we wake up, we'll be all rested and everything and we can find a way to escape, okay?" She sneezed. "I'll be right here, right beside you. Right here." Stretching out on the cold, hard, moist cave floor next to the tumbling water, she made a pillow for herself out of one of the backpacks. The leather jacket had protected her somewhat from the mists of the waterfall, but her head and neck and legs had gotten wet, and she was cold all over. She tightened the jacket around her, spread out the small sweater over her legs, and laid her heavy head on the backpack. "Don't forget, Jeremy," she whispered, "I'm right here."

She turned out the light. This time Jeremy didn't whimper. The sudden blackness was disorienting, but the gurgling, rushing water was soothing. As long as she kept her eyes closed, she could pretend she was in a beautiful forest next to a lovely stream. Or better yet . . . sleeping out with Caleb right behind the house on the sloping green lawn beneath a bezillion stars, while the gentle waters of the stream rushed over her and Caleb's dam.

Then she fell into a deep and unfortunate sleep.

THIRTY

Chris Helmon studied each note while Dylan explained where they'd been found and how. "Okay. Here's the deal," he said. "I think he's taking buildings and stuff from right here in Kerrville and using them in the poems. Like you were telling me about the 'riverside wall.' Come to find out, it wasn't a wall by the river at all, but a small dam near Riverside Drive."

"So you think this part, here, where he says, 'After searching the Castle high and low; She will find a message from the Shadow,' could mean a house here in Kerrville? Maybe his own home?" asked Matt.

"I don't know. Maybe."

"But you don't think so," prompted Dylan.

"Tell the truth, no. You gotta think like this guy thinks. If he says 'castle,' he *means* 'castle.'"

"But there aren't any castles around here." Matt clawed his fingers through his hair.

"No, not literal castles. But you got to think, is there a building somewhere that might *look* like a castle?"

Dylan and Matt shared feelings of mutual frustration. They stared at each other blankly.

"Think about it." Helmon was grinning.

Dylan realized that Helmon already knew what Shadow was talking about and was enjoying his power—*real* power for a change. She didn't have much patience left and even less temper. "For Christ's sake, you little twerp, tell us what you know or leave us alone!" she cried.

Matt frowned at her. She ignored him.

224

"There's no need to be rude," he said. He sounded genuinely hurt. Dylan wanted to kick him. He not only looked like a kid, he *acted* like one. She glared at him.

"Okay," he said with a note of resignation in his voice. "You know about a place called the Hill Country Museum, over on Garrett Street?"

Dylan and Matt shook their heads.

"It used to be the home of a guy named Captain Charles Schreiner. It was built about a hundred years ago, in the Romanesque style." He sat back, beaming triumphantly.

Dylan still wanted to kick him, but Matt straightened excitedly in his wheelchair and said, "Wait a minute! I know what you're talking about! It's a building downtown—" He turned toward Dylan. "It looks like a fucking castle!" He started rolling toward the door, and Dylan scrambled after him, stuffing the poems in her bag.

Helmon didn't move. "Come on!" she shouted. "We're going to the castle to find the next scroll!" He jumped up and followed them.

They all headed for the front door to take the van. Dylan could see they were hemmed in by one of the ladies in the kitchen. She needed to ask the lady to move her car, and she wanted to check on Caleb and tell him what they were doing before she left. On her way back through the house, she stopped for a moment and glanced out the French doors toward the deck, where rain pounded so hard on the roof that . . . she hesitated. The quality of sound from the downpour had made a subtle change. It was deeper, heavier. Something wasn't right about it.

Dylan pushed open the door and stepped out onto the deck, just under the overhang. There the noise came to her full force: rushing and plunging. For a moment when she recognized the sound, her heart seemed to stop.

It was the little stream out back . . . only now it was a raging torrent many feet over the top of the little dam lovingly constructed by her children just a few sunny days ago. The waterfall had disappeared. The gnarled roots of the cypress trees lining the banks of the stream were already underwater.

The ominous sky pressed ever closer, swollen, bruised, and angry. And the rains poured relentlessly down, threatening all that Dylan held dear.

Aidan woke with a start, but even though she opened her eyes, everything was still black. Thrashing her arms, she cried out. A soothing hand closed over her arm, and a moment later a flashlight was pressed into her hand.

Then she remembered.

It wasn't just the remembering that was bad; Aidan felt terrible. Her neck was incredibly stiff and her head ached. It felt as if every muscle in her body was sore, and she felt so very heavy. Oddly enough, she felt hot, too. She'd gone to sleep feeling cold, but now she felt hot.

There were so many things she and Jeremy needed to do! But she didn't want to do anything just yet. Maybe rest a little more.

She flicked on the light and was immediately comforted. Jeremy sat close by. "Boy, you really are Tandy," she said, but her tongue seemed a bit thick and it was hard to talk. "I mean, you had to wake up time after time and there was nobody here and you didn't have a light. No wonder you don't want to talk to anybody." She shivered. Why was she shivering when she felt hot? "I feel lousy," she said and closed her eyes.

Jeremy got up and left her side. A moment later he returned, holding out a Batman cup from some kid's lunchbox. She took it from him and drank gratefully. The water was crisp and cold and tasted better than any she'd ever had.

But she was so *tired*. She could hardly hold up the cup! "Do you think I could have some more?" she asked. Her neck really hurt.

Jeremy got to his feet and went back to the stream. He didn't need the light to navigate at all and wasn't the slightest bit hesitant in his movements. He really had learned to move like the blind. She wondered what it was like to be alone in total darkness for two weeks. Most people, she figured, would go crazy.

But there were the bats, who, she remembered from a science report, really wouldn't hurt you—they were a kind of company. And there was that wonderful singing waterfall. Then—way, way up high—was that thin shaft of light, like a tiny glimmer of hope in the darkness. The water and what little food he'd been able to scavenge had kept his body going, but Aidan suspected it was that tiny beacon of hope that kept his spirit alive.

She wondered if he was ever going to talk again, and felt sad for his parents. That reminded her of *her* parents, and she felt heartsick at what they must be going through.

There was one thing she didn't like to think about, though, but she couldn't seem to help it. Would they all just assume that she was dead and stop looking?

A shudder took her over and lengthened into a spasm of shivering. Jeremy returned with the water, and she gulped it all down. "We've got to plan our escape," she said weakly. "It's just, I think I'm getting sick or something. I feel really yucky." She sighed. "You gotta tell me, Jeremy. Have you tried to find another way to climb up to the hole the bats go out of?" She shone the flashlight's beam somewhere in the neighborhood of his chest, and he nodded. "You know, I probably should turn this flashlight off and save the batteries. Won't do me much good, though, if you won't talk to me. I can't see you nod in the dark."

She waited. He said nothing.

Exasperated, she turned off the light anyway. The sound of the water falling was soothing. She found herself drifting off to sleep. Her last weary thought was that the waterfall seemed noisier somehow, like maybe there was more water coming down the cave wall and into the underground stream.

Aidan fell into a restless, feverish sleep, short-circuited by dreams of swimming for her life.

"Mom, I'm going with you," said Caleb, planting his feet apart and crossing his arms over his chest in a purely Dylanesque stance.

"Caleb, there's really nothing you can do."

"How do you know? I might have some good ideas." He turned and dug around in his closet for a windbreaker. When he spoke, his voice was muffled. "Aidan's my sister," he said, "and if I have to sit around this house in the rain with all these people hanging around for one more minute, worrying about her, I'll go nuts." He faced her and shrugged on the windbreaker. His twelve-year-old jaw was set in a way she'd never seen, his chin high with determination. Dylan had no doubt that, if they left without him, he'd follow through the mud and rain on his bike.

She had never been prouder of him. "Let's go, then," she said and turned away quickly so that he wouldn't have to hide his relief from her.

Caleb dashed out the door, and Dylan followed, running through pelting rain to the van. Along the way to the museum, Chris told them some more about the Schreiner home. Construction had begun over a hundred years before, and it had taken nearly twenty years to finish. Built of thick native stone and complete with bays, rounded arches, and turretlike spires, the house was the closest thing Kerrville had to a medieval castle.

Flash-flood warnings were in full effect when they pulled up to the historic landmark building. It seemed to brood in the mist beneath gray, lowering skies. They stared through drizzled windows at it.

"The poem said, 'start in the middle,'" said Dylan. "What do you think he meant by that?"

"Could be a middle room."

"Or a middle archway."

"Or a middle floor."

"Let's get going," Dylan said. They piled out, waiting impatiently for the apparatus that lowered Matt's chair. Passing through a black wrought-iron fence with spikes, they confronted a stairway leading up to the front porch, but no ramp. Dylan gave Matt a hand with the stairway, and then they split up.

The underlying sense of urgency made the task seem almost overwhelming to Dylan. They had already lost so much time! Who knew how long the scroll had been hidden here? And where were they to start looking?

She almost went back to the car and phoned Dickerson. He could have officers and agents swarming around this place in five minutes. But something held her back. The Shadow wanted to confront her alone. It had been so from the beginning. Dylan was beginning to think that the only way they were ever going to find the elusive child-snatcher was for her to go it—one on one—with Shadow.

Standing there on the porch, trying to think where to start, Dylan was amazed by a triumphant shout from over her head.

Caleb had found the scroll.

It had been jammed into the wrought-iron balcony beneath the middle archway on the second floor. Had no one been specifically searching for the small roll of paper, it might never have been found.

They huddled together in the van to read it. To Dylan's dismay, it had been soaked by rain, and the drenched ink had bled. The words were almost illegible. Laboring over it like a team of Dead Sea manuscript experts, they finally managed to piece together the rhyme:

> *Congratulations to the Dragon Queen,*
> *Who finally figured out what I mean.*
> *To follow the path of the trolls' last journey,*
> *Look to the enchanted beasts for the pass key.*

"His rhythm's all off," pointed out Caleb. "He'd flunk English."

Dylan and Matt turned toward Helmon. He said, "I guess you're wondering what he means by enchanted beasts, huh?"

"It would help," said Matt dryly.

"Hmmmm." Helmon turned to gaze out the window. In the ensuing silence, rained drummed loudly on the van roof.

"This one bothers me more than the others," said Dylan. "Look here—he's talking about *I* rather than about *Shadow* or *the Shadow*."

"First person then, rather than third," mused Matt. "What do you make of it?"

"I'm not sure, but I'd guess that Shadow is no longer a fantasy character to him, but he now *is* the Shadow."

"Which means he's now completely out of touch with reality."

Dylan fought the gloom of despair. "That's the way I figure it."

"I got it!" cried Helmon.

They all turned to him. Dylan took her bottom lip between her teeth.

"I figured out what he means by 'enchanted beasts,' " he said. "And you'll never believe it."

THIRTY-ONE

The next time Aidan woke up, she felt even worse. At first she panicked again, especially when she couldn't find Jeremy. But a flashlight search revealed him prone on his stomach beside the stream. Both his arms were extended in front of him, and he seemed to be holding something underwater.

She got dizzily to her feet and staggered over to him. Suddenly he scooped up what appeared to be a school lunchbox, reached inside, and pulled out a tiny flopping fish. To her shock, he swallowed it whole, then turned and grinned at her. Dipping a brick-red hand back into the lunchbox, he produced another fish and offered it to Aidan.

She nearly threw up. "Oh, gross, Jeremy! Yuck! You're eating them alive! Uncooked! Eeew." She turned away and returned to her "bed," where she plunked down, thinking that this must be the positively absolutely yuckiest thing she'd ever seen in her life.

Then again, what else did he have to eat? After all, there couldn't have been that much in the three or four backpacks she saw. She looked back at the boy with renewed respect. Who would have thought to go fishing with a lunchbox?

"What are you, some kind of Cub Scout or something?" she asked with a grin. But her throat hurt when she talked, and her head was beginning to spin. She turned off the flashlight, heard another splash, and assumed that Jeremy had gone back to fishing.

A remarkable kid, really. She'd like him to meet her dad. They'd like each other.

But first, they had to get out of here.

She rested until Jeremy came back to sit beside her. "Jeremy, have you explored this whole room? I mean, I know you didn't have any light or anything to help you. Why don't we look around with the flashlight, okay?"

He nodded. She started to get up, hesitated, then said, "I feel so clumsy and yucky." He reached down and took her arm to help her up. She stood, shivering, took a step, then reached back her hand toward Jeremy. He took it and they were both comforted.

Moving slowly because of the slippery floor and Aidan's bouts of dizziness, they worked their way all around the room. At one point they jumped the narrow stream and searched the other side, especially the wall beneath the opening high above.

They could see no way out.

After a long search, which exhausted them both, they sat down to rest. Aidan suddenly remembered the beef jerky Shadow had given her. She handed a piece to Jeremy, who marveled at it before wolfing it down almost whole—just as he had done the fish. Aidan, thinking of the fish, decided to save hers for later. "You know Shadow, that crazy guy? I think he's moved in. There was a sleeping bag and stuff. If we go back into the Trove Room, we've got to sneak past him in order to get to the tunnel that leads out of the cave." She sighed. Her neck was so stiff she could hardly move it, and her head was pounding. A shiver possessed her and would not go away. She looked at Jeremy. "We've got to do it. You're starving to death and I'm getting sick. Besides, they'll never find us in here."

Aidan turned out the light to save batteries, and Jeremy moved closer. Leaning her head heavily on his shoulder, she said, "He can't stay awake forever, can he?" Jeremy, as usual, was silent. Aidan wished she knew what time it was. She wished somebody could somehow figure out how to find them. She thought of her parents, who must be desperate by now. Her head hurt and she felt awful and she wanted to cry. Then she remembered something her dad had told her once, when she felt sorry for him. He said, "Count what you have left, not what you have lost."

There was one thing Aidan had in this cold, dark, and barren place that she never would have expected to have, and that was a friend. Maybe, together, they could outwit Shadow. But they had to act soon. If she got much sicker, she didn't think Jeremy would be able to carry her out.

The image of the little crumpled boy, covered in blood and dumped in a tunnel, flashed clearly into Aidan's mind, and she was suddenly more frightened than she had ever been in her life. *"This is what happens to trolls who defy me,"* Shadow had said.

And Aidan had definitely defied him. Her shivering grew worse, almost uncontrollable now, and her teeth began to rattle together. Jeremy got to his feet and pulled her up with him. She turned the light back on.

In spite of the light he began feeling his way along the cave walls—all around—until he came to a hole about waist high. She followed and shone the flashlight beam into it. From the looks of it, it was the short tunnel that led to the bat room. For a long moment they stood in front of it, weighing their fears against their courage. Finally Aidan said, "We have to be Tandy." Jeremy nodded.

Jeremy, who was more used to finding his way through the tunnel, went first. Aidan followed closely behind. The first little stretch wasn't easy, because it was on a slippery incline, but soon enough they were in the chamber that had once been alive with bats. Aidan remembered from her science report that the bats would return, and she wondered when. In spite of the fact that she knew they weren't dangerous, she still didn't want to be here when they came back.

Jeremy groped his way around the wall of the bat chamber until he came to the tunnel leading out. She wondered how many times he'd gotten turned around in the hollow blackness and wound up back in the waterfall room.

But he seemed to know what he was doing, and she followed, feeling as claustrophobic as before, when the narrow walls closed in around her shoulders.

Soon they were able to get to their hands and knees. Aidan was still carrying the flashlight, but Jeremy reached back and made her turn it off. She realized that he was right, but she really hated being in the tunnel in the pitch dark and hurried along, bumping her nose against his butt from time to time. She did not want to find herself alone in the dark tunnel, and wondered, again, just how the boy had managed to keep his sanity.

Eventually they got to their feet and crouched, and her heart began pounding in rhythm to the beating in her head, because she knew they were drawing nearer to the Trove Room, where Shadow almost surely must be waiting. Instinctively she walked on the toes of her sneakers, holding on to the waistband of Jeremy's pants. When they stood up, she knew they were almost there. She felt faint and struggled against it.

Almost there.

Jeremy stopped. She stumbled up against him and waited until her breath calmed and her heartbeat slowed back down. He was listening for something, and she listened, too, straining in the profound cave silence.

Then she heard it . . . a gentle snoring! Shadow was asleep! She grabbed Jeremy's arm and squeezed it. She couldn't believe the ordeal was almost over.

Walking abreast now, they tiptoed along to what their senses told them was the mouth of the tunnel, though they were still surrounded by total blackness.

Aidan took a step.

Too late, she felt the trip wire give way against her ankle, and before she could even register the thought—the silence was jarred by an unholy jangling racket that sent electrified sparks of terror through Aidan's body. Like a deer trapped in headlights, she froze.

Jeremy yanked the flashlight from her hand and turned it

on. Dragging Aidan by the hand, he took off in a dead run
down the tunnel . . . with the bellowing Shadow close on
their heels.

When the van pulled up in front of the shop, they all
exchanged sheepish glances.

"What do we say to the guy?" asked Caleb. "I mean, he'll
think we're crazy."

"We don't say anything," said Matt.

"Right," agreed Dylan. "We just say we want to look
around. And you understand what we're looking for."

"Right."

"Okay. Let's go."

They made their way into the dreary rain. Matt had to
jump a curb, which was usually no problem to him, but the
gutters were awash with rain. Dylan and Chris hefted his
wheelchair between them and set it up on the sidewalk.

They hurried into a shop called Hill Country Taxidermy.

Between Ingram and Kerrville, there had to be half a
dozen taxidermy shops, catering to everything from the
exotic to the mundane. YOU SHOOT IT, WE'LL STUFF IT read the
sign over the door.

Dylan had never been in a taxidermy shop before. She
was amazed at the quality of workmanship, and at the
tasteful and beautiful displays of wildlife, similar to what
she'd seen in museums, set in glass cases and surrounded by
natural plants and rocks.

They didn't find any scrolls.

Discouraged, they trooped on out into the rain and headed
for the next shop.

And the next.

"Maybe you were wrong," commented Matt, splashing
the van through a low-lying street. "Could there be any
other kinds of enchanted beasts?"

"I don't think so," said Chris. "You have to think in terms
of fantasy, of casting spells and enchantments and stuff like

that. The animals in a taxidermy shop look like real animals that have had a spell cast on them.''

He had a point.

Wilderness Taxidermy was their last stop in Kerrville, before heading down the road to Ingram. Dylan was feeling damp and cold and miserable. She still wasn't convinced that they were doing the right thing by trusting Chris Helmon, but she didn't see that they had any choice.

She was feeling light-headed and knew she would have to eat something or pass out cold, which would be no help to anybody. She wondered if her baby was being fed, and her heart cracked. As if reading her mind, Matt reached over and squeezed her hand. It gave her strength.

Animals, frozen in their magnificence, stared at Dylan with moist and artificial eyes. It spooked her. She especially hated the severed heads, mounted on carved wooden frames and lining the walls. It seemed like such a barbaric custom to her, and she kept fighting the image of a row of human heads, mounted and lining the cave walls of the den of some mountain grizzly bear someplace.

"Dylan." Matt's hiss held excitement. Dylan hurried over to him. "In the bear's mouth," he whispered. She looked up. It was way out of Matt's reach.

"You take point," she said. He nodded and wheeled over to the proprietor, who'd been watching them keenly since they arrived. Gushing over a display at the other end of the store, Matt led the man away and kept him occupied while Dylan stood on tiptoe and reached her fingertips into the mouth of the bear, just barely grasping a smidgeon of purple velvet material.

She gave it a little yank, and a purple pouch fell out and hit her on the head before bouncing onto the floor. She scooped it up and dropped it into her bag, waited for a few moments, then headed for the door. "Matt, we really have to be going," she said.

He joined her and they all bumped eagerly out the door, racing through the pummeling rain for the van. Dylan's heart was pounding. This was no scroll. Whatever was inside the pouch, it was *heavy*.

Gathering together in the van, they peered at Dylan, who opened the purple velvet pouch with trembling, cold fingers. She reached inside and pulled out a small piece of cardboard, on which were pasted three round smooth stones, all in a row.

The first had painted on it what looked like the letter *M*. The second, the letter *R*, and the third one was blank.

Chris sucked in his breath, and they all looked at him expectantly.

"More runes?" asked Caleb.

"Yeah."

There was a reluctant tone to his voice that Dylan did not like. *"What?"*

He groped in his roomy fatigues pocket and withdrew the small book on runes. "We have to take them in order," he said slowly. "It's just . . ."

She held her breath. She didn't want to hear, but she did.

He gave her a long look and his eyes appeared hooded, shadowed. *"What? What?"* she cried.

"Well, I mean, you have to take them in order—"

"Talk or we'll break your neck!" said Matt.

"Okay. It's just that last one."

"What about it?" Caleb's voice was also sharp and irritable.

"It's blank."

"Yeah, so?" Dylan's mouth turned to cotton.

He still hesitated. "It usually means death."

THIRTY-TWO

Aidan pushed herself to run as fast as she could, but her legs seemed to have turned to pea soup. It had taken Shadow only a moment to spring to his feet and chase after them, and he was so close behind that she was afraid to look around. Their only hope lay in reaching the crawl space just ahead of him and squirming through just out of reach. They both knew his shoulders were too broad to fit.

Once they dropped to their hands and knees, it was painful going. She could hear Shadow grunt—it was a narrower fit for him. Jeremy hit the smallest tunnel first and slithered through like a snake. Aidan's legs ached so badly and felt so heavy that she was ready to collapse by the time she had to stretch out. Whimpering in pain and fear, she dragged herself along, but she was too slow.

A hand clasped her foot.

Screaming and kicking, she fought to get loose, but he began pulling her backward. Jeremy could do nothing to help her. Sobbing, struggling, Aidan summoned up her last resource of strength, gave her foot a mighty heave—and the Keds sneaker came off in Shadow's hand. Before he could drop it and grab her foot, she'd yanked her body just inches out of his reach.

His furious screams of frustration careened off the narrow tunnel and assaulted the ears of the two children, who didn't stop until they'd reached the waterfall room, where they dropped in a heap to the floor, clinging to each other and panting as much from terror as fatigue.

When Aidan could talk, which wasn't easy over her fear

and trembling, she said, "I should have known. Booby traps."

"Take it from the top," said Matt grimly. They all huddled together in a booth at the Bluebonnet Café, where Dylan was forcing herself to eat while the others drank coffee. Caleb had a Coke.

Helmon tapped the first stone with the tip of his finger. "I guess you think that's the letter *M*."

"Not necessarily," said Dylan, her voice heavy with sarcasm. She was beyond impatience with Chris Helmon.

"Okay." He flipped through the book on runes until he found the one painted on the stone. "It's called *Ehwaz*," he intoned, "and it is the rune of transit and transition. It can be like, a new dwelling place, or a physical change, or just a steady spiritual growth. Usually growth means improvement."

"Well, we can count that out, can't we?" said Dylan irritably.

He ignored her. "This second one, here; it looks kind of like a jagged *R*, right? No rounded edges or anything. It's called *Raido*, and it means 'journey,' or more specifically, a reunion after a journey. It's a spiritual union. It can also mean '*quest*.'"

Matt frowned. "You figure this guy thinks he's having some sort of spiritual reunion with these kids?"

"Geez, Dad, do you mean like in heaven?" Caleb blurted.

Dylan shot Matt a stern look. They had to be careful what they said around the boy. This whole thing was frightening enough for him.

"I doubt it," offered Chris. "The runes really don't have anything to do with heaven and stuff."

"Then what are they?" asked Caleb.

"Okay. There are twenty-five total runes in a set, see. You're supposed to keep them in a pouch, and then, like, whenever you've got some big decision to make in your life, or you have some real doubts about something or whatever, you consult the runes."

"How do you do that?"

"You shake up the bag real good, then you reach inside without looking and pull out three runes. Each rune has a special meaning, and when you put them together, it's supposed to give you some kind of spiritual direction."

"Like a sign?"

"Kinda. Also, in Viking times and other ancient times, runes were used to communicate messages along roadsides or whatever. In fantasy books, like *The Lord of the Rings* or what have you, you'll see runes around the border of a map, or placed along a trail in the woods."

Caleb nodded. "Cool."

"Can we get on with this?" Dylan had to admit that Helmon's knowledge was impressive, but it didn't improve her mood.

"Okay. The last rune, then, is the blank rune. That's supposed to be a tremendously powerful rune. It can mean the Unknowable, or it can stand for Odin, which can portend death."

"What does *portend* mean?" asked Caleb.

"Like, predict, in a way. But mainly, it just means your destiny. Let's see here . . . It says that 'nothing is predestined.' Mainly, the Unknown beckons."

"So, what do you think it all means?" asked Matt.

"He obviously meant for the Dragon Queen to find it, so it's a message for her. Now, I don't know if this guy really consulted the runes, here, or if he just picked out the ones that said what he wanted to say. Anyhow, I think he's warning her that her life has undergone a tremendous change—"

"He's got that part right," said Dylan gloomily.

"And that she is going to have to embark on a quest to seek her destiny."

"A *quest*?" asked Matt. "You mean like Don Quixote?"

Helmon shrugged. "I don't know. I'm not the Dungeon Master here. All I can say is that the end of the quest is always unknown. Or maybe he intends the other meaning. Maybe the kids are dead already. Who knows? It's his game."

Dylan put her head in her hands. After all, that's all it was to some psychotic freak out there who was destroying the lives of innocent children and their families.

A game. Just a game.

Caleb took the card with the stones glued on from Helmon and began to toy with it. He turned it over in his hands. "Guys! Look!"

They all leaned forward.

Drawn lightly in pencil on the back of the card, so casually as to be almost missed altogether—was a map.

Shadow no longer owned himself. Instead, rage possessed him. He wanted to hurt somebody and, thwarted in that desire, he wanted to destroy. Jerking his dagger from its scabbard at his waist, he pawed through the Treasure Trove. He'd grab up a journey-pouch and start slashing. When he could do no more damage there, he'd discard it and rip into another one.

It was as if he had superhuman strength, and his fury knew no bounds. Every little frustration he'd ever known, every denial of his heart's desire, every pent-up resentment, spewed forth from him like hot molten lava from a volcano.

He wanted to kill.

In spite of every logical thought he'd ever held, Shadow was certain he'd heard *two* trolls running away from him! That could mean only one thing: The Secret Caverns had allowed the first troll to escape from the bats. However, the moronic trolls' pitiful attempt to escape had told Shadow something else, loud and clear: There were no tunnels leading out of the chamber they now occupied, nor was there an escape route.

Chest heaving, heart hammering, Shadow straightened his body over the shredded and slashed remains of stolen booty. Tattered bits of material clung to his velvet cloak, and tufts of cotton batting floated and swirled around him, settling softly to the floor of the cave like snowflakes.

He smiled.

They could not stay in there with the bats forever, he knew. Sooner or later they would have to come out, and when that time came, the *mazemaster* would be waiting for them.

Aidan dozed fitfully, while fever tricked and teased at her brain and all the collected aches—her head, her neck, her legs, her stomach, her throat—melted into one hot bodypain and settled in for the duration.

Once, she awoke with a start. The flashlight had been turned off, and she searched the far reaches of the cavern ceiling for the thin shaft of light that kept hope alive and despair at bay.

She couldn't find it.

"Jeremy!" she cried. "Where's the light? I can't see the light!" She fumbled for the flashlight and beamed it in a general arc, expecting to find her friend huddled down close by. Instead, he was standing strangely erect over near the waterfall, his head cocked as if listening fiercely.

She turned off the flashlight and listened.

It *was* noisier!

"Jeremy . . . what's going on?" She waited nervously for the sounds of his shoes padding over the moist cavern floor to her. She reached out her hand in the darkness until they found each other, and he helped her to her feet. Wordlessly he led her toward the water for a few feet, then stopped. Groping for the flashlight, he shone it down, toward the water.

The little stream they had jumped over just hours earlier now stretched three times the width. Even as Aidan watched, horrified, the water crept up a few inches more.

• • •

They took Caleb home, and the first thing Dylan did was step out onto the deck to see if the creek had risen further. To her horror, it had already flooded its banks and was creeping across the sloping lawn toward the house.

Matt joined her on the deck to survey the threat. The first thing they did was send home all the neighbors so that they could tend to their own property and animals.

"My house is on pretty high ground," Helmon assured them, and settled down on the couch with Caleb and Pandora to study the crude and confusing map they'd found on the back of the runes card. He thought it might be the map of a cave, but it was too incomplete to say for sure.

Matt and Dylan held a furtive conference in the breakfast nook. "I feel like we're under siege," said Dylan, twisting her hands together. "All I want to think about is Aidan, but I have to think about Caleb, too, and our home. I don't know what to do."

"C'mon, Red, you're stronger than that. It's not like you to wring your hands and play the helpless female."

She sighed. "I don't know. Where does strength come from? I always believed it came from within, or from God, or whatever, but now I wonder if it doesn't come from home and family, too. Without those . . . then who am I, after all?"

"You're still Dylan Tandy. And you haven't lost your home *or* your family. Not yet, anyway."

She gazed out the window at the endless, slashing rain. Five inches had fallen the day before, and they were expecting at least another five today. Even more worrisome was the fact that even heavier rains had fallen farther north, near the headwaters of the Guadalupe, which meant that swollen floodwaters would begin spreading down and overloading what was already a high-water area. Barricades had been set up in the lowest-lying areas to keep people from trying to drive though, and warnings had been posted to prevent people from pushing their vehicles into unsafe areas. The police were forced to set aside their investigation on Aidan's case, for the time being, in order to deal with the more immediate crisis of evacuating families from harm's way.

Dylan felt fractured and unfocused. There seemed to be so many different crises pulling at her at the same time that she was having difficulty deciding anything. Something was nagging at her. She stood in the middle of the kitchen, thinking.

Matt, sensing her uncharacteristic confusion, called Caleb into the kitchen and told him to pack up a few clothes for himself and Aidan as well as a very few of their most precious possessions. He sent Chris out to the utility room to fetch Pandora's carrying case and a sack of dry cat food.

"We've got to get out of here," he told her. "We'll go to the police department, and they'll send us to the nearest safe shelter." Caleb entered the kitchen and gently placed Aidan's stuffed mouse, Squeakers, on the table. It looked alone and forlorn. "Throw a few things in a bag, Dylan," Matt said, forcing her attention. "Scrapbooks, photo albums, whatever. Things we can't replace. Okay? We haven't much time."

Scrapbooks. Matt said to get scrapbooks. Dylan headed slowly for their bedroom, trying to make herself think about scrapbooks when something else . . .

Judging from Chris Helmon's behavior, Dylan was having a hard time continuing to think of him as a kidnapper and possible murderer. A nerd, maybe. Definitely a nerd, but a bad guy? Cop instincts were overcoming her own suspicions, telling her to look elsewhere.

Who else knew about Dungeons & Dragons, and about runes, and fantasy literature?

Marty, certainly, and Peggy. People she'd played with that night when she had become "Rowena" and had helped to save the Princess Aurelia.

Dylan reached the bedroom and sat on the edge of the

bed. She had to hurry. Had to gather up some scrapbooks and stuff . . .

Who else had a problem with the restrictions of the game, with the power of the Dungeon Master? She pulled out a couple of photo albums from a shelf.

The two boys who had left the group. David Elliott. Jason Crandall. But they were just kids themselves, for God's sake!

"Dylan! Hurry up!" Matt's voice, drifting from the kitchen, lended urgency to her reverie. But instead of gathering more mementos, she leaned across the bed to grab for the phone, fumbling in a bedside drawer as she did so for the Kerrville phone book.

It was a long shot, but she had to check it out.

She found the number but, to her immense frustration, wound up listening to a recording: *"You have reached the Elliott residence. Please leave a message at the tone."* She slammed down the phone and dialed again.

A cultered male voice answered. She said, "Mr. Crandall, this is Dylan Tandy. It's urgent that I talk to you about your son—"

"Ms. Tandy!" he interrupted. "Thank God it's you! How did you know I was looking for Jason?"

Dylan shook her head. "What? Is this Mr. Crandall?"

"Yes."

"Mr. Crandall, I'm a private inves—"

"I know who you are. I've read about you in the paper. That's why I'm so astonished that you would call. I've been so frantic, I almost called you myself."

Dylan got to her feet and carried the portable phone toward the kitchen. "I'm not sure I understand—"

"Well, I thought perhaps the police had called you when I reported Jason missing."

"No." Entering the kitchen, Dylan gestured to Matt, who picked up the extension. "I'm afraid I wasn't aware your son was missing."

"You've got to help me." Something about the urgency in

the man's voice rooted Dylan to the spot, gripping the receiver with sweaty hands while all other sounds save his voice faded away.

"I got home from a business trip—I've been away about a month—to discover that Jason was gone. At first I didn't worry about it too much. He's a very independent boy. I thought he might be camping out on the property or visiting friends or something."

Matt raised his brows at Dylan, and she jotted him a note to fill him in while Crandall continued. "After a couple of days I started to get really worried. So I called the police. They told me about the other children who were missing. They said they'd be out as soon as possible, but with the storm and all . . ."

Matt frowned at her and tapped his watch. Dylan held up a forefinger.

"That was a couple of hours ago. While I was waiting, I read all the back newspapers. So I read the article about your little girl and those poems. And I went into Jason's room, to see if he had packed any clothes. The police had asked." He sighed. Dylan wanted to scream. "I make a point of staying out of Jason's room. I figure he's entitled to his privacy, and anyway, you wouldn't believe the mess. But I went in there to look around, and, well, frankly, I think you'd better come over here. You'd have to see it to believe it."

"What do you mean?" she asked in a small voice.

"I mean . . . it seems my son was obsessed—and I mean *obsessed*—with Dungeons and Dragons."

"Excuse me, Mr. Crandall. Just a minute." Dylan flagged down Chris Helmon and covered the mouthpiece of the receiver with her hand. "What can you tell me about Jason Crandall?"

Helmon rolled his eyes. "Guy's a dweeb. He tried to join our group a few months ago, but that dude was really weird, man. He wanted to get all the powers right away, see, without *earning* them, like you're supposed to. And he kept wanting to take over the game and run everything. The other players really resented it, and eventually we asked him to leave." He set the purple pouch on the kitchen table. "Don't forget this."

So it wasn't as Dylan had assumed; that Chris was the power-hungry player who had disgusted and eventually run off Jason Crandall from the game. Why hadn't Marty explained things better when she'd first asked him about Jason and David Elliott? He'd acted as if the whole thing were Chris's fault. Why hadn't she checked further? *Because—you were deafened, dumbed, and blinded by your own stubborn self-assurance that Chris Helmon was the kidnapper.*

Forget it. Water under the bridge. It wasn't the first time she'd been proved wrong in an investigation. It's just the first time it had ever been so intensely personal. How did the saying go? *Any lawyer who defends himself has a fool for a client?* How about, *Any investigator who investigates her own case has a stupid, bullheaded . . .* Dylan's hand began to shake so hard she nearly dropped the phone. *Get with it. Finding Aidan is all that matters.* Dry-mouthed, she managed to ask, "Mr. Crandall, where do you live, exactly?"

"I've got a country estate near the river. In fact, I may have to leave here myself, before long. Do you want directions?"

"In a minute. One more question."

"Anything, but hurry, Ms. Tandy. I'm worried sick about my son."

She swallowed and gazed up toward the ceiling, trying to slow her own heartbeat. Dimly she was aware of Matt and Caleb hovering at hand. "Mr. Crandall. This is very important. Do you know of any *caves* in your area?"

"Yes, of course!" he cried. "I completely forgot, until you asked."

"What? *What?*"

"We do have an unexplored cavern located on our own property. I've been meaning to have professional spelunkers come out and map it out so that I would know how dangerous it might be. Jason isn't supposed to go there, but . . ." There was an electric pause. "God help us, Ms. Tandy. You better hurry over here. That whole area's directly in a flood path."

THIRTY-THREE

When Dylan hung up the phone, she didn't have to say anything. Matt said, "You found Shadow, didn't you?"

"I think so." She explained in more detail.

"*Jesus!* Are you kidding me? Are you actually telling me that a *kid* has held this whole town hostage, confounded every law enforcement agency imaginable, and managed to get away with three—no—four children within one month?"

Dylan shook her head slowly. "It's hard to believe, on the one hand, but on the other hand I can see why the kids went with him—especially Aidan. It explains a lot of things."

"He's just a couple of years older than Caleb!"

"I know." They considered this for a long, incredulous moment. Then Matt shook himself.

"So, what are we going to do now?"

"I've got to go to Crandall's, Matt, you know that."

"Of course. I'll take Caleb to a shelter."

"*No.*"

They turned and stared at their son. They had almost forgotten he was there. "Dad—you've got to go with Mom. She'll go to that cave, and there's no telling what she'll find."

"Mom won't go alone, son. We'll contact Sergeant Dickerson and get some emergency personnel down there."

"I don't care. I want you to go with her."

"Caleb—"

To his parents' astonishment, the boy burst into ragged,

pent-up sobs. "You have to go together. You *have* to! You'll never find Aidan if you don't. She's my *sister*!"

They didn't know what to say. Neither of them wanted to point out the difficulty of getting Matt into a cave, or the possibility that a flash flood could take both their lives. Dylan looked at Matt helplessly. "Honey," she said soothingly to Caleb, wrapping her arms around his tense shoulders, "this is a very dangerous area we're talking about. Besides, you are in danger here yourself. Dad has to take you to safety."

"I'll take him," interrupted Chris Helmon. "My house is on high ground. It's never been flooded. He can come home with me."

Dylan took her bottom lip between her teeth. She didn't like Helmon much, and there was still that residue of suspicion that tugged at her. Could he be trusted with her son?

Caleb turned in her arms and stared up at her with a tear-streaked face and runny nose—not too far up, anymore, growing as he was—and said, "Mom, I *know* it's dangerous. That's why I want Dad to go with you."

"I can take care of myself—"

"Yeah, I know. But even a good cop needs backup now and then."

She rolled her eyes. Of course he was right. Still . . . "I'll tell you the truth, Caleb. I don't want to risk both our lives. You could be left all alone."

"I don't think so," he insisted. "You guys are too good. And . . . I asked God to help you out." He glanced away shyly.

"Let me help, too," said Chris. "I want to do it for my kid sister."

"I didn't know you had a sister," said Matt.

"She died. Leukemia. She was ten."

"I'm sorry," said Dylan and Matt together.

"It happened a long time ago. Thing is, your daughter reminds me of her."

Dylan stared at him. "Is that why you were so nice to her that day in the comic book store? When you took five bucks off the price of the unicorn necklace?"

He nodded.

That decided it for Dylan. All along she'd been worried about the way Chris had stared at Aidan that day; she hadn't trusted his kindness. She'd arrested a few pedophiles in her day, and they all looked like your favorite uncle.

This was the final piece in the puzzle, and the relief was palpable. For the first time she began to believe that Chris Helmon was who he said he was.

"We don't have much time," said Matt.

Dylan took Caleb's smooth wet face in her hands and looked deep into his eyes. "Are you sure, sweetheart?"

"I won't worry as long as you guys are together. You're a team, right?"

She pulled her son close to her breast and buried her face in his rumpled hair, love for him as powerful within her as any storm outside.

"Hurry," he murmured.

She released him and the room became electrified. Caleb chased down Pandora and stuffed her, over great protest, into her cat carrier. He added her favorite toy and a towel to curl up on.

"We'll need this," said Chris wryly, standing in the door with the litter box in his hands.

Matt bolted for the office, where he crammed as many floppy disks and videotapes as he could fit into a cardboard box.

Dylan quickly changed into jeans, a khaki shirt, and a sturdy pair of thick, lace-up boots. Then she grabbed a backpack and piled in a small first-aid kit, two powerful flashlights that operated on nine-volt batteries, extra batteries, a container of water, and anything else she could think of that she might need to search for possible injured children in a cave. Next she got out her nine millimeter semiautomatic, put in a fresh clip, and packed more ammo. She strapped the gun into a shoulder holster.

God knew, she didn't want to have to use it against a kid, but he was unbalanced and had done great harm already. Who knew what he might do when directly threatened by the Dragon Queen?

Matt still preferred his .38 special revolver. She got it down from its safe hiding place as well and grabbed a handful of speed loaders. She also added his strap-on, plastic protector, which he used as a sort of sled when dragging himself over rough country where the wheelchair didn't fit. One open sore on the buttocks of a paraplegic could take weeks to heal—sometimes requiring surgery. Her active husband always took care that that didn't happen.

After stacking everything up on the den couch, she remembered something else and dashed for the bedroom, where she pulled out as many scrapbooks and family photo albums as she could carry. On the way through the kitchen, she stopped and peered out the bay window toward the creek. Water reached halfway up the cypress trees and had crept up about one third of the backyard. For a moment she gazed around her warm and wonderful kitchen, blinking back tears, then joined the others as they loaded the van and Chris's car.

Her last chore would be to call Campbell Scott, brief him, and tell him to contact the police and emergency rescue squads. She would have to do that in the van on their way to the Crandalls'.

Matt was waiting in the van, engine running. Dylan glanced around to make sure she hadn't forgotten anything. The neighbor women had polished and scrubbed until the old limestone house gleamed, its parquet floor shining, all their precious old collectibles shown off just so. She took a last, heartbroken look, memorizing everything; then dashed through the rain to say good-bye to Caleb, where he sat stiffly in the front seat of Helmon's car, his face showing pale and strong through the swishing windshield wipers.

He clutched Squeakers to his chest. She leaned through the window and hugged him fiercely. "I'll see you all later," he said. "Tell Aidan I brought her favorite books."

His courage made her weep. *And a little babe shall lead them*, she thought, and fixed the bravery of her child in her mind like a beaming lighthouse in the storm.

"Jeremy! What's happening! I can't see the little light anymore, and the stream's getting bigger!" Aidan struggled to get her feverish mind working. "You know something else? The bats haven't come back." She thought about this. According to her science reports, bats left their dwelling places in the evening to roam over the countryside, devouring thousands of mosquitoes and other insects, and returned in the morning.

Could be it wasn't morning yet. But then, they *had* flown out that hole that let the light in up over the waterfall. And now the light wasn't coming in. *Think*.

Maybe it was still night. Or maybe the waterfall must be like a stream outside that fell down into the cave and made an underground stream. Only it was getting bigger. Could it be stopping up the hole now so the bats couldn't get back in?

And if so, then why was that happening? And where was all this extra water going to go? What if the waterfall room started to fill up? She looked over at Jeremy. He was watching her. She knew that he knew what she was thinking.

If the waterfall room started to fill up, then she and Jeremy had only one way to go, and that was into the bat room.

And if the bat room started to fill up . . .

"Jeremy," she said, "we've got to start thinking of some kind of plan. Shadow's waiting for us. If all this water keeps coming, we'll have to go right toward him."

Jeremy nodded.

"We can't just walk right into him."

He shook his head.

"So we gotta have a plan." Just standing around talking had weakened Aidan. All she wanted to do was sleep. She crouched down beside the water, made a cup of her hands, and splashed her face. The water was ice cold. She took a long drink. Then, wearily, she said, "Let's sit down over here and turn the light off. I'll throw out some ideas. If you like them, squeeze my hand, okay?"

He nodded.

They gathered up the backpacks and made their way back from the water, near the opening to the bat room, where Aidan lowered her aching body to the floor. Jeremy joined her. She took his hand and turned out the light.

And the whole room, it seemed, echoed with the sound of water.

Shadow pulled back the soaked boughs shading the cave entrance and gazed out, dumbstruck at the powerful flood of water that plummeted through the grotto, dragging brush and debris in its path and almost completely cutting off the entrance to the Secret Caverns.

In all the months Shadow had been coming to Shadowland, he had never seen anything like this. He had not even known that water ever flowed through the area. The sight of the raging, miniature river, which had long since covered over the trail he took every day to get to the Secret Caverns, terrified him. It occurred to him that the caverns themselves could eventually be flooded.

What should he do? Should he leave and come back when the waters receded?

No. The Secret Caverns were his friend. Their labyrinths extended deep underground. He would be just as safe, hidden in the maze, as he would be anywhere else. The Secret Caverns wouldn't let anything hurt him.

As for the trolls, well, they could take their chances: deal with a flood, or face the *mazemaster*.

With a nod of satisfaction he retreated into the bowels of the caverns to await his destiny.

Even a drenching and dreary downpour couldn't hide the opulence of George Crandall's house, located on over a hundred acres of choice riverfront property between the nearby villages of Ingram and Hunt. Dylan and Matt had to pass through an electronic gate to gain access to the curved drive leading to the columned, multistory house. It perched on a craggy riverbank that normally provided a natural rocky "seawall" to the water. On this day, however, the swollen Guadalupe had reached the top of the drop-off and licked wickedly at the lush lawns.

A maid let them into a spectacular foyer, open to a living room that looked out of two-story corner window-walls to a sculptured yard, pool, and on to the river, though the sheets of water sliding down the windows cut short that part of the dramatic view. The sunken living and dining rooms, decorated entirely in black and white, were delineated by columns rather than walls. To the left of the front door was a book-lined study, only one story high. Over the study was a balconied loft. To the right, a similar room revealed a big-screen TV and massive stereo. It, too, provided a scenic overlook from its "roof" to the luxurious rooms and windows beyond.

A handsome, well-dressed man with salt-and-pepper hair crossed the spotless black-and-white floor tiles to shake their hands. "I'm George Crandall," he said in a voice unmistakably rich. His deep brown eyes were the only part of him which betrayed his anxiety. He led them over to a curved wet bar near the flawless living room. When they declined a drink, he poured himself a stiff Scotch on the rocks. Dylan noticed a slight tremble to his hand and wondered how many he'd had before their arrival.

They followed him into the living room, where Dylan sat on a white suede sofa beneath a spectacular signed Ansel Adams print. Matt parked next to her. Crandall moved over to the window and looked out without seeing. After a moment he said, "I figured you'd want to see this. I found it in Jason's room." He leaned forward and handed a piece of paper to Dylan. As soon as she spotted the familiar scroll and handwriting, her heart seemed to thrust itself into her throat. "To see that the *mindslayer* has won over all" was completed by the following lines, all of which had been scribbled out: "the Dragon Queen down the pit of defeat will fall; the dragons, their Queen will disaster befall; and the Dragon Queen to the mazemaster will crawl." The final line had not been scribbled out, and leapt out at her: "check for the journey-pouch 'neath the riverside wall."

With a shaking hand she passed the note on to Matt. Numbly she said, "Mr. Crandall, I am so very sorry about all that has happened. But I'm afraid your son has crossed completely over the line of reality. I believe he has taken all those children, including our daughter, to the cave on your property to play some sort of fantasy game; and we think he is hiding out there now. If a flash flood hits your property, they'll all drown. I've had Jeremy Scott's father call emergency rescue personnel, but it's going to take them a while to get here because they are so busy saving idiots who drive their cars through flood zones."

She got to her feet. "We don't have a single moment to waste. Please take us to the cave now. And hurry."

"I've got a Jeep," he said. "Come on." He glanced back at Matt. "Can you manage?"

"It's my little girl," said Matt grimly. "Nothing can stop me."

They headed for the garage.

"I've done everything wrong," he said as they climbed into the jeep. Dylan wasn't sure she wanted to hear a maudlin, drink-induced confession, but as rain thundered on the canvas roof of the jeep and lashed against the plastic zip-up windows, she let the man talk. Matt reached his hand around the side of the front seat to where she was sitting in the back, and she squeezed his fingers.

"Jason was always a disappointment to me," George Crandall said sadly. "He doted on his mother—so much so that I knew he was going to grow up a wasted mama's boy, but she would never let me discipline him or interfere with him in any way." He shifted gears. "They were so complete, you know, together. From the day that boy was born, there was just no room for me in her life." He squinted into the windshield, and Matt wiped at the mist with his handkerchief. "We were living in Houston then. I was a workaholic anyway, but that gave me an excuse to stay gone most of the time, working."

Even with four-wheel drive, the wheels of the vehicle strained through the mud. Dylan tried to see out the side spaces but couldn't. It was as if they were encased in a cold, sorrowful tomb. She shook the dreary thought from her mind and tried to concentrate on Crandall's words. "I won't lie to you," he said. "There were affairs. I had to find some comfort somewhere. I think Lydia knew, but she honestly didn't seem to care, not as long as she had my money and her son." He shook his head and seemed to look inward even as he turned up the windshield wipers to full speed.

"I worried about him. I did. I'm not completely heartless. I mean, he never had any friends his own age. He didn't seem to need any. I wanted to send him away to school, you know, to force him to make the break from her and bond with his schoolmates. Of course, she thought I was a monstrous bastard to even suggest it."

Dylan could imagine the scene between mother, father, and boy. "A year ago Lydia died. Just like that. No warning. We knew she had high blood pressure, but she took medication for it and the cook had her on a special diet." The jeep jounced into a deep hole with a jarring *thump* followed by a loud splash. Dylan felt her head hit the roll bar of the jeep. "Cerebral hemorrhage," Crandall went on, as if he hadn't noticed. "Poor kid came home from school and found her dead on the bathroom floor." Matt caught Dylan's eye with a warning look. It looked as if they were driving in circles, and Dylan wondered if Crandall was sure of his way. She lifted her eyebrows as Crandall continued. "Of course, I was out of town at the time." He gave them a challenging look, but they wisely said nothing.

"Secretly I thought it might turn out to be the best thing for the boy. I know that sounds terrible, but I thought it would help him grow up, in the long run. But I handled it all wrong. I did all the wrong things. At first he just moped around in his mother's room all the time—it was creepy.

"So I sold the house. Sold all of it. Moved us down here. I thought a fresh new start would be the best thing for both of us. Instead, it was a disaster. An unmitigated disaster."

"Uh, excuse me, Mr. Crandall, but are you sure we're heading in the right direction?"

Clearly annoyed at Dylan's interruption, Crandall said, "Of course I'm sure. It's my own land, isn't it? This is a roundabout road that I have to take because of the high water." He lapsed into silence. Dylan, embarrassed, urged him to continue.

"I sent him to a therapist. Five times a week. I mean, I did everything I could. It didn't help. Nothing did." The jeep turned onto a firmer, but still sloppy, road, and Crandall accelerated. "I was still working as much as ever. By that time I didn't know how *not* to. One day I found a Dungeons and Dragons manual on the dining room table. I looked through it a little, then I asked Jason about it. From what he told me, it sounded harmless enough, and Lord knows I was thrilled that he finally had a new interest. He did seem to perk up after that, and when I gave him a dirt bike for his fifteenth birthday, he was overjoyed." A brief smile crossed his face.

Dirt bike. Dylan and Matt exchanged glances. The witness who'd seen a child in a Jurassic Park jacket leave the park on the back of a "motorcycle" had been right, after all.

"When he asked if he could stop therapy, I figured he was working his way through his mother's death pretty well, so

I said sure. It never did seem to help, anyway." A heavy sigh escaped him. "Things rocked along for months. I still traveled a lot, but he wasn't completely alone. There was the maid and the cook. Besides, he's an independent kid. He was getting by in school. He rode his bike. He made a fuss about keeping the maid out of his room, but I thought that was pretty normal."

Dylan looked down at her hands in her lap. Apparently, this man had had no one to talk to since his wife's death. It was a relief to him to unburden, and she didn't figure he'd hold back much. Still, time was running out. She *willed* the jeep to go faster even as it slowed, left the road, and abruptly turned up an incline.

"So I stopped worrying about Jason. God help me, I never would have thought . . ." At last Crandall fell silent, gripping the steering wheel as the jeep earned its rugged reputation, groaning and sliding up the incline. Reaching the top seemed an impossible task. Dylan gripped the sides of the backseat and said a little prayer of her own: *Please, God, don't let us be too late.*

THIRTY-FOUR

When the water reached their toes, Aidan and Jeremy clambered through the passageway leading to the bat room, dragging the four backpacks with them. For a while she was as quiet as the speechless boy. She remembered reading somewhere, though she couldn't remember where, that children who spent the night in underground shelters while England was being bombed during World War II were always unnaturally silent. The mental picture of it had stuck in her mind, and now she understood why.

She felt alternately hot and then chilled to the bone. Her chest had tightened up, and she was having trouble breathing. Her head swam and her stomach rolled. Yet even her illness could not distract her from the thought that she had never been more frightened in her life. From the look in Jeremy's rounded eyes, she could see he felt the same way.

Their only hope was to somehow get away from the Shadow and make a break for the cave entrance. If they were forced down the other tunnel, the one leading deep into the cave itself, Aidan knew they'd wind up hopelessly lost in the maze. After all, the flashlight wouldn't last forever.

And if Shadow *caught* them, well, that was something she would not, could not, think about.

The cave was even colder than usual. Aidan's clothing had never completely dried out, and its dampness made her miserable. At home her parents always fussed over her when she was sick, permitting her to make a bed on the couch and watch movies on TV all day. Dad would bring her chicken broth and Gatorade, and if Mom was out working, she'd always bring home some kind of treat, usually a new book. Desperately homesick, Aidan wanted to cry, but she didn't want to make things worse for Jeremy.

She even missed Caleb, who might have had all sorts of clever ideas for handling Shadow. She sighed and leaned against the cave wall. She was so very tired. . . .

A hand shook her awake. Confused, she rubbed her eyes. Jeremy had the flashlight, and she stared in mute fascination in the direction of its beam. A trickle of water dribbled, then streamed out of the passageway and into the bat room.

The children sprang to their feet. Aidan swayed and steadied herself on the wall as she hurried over to the tunnel leading out. She didn't want to think about what would happen if water suddenly came flooding into the passageway and trapped them in that narrow tunnel.

They scrambled through the pipelike tunnel, pushing their backpacks in front of them. Aidan felt as if demons were at her feet and almost forgot how sick she was in her haste. As soon as they emerged into the section where they could crawl, they crouched down together. "Time to put on our bulletproof vests," she whispered. Jeremy nodded.

First they slipped their arms through the straps of a backpack and put it on normally. Then they each took one more backpack and slipped it on *backward*, with the pack in front. It was cumbersome and awkward, and a tight fit in the passage; but while not exactly bulletproof, Aidan figured the packs would provide some sort of shield if Shadow started swinging that dagger around.

Nervous and big-eyed, she stared a moment at Jeremy, then held her palm up in front of her. His brows crinkled, then a grin broke over his face, and he silently high-fived her. Then they turned and single-filed down the tunnel until they could stand and walk abreast. Jeremy groped for her hand and killed the light.

The silence was so profound that Aidan could hear a high-pitched ringing in her ears. The velvet blackness was completely disorienting, but she did as Jeremy and trailed one hand along the wall to keep her bearings. Her pulse thudded in her ears. She felt as though she were dragging her legs through a swamp, and her tongue burned with fever. If it came to it, she wasn't sure if she would be able to run at all.

Jeremy came to a halt, and she stumbled next to him. She felt him tug at her hand and stooped down. It took her a moment to realize that he was stealthily feeling along for the trip wire. She did the same on her side. She held her breath.

They found it.

Straightening, she let out her pent-up breath slowly and silently. Jeremy took her hand and closed it around his fist, then he touched the palm of her hand with one finger, two, then three. She moved her hand up and down in confirmation.

One. Two. *Three.*

In unison they each pulled a knee up high and stepped over the trip wire. On the other side they held on to each other. Aidan felt sure she was going to faint. Which way now? She was completely mixed up.

Jeremy tugged at her left hand. Trusting him, she headed in that direction. They took about three steps toward freedom before their heads crashed into a number of tin cans which must have been suspended from the cave ceiling. *Bangclangcrash.*

A bold light blinded their eyes, followed by the sound of demented laughing.

"*So.* You thought you could outwit the *mazemaster*?"

Aidan shaded her eyes. She couldn't see anything.

"You'll never get out of here," said the voice. "Never. And don't expect mommy and daddy dragons to come save you, know why? It's been raining outside for *days*, and the whole area is flooded! They couldn't get to you if they tried!" More laughter. "So now the stupid trolls must face the *mindslayer* in the Secret Caverns, and when the *mindslayer* is through with you, he will *truly* have earned the title of *mazemaster*!"

They turned and ran. Jeremy still held the flashlight, and he flicked it on so that they wouldn't take the wrong tunnel and wind up back in the flooded bat room. Running footsteps thudded right behind them.

Aidan *willed* her leaden feet to move, and Jeremy yanked her along by the hand, practically dragging her. They spotted a tunnel to the right and took it, with Shadow hard on her heels.

Aidan stumbled, letting go of Jeremy's hand. He blundered forward a few steps while she staggered dizzily, struggling to right herself against a teetering equilibrium.

A hand grasped her backpack from behind, lifting her feet off the floor. The big light that had shone in her eyes clanged to the floor and pointed crazily up at the cave ceiling.

Aidan screamed. Her body was slammed back against the cave wall. *"Jeremy! Run! Run!"* she yelled.

Something thudded against her frontal backpack, and she heard a wild bellow of rage. Kicking, screaming, she squirmed until she felt another *thud*.

Only this one carried with it a soft ripping sound; and Aidan realized, perhaps for the first time, that she might die.

Dylan and Matt stared in dismay from the top of the bluff that led down to the grotto. "Does that creek always run that high?" asked Matt.

"Hell, there *is* no creek here, normally!" cried Crandall. "This entire area here is really awash. We've just never seen it flooded before."

"I hate to sound like a city boy," said Matt. "But what's a wash?"

"It's kind of a natural runoff for high water. Like a gutter." He pointed past the torrential stream. "See those willow boughs hanging down? Looks like a curtain?"

They squinted through the rain and mist.

"That's the cave entrance. You go in about, oh, twenty, thirty feet, you'll come to a large room. Two other tunnels branch off from that room, but I never explored them. I decided to leave that up to the professionals. Just never got around to calling them."

"And you had no idea your son was down here?" Water poured off Dylan's floppy rain cap.

In answer he ducked his head.

Matt had strapped on his plastic protector and lowered himself from his wheelchair onto the ground. He squirmed around until he was facing downhill, backward.

Dylan said, "Mr. Crandall, I'd like you to put in another call to the authorities and rescue squad, then wait for them at your gate so that you can lead them to us whenever they get here. We're going down."

"Can't I go with you?" he asked, no longer the confident businessman but a confused and frightened parent.

Dylan glanced at Matt, then shook her head. "Better not, Mr. Crandall. There's no telling what we may find there, or how the Sha—Jason—would react to seeing you in this fantasy world he's made for himself."

He nodded reluctantly, but Dylan could detect a note of relief in his voice when he said, "I guess you're right. The kid hates me anyway." Before she could say anything to that, he headed for the Jeep. Turning back, he said, "I'm sorry."

Dylan shrugged. "So are we." She placed her hands underneath Matt's arms and began their cumbersome trip down the hillside. She would back stride by stride, dragging him after her. He helped as best he could. The mud was a help and a hindrance. It made it easier to pull Matt, but it also caused her to slip a number of times. Before long they were both soaked and mud-covered.

The water ran catty-cornered to the cave entrance. Luckily, the hill they were clambering down was on the near side of the wash. Once they reached the bottom of the hill, Matt took over, dragging himself rapidly along beside her with his powerful arms. The water raged past, only a few feet away. If it gained very much in width, it would flood the cave entrance.

Dylan removed rocks and other impediments out of Matt's way until they reached the cave entrance, where they both rested a moment, panting heavily.

"Okay," she managed. "Now what?"

"I figure the Shadow may be expecting the Dragon Queen, but not her assistant, right? So I'll settle in just inside the cave mouth. That way I can stop anybody trying to run out—even if it's one of the kids."

She nodded.

He gave her a long, regretful look. "You know I'd rather go all the way in with you."

"I know."

"I just don't want to slow you down."

"It's a tremendous relief, just knowing you're here. Caleb was right. Even a good cop needs backup from time to time."

He gave her a one-sided grin. "If you are in there longer than"—he consulted his watch—"say, a half hour—"

"Give me forty-five minutes."

"Okay. Forty-five. The emergency people should be here by then, but if they aren't, I'm coming in after you, no matter what."

She nodded. "What if the water rises? We need some kind of signal."

"I'll fire my gun out the cave door. Wouldn't want to bring the whole place down on your head."

From her backpack she withdrew one of the strong flashlights and handed another one to Matt, along with an extra battery.

He grinned sheepishly. "Didn't even think about that."

They moved through the sopping greenery into the cavern entrance. Dylan flicked on her light. Even then the place was spooky.

Poor scared babies, she thought. "Well, I'm on my way," she said. She leaned down and kissed him. "See you."

"I'll be waiting."

Dylan headed down the tunnel, gripping her flashlight. It was surprisingly cold, and she worried about the children in their thin summer clothes.

She wondered what she might find, and shivered.

When the tunnel crooked to the right, she turned off her light and listened. Velvety black silence cocooned her like a tomb. She waited, holding her breath, realizing that to turn the light back on would make her stand out like a beacon if Shadow was waiting in that first room.

Touching the wall, she continued on her slow blind way, fighting disorientation. Experienced spelunkers, she knew, could be forever lost in a cave without light.

She thought of Jeremy Scott, and of the other boys. If Shadow had kept them hostage somewhere in total darkness and silence, they'd have gone mad by now.

She tried not to think about Aidan.

On she crept. Twenty or thirty feet, he'd said. She cursed herself for not counting her steps.

Clangbangcrash!

Something racketed against her head. Dylan's heart leapt to her throat, and she snapped on the flashlight in spite of the risk.

Tin cans, filled with pebbles, had been suspended from the ceiling.

Heart still jackhammering, Dylan sought to calm herself. It had simply never occurred to any of them that the boy could have set out warnings. She would have to be more careful.

Breathing deeply, she flashed the light around the room, making out a sleeping bag, some canned goods, and other camping supplies. The beam settled on a huge pile of something against one wall, and she went over to investigate. With growing horror Dylan stared down at the shredded and savaged remains of children's belongings.

Then she heard a scream.

THIRTY-FIVE

Aidan kicked Shadow as hard as she could in the knee. He dropped her; and as soon as she hit the floor, she kicked him again, this time in the groin. With a scream of pain he hunched over. Jeremy, who had not run away after all, grabbed her hand, and they took off down the tunnel.

"Wait!" cried Aidan. "I remember that big stalactite. There's a tunnel to the right of it. Go. *Go!"*

Tiny sticky cobweb fingers grasped at their faces. Sputtering, they floundered through and started to run—and then Jeremy tripped over something and fell headlong. The flashlight flew from his hand, struck the floor with a sickening crunch, and went black.

Aidan skidded to a stop. What had he tripped over? She groped around, feeling her way . . . until her hand nudged something soft and cold. Bile rose in her throat and she gagged.

She'd forgotten. She had *made* herself forget.

Fighting hysteria, she clambered over the body and crawled around until she found Jeremy. He was shaking. She didn't know if he'd had a chance to see what he'd fallen over or not.

Slowly he began to investigate. Aidan tried to hold him back, but she was too late. A strange, choking sound erupted from the boy. Flinging himself away from her, he began crawling rapidly down the tunnel in a frenzy.

"Jeremy! *No!"*

He kept making that weird dry sound deep in his throat. Aidan stumbled along in his direction. To her horror, she

267

heard him get to his feet and begin running frantically into the black unknown.

"Jeremy! Come back! Don't leave me here!" Aidan sobbed. She stood up and started to follow as best she could. "You'll get lost, Jeremy! *Please!*" Terror sent her plunging into the coffin-darkness, blubbering for Jeremy. She could handle most anything, she thought, but losing him.

Suddenly she slammed into something and nearly screamed before she realized that he had stopped and she had blundered into him. He was trembling violently. She put her arms around him. "It's gonna be all right," she said, trying to believe it herself. His face was wet, and she realized that the strange choking sounds she'd heard had been sobs. "We're still alive, Jeremy. We've gotta be Tandy, you know. We can't go running off down these tunnels without a light, or we'll be lost in here *forever.*"

Slowly she pulled him down to the floor. "Let's sit right here for a while," she said, "and think about what to do, okay?"

Jeremy sat, but he was stiff, silent, and unyielding. Deep in her heart, Aidan felt that she might truly have lost him this time. She held on to his cold fingers and tried very hard not to cry.

Dylan raced down the opposite tunnel toward the sound of the scream, holding the flashlight up ahead of her and withdrawing her gun as she ran. A tunnel opened up to the right, but she continued on straight ahead. No point in getting any more turned around than she had to.

A stitch in her side forced her to slow to a brisk walk. The tunnel bent to the left and dead-ended in a small, earth-encrusted alcove. To her surprise, an opening near the top of the alcove dripped rain. Panting, she flashed the beam of her light up to the opening. Could it have been an escape route for the children?

If so, where were they now?

While she stood, perplexed, a sound came to her that sent

chillbumps swarming all over her body. The sound was repeated several times in unison.

It was the cold, deadly *br-r-r-r* of rattlesnakes, rudely awakened in their den.

Shadow crouched, clutching his privates and trying not to throw up. *The little witch!* How dare she bring harm to the *mindslayer!*

He would punish her. He would hurt her. His rage was no longer a thing separate from him; it had *become* him. He could no more act now without it than a rocket could climb into space without being propelled by jet fuel. Growling, he limped over to the bright flashlight, retrieved it, and hunted around until he found his dagger. Then he tore through the cobwebs, stepped over the body of the troll, and started down the tunnel after the treacherous Dragon Princess.

Dylan froze. Slowly she moved the beam of the flashlight around the room. Snakes were piled, one atop the other, around the perimeters of the small antechamber. Apparently they'd found the place through the opening outside and came and went through there without ever going too deeply into the cold cave.

Two or three were coiled at the base of the pile, rattling furiously at the intruder, their evil little black eyes glaring at Dylan, forked tongues testing the air for heat or movement—their signal to strike.

She knew that snakes could strike the entire length of their bodies. Clearly, they had the advantage. Fingernails of fear clawed at her skin.

She was terrified of snakes.

The flashlight jerked convulsively in her trembling hand. The rattles jittered hypnotically.

She could begin firing at will, hoping to hit them all before she was bitten, or she could try something her grandmother had once told her while warning her about snakes down at the creek.

She'd never had to try it before.

Slowly . . . ever so very slowly . . . she began to back out of the rattlesnake den. She did not know if there were any snakes behind her. One step. Two.

A big one in the nearest corner lifted his flat, wicked head from his high coil and stared Dylan down, tongue slipping in and out, rattle blurring, body tensing.

Squeezing Jeremy's limp hand, Aidan spotted the light before he did. For a wild improbable moment, she thought it might be rescuers.

But she knew who it was.

If there were just a side tunnel they could hide in! A whimpering sound came out of her own mouth, and she bit her tongue to quiet it. Her heart was a wildly fluttering moth, caught in a jar.

Aidan huddled close to Jeremy, as if somehow, together, they could fight off Shadow. She thought Jeremy had seen the light by now, but he didn't seem to care. It was as if he'd lost the will to live. It made her feel more alone than if he'd left her in the tunnel.

The light drew closer.

Dylan put as much room between her and the rattlesnake den as possible, hurrying back down the tunnel to the big stalactite which seemed to mark a turnoff, now to her left and curtained by cobwebs. Leery of poisonous spiders, she shone the flashlight around the web, then pointed the beam down to the floor, where her breath whooshed out of her and her knees went weak.

She dropped to the floor and touched the small, cold body, turning it toward her with dread. She knew by the clothing that it wasn't Aidan, but she felt heartsick all the same.

Eric Rathbone. Bludgeoned to death.

Nausea washed over Dylan. If one child was dead . . . then what of the others? What of Jeremy?

What of Aidan?

Tears washed her eyes and splashed to the child's arm. They'd been too late.

Snuffling, she raised her head. *A light.*

Gathering her wits about her, Dylan sprang to her feet, leapt over the inert form, and tore down the tunnel. A voice echoed to her: *"No!"*

Aidan!

"Aidan!" she screamed, her voice reverberating down the tunnel.

"Mom!"

The light swung around. Dylan skidded to a stop, stooped, placed her light on the floor, and assumed the position, pointing her weapon straight at the light. "Make one move," she cried, "and I'll kill you!"

"Mom! Don't shoot! He's making me hold the light!"

Confused, Dylan let go of her gun with one hand and reached for her flashlight. Too late, she heard the soft-soled creeping at her side, the swirl of velvet, the rush of a body, hurling toward her.

They hit the floor together, grappling and rolling. Dylan's gun went clattering off somewhere. She couldn't see anything and groped for a handhold or a place to kick. A bright light gleamed in her eyes.

"No!" she cried. "You're blinding me!" The light immediately shifted.

This kid was surprisingly strong for his age, and he growled like some sort of supernatural creature. Dylan bit and clawed and pulled hair—all the dirty fighting techniques she'd ever known. "Jason!" she hollered. "It's time to give it up, son. Your dad and we all want to help you. *Ouch.*"

She felt the boy hesitate, then she was shoved aside and heard a wild scrambling. Before she could right herself Dylan was pushed back down to the cave floor by a blessed, familiar form, covering her face with wet kisses.

"I knew you'd never give up," said her little girl.

Dylan clutched the child close to her breast, sobbing tears of tremendous, almost unimaginable relief. After a moment Aidan pulled back slightly and groped through the darkness for something. To Dylan's astonishment, she felt another little hand pressed into her own.

"Mom, this is Jeremy," said Aidan.

Dylan let go of her child just long enough to find the light, which she shone upward, revealing, first a pair of filthy baseball uniform pants, two backpacks worn mysteriously front and back, then a whole collection of windbreakers, and finally a weary, defeated little face that only vaguely resembled his grinning school picture.

"I found him," said Aidan proudly. "He survived all this time in the waterfall room, and he helped me escape."

"I'm very proud of you," said Dylan, then she got to her knees and enfolded the quiet little person in her arms. He didn't say anything, but when he twined thin arms around her neck and squeezed, Dylan knew he was going to be all right.

After a moment she placed one arm around each child and gave them both a tight squeeze. Aidan was also wearing two backpacks, only one of hers had been slashed—something she'd have to ask about later. "Okay," she said. "How do we get out of here? I'm completely turned around." She glanced around into the velvety darkness, wondering where the Shadow might lurk.

"Don't worry, Mom," said Aidan. She took the flashlight from her mother and beamed it back and forth along the cave wall, near the bottom. A tiny white scratch appeared and she stopped. "We'll just follow my trail," she said.

Although Dylan couldn't see her daughter's face, she didn't have to; she could have traced that big grin in her sleep.

Shadow staggered wildly down the cave tunnel toward the Trove Room. *What had happened? The Dragon Queen had found him after all! The Secret Caverns were going to be so angry!*

Sobbing, stumbling, he scrambled into the Trove Room and began pawing through things. *Where was the Magic Amulet? He had to find it! He had to!* Whimpering, he flung one thing after another all over the room, but the Magic Amulet was nowhere to be found.

They must have stolen it! No! NO! The Secret Caverns would punish him for sure!

Shadow grabbed up the flashlight and hurried toward the exit tunnel, ducking his head to avoid the cans. Running full speed, he took two or three giant steps before tripping headlong across a log or something that blocked the tunnel.

Hands skidding the tunnel floor, Shadow's light bounced out of reach. Bewildered, he shook his head and, in the next moment, felt strong, muscular arms grab him around the neck and throat and yank back his head until he choked.

"Sorry, Jason," a deep male voice growled in his ear. *"The game's over. Finders keepers, losers weepers."*

By the time Dylan and the children reached Matt, who had moved himself to just outside the entrance to the Trove Room, Jason Crandall rested stomach down on the cave floor, his hands cuffed behind his back.

"I see you've got everything under control," Dylan said wryly. "But then, I wasn't worried."

"Piece of cake," Matt said with a big grin.

"Dad!" Aidan raced for her father and flung herself over him, showering him with kisses while Dylan stood back, her arms around Jeremy's shoulders.

When Matt could get a breath, he looked over the top of his little girl's head at Dylan, and she could see by the flashlight the tears streaming down his face.

They gave each other the Look; that glance between parents over the head of their child that needs no words.

He gestured toward her. "I see you found Jeremy," he said.

"No, Aidan found him."

"I'll tell you all about it later, Dad," Aidan said importantly. Matt squeezed her.

"Any more?" he asked Dylan hopefully.

"Eric Rathbone." She gave him a warning look and a slight shake of the head; a gesture that any cop would immediately comprehend. He ducked his head. After a moment he said, "Any others?"

"No. I thought we'd get a team of spelunkers in here to search."

"Well, we're going to have to wait a little while on that, because we seem to have a little problem."

Dylan cocked her head at him. "What's that?"

"Now, don't freak out or anything, but it seems as if water is lapping right at the cave door. In fact, it's working its way down this tunnel even as we speak. Personally, I found it prudent to move."

Dylan knew that she should be dismayed at the news, but with her arms around Jeremy and Matt's arms around Aidan—and with the great and all-powerful Shadow captured and right there on the cave floor between them . . . well, it was awfully hard to get too worked up about it.

She shrugged. "Piece of cake."

PART IV   COPYCATS

"That name even you hobbits have heard of, like a shadow on the borders of old stories. Always after a defeat and a respite, the Shadow takes another shape and grows again."

"I wish it need not have happened in my time," said Frodo.

"So do I," said Gandalf, "and so do we all who live to see such times. But that is not for them to decide. All we have to decide is what to do with the time that is given us."
—J.R.R. Tolkien
The Fellowship of the Ring

Imitation is a form of suicide.
—Ralph Waldo Emerson

THIRTY-SIX

By the time rescue workers had extricated Dylan, Matt, and the children from the cave, Aidan's fever had shot up to alarming heights. She was immediately hospitalized with pneumococcal pneumonia, but responded strongly to anti-biotics and began a rapid recovery.

Jeremy Scott was treated for exposure, weakened vision, and a throat badly swollen from the cold and damp, but he was released after a couple of days. To his parents' dismay, his worst wounds appeared to be hidden, for he steadfastly refused to talk. They figured the only alternative open to them was to put him in art therapy, where he drew horrifying pictures, all in black.

To receive a child back from the brink of death is a wondrous miracle almost beyond description, but dealing with the aftermath of the trauma is an entirely different thing. Jeremy seemed to have lost interest in everything that had ever mattered to him before, and his continuing silence was maddening. He seemed to have drifted into some misty netherworld beyond the reach of those who loved him. His parents began to despair that he would ever return to them.

One night, a few weeks after his ordeal, they were awakened by the eerie sounds of a baby screaming. When they rushed to Jeremy's room, they were dumbfounded to find him thrashing in the throes of yet another nightmare, screaming in a voice they hadn't heard since his infancy. His mother clasped him to her breast while his father gently patted his face, but it seemed as if they could not bring him back from wherever his night terrors had taken him.

Campbell Scott began talking in a slow, steady voice, cutting through the screams. With tears streaming down his face, he told the child all his parents had gone through in the desperate search for him, all the sleepless nights and dark days, all the futile police searches and the stupefying misery of confronting the Shadow. He told his son how Dylan Tandy had given them hope, and how their hopes had been shattered when Aidan disappeared. And how they had fallen to their knees, weeping and thanking God, when their little boy was found again.

At some point during the story, Jeremy stopped screaming and lay very still in his mother's arms. And when it was all over, he drew a shuddering breath and said, "I thought you had forgotten all about me."

And so, he finally returned from Shadowland.

Aidan, too, was plagued by nightmares, but every time she opened her eyes, the first thing she saw was either her mother or her father. Once they even sneaked Pandora in to the hospital room to see her, and Caleb came every day. She told her parents that if she could just go home again, she thought she would be all right.

Caleb was particularly gentle with his little sister, but Dylan needed to remind herself occasionally that the boy had been traumatized as well. She encouraged him to talk about it often, but the sad thing, to Dylan, was that he seemed to have lost his little-boy softness forever.

They chose not to tell Aidan how close she had come to losing her home, how the floodwaters had risen all the way to the bottom step of the deck before cresting and beginning to recede. For the time being, they were content to leave her in the hospital, until the waters dropped down to a more creeklike level again. The family had agreed that Aidan had been frightened enough as it was; she did not need to fear the loss of her home on top of it.

Once she was home, she was treated like royalty, complete with a couch-bed and the TV, but she was beginning to be bored with lying around all day and started to pick fights with her brother. That's when her parents knew she was going to be fine.

One day she had a special visitor. Jeremy Scott came to see her. He was almost unrecognizable to her. He'd put on some weight and had a haircut. He had a gift for her. It seemed that a favorite aunt—over his father's protests— had taught the boy cross-stitching once during a bout with the flu. Jeremy proudly handed her a crudely stitched but nicely framed little sign that read: AIDAN: THE MOST TANDY OF ALL.

While she marveled at it, he surprised her again. "I just wanted to say thanks," he said and gave her the high-five.

Neither one of them saw Dylan duck into the bathroom for a quick bawling session. Only Colleen Scott noticed, but nobody had to explain anything to her. Not anything at all.

It was a different story altogether with Jason Crandall. When the police and FBI could make no sense whatsoever out of what he was telling them about trolls and Shadow-land, they invited Dylan Tandy to sit in on the questioning as a sort of interpreter.

Only then did the full horror of the story begin to unfold. It took them all a while to figure out what he meant by "the beast within," but a child psychiatrist helped the authorities to decipher that part to mean all the rage and grief he had pent up inside himself since his mother's death. Part of the anger was directed at her, for leaving him; part toward his father, for ignoring him and for moving him out of his mother's house; and part of it was aimed at himself. When the burden of it all became too great, he started to escape it through fantasy.

It would have been easy at this point, Dylan thought, to have blamed the Dungeons & Dragons game itself for the tragedy. But it was her belief—backed up by the experts— that Jason Crandall was a time bomb, ticking away to explode one way or the other. Dungeons & Dragons merely gave him a convenient excuse. In other words, it was the boy who was disturbed, not the game. If Dungeons & Dragons hadn't set him off—something else would have.

She remembered reading once that John Lennon's assassin had gotten his "message" to kill from the book *The Catcher in the Rye*. Others blamed satanism, heavy metal music, or drugs for their crimes, but the truth was that the *rage* came first. If someone, somewhere along the line, had recognized that and had given the boy a healthy outlet for his anger, or had just reached out to him in sympathy and comfort, then perhaps the entire tragedy could have been averted.

Because Jason Crandall was a juvenile, and a wealthy one at that, the judge agreed to have him committed to an expensive private psychiatric facility for treatment, where the attending physicians agreed that his stay was likely to be a long one. One psychiatrist told George Crandall that he was going to have to bone up on his Tolkien, or he'd be unable to converse with Jason at all. The Rathbones, numb with mourning for Eric, protested but were overruled.

The police and FBI were content to close the case at this point, but something bothered Dylan tremendously. Throughout his questioning, Jason vehemently refused to take credit for the disappearance of the first victim, Timmy Castillo. He kept claiming that he had been hiding in the bushes and had seen someone he called the "Troll Master" murder the boy.

The questioning officers assumed that his fantasy world had gotten the better of him, but when a thorough exploration of the "Secret Caverns" by professional spelunkers revealed no further bodies, Dylan wasn't so sure. It made no sense to her that the boy would lie at this point.

She convinced Sergeant Dickerson to give her the full case file on the Castillo disappearance for study, which she read deep into the night.

Timmy Castillo had gone outside to play with several friends around five P.M. one hot summer evening. Though his mother had often warned him to stay away from the

construction site, the boys found it an irresistible playground, once the workers had left for the day. They played
chase and hide-and-seek, and went on various adventures.
About six-thirty, two of the boys went on home. That left
Timmy and another boy named Kevin Edwards.

Kevin Edwards maintained that he had been hiding from
Timmy. He intended to jump out and frighten Timmy, he
said, which was something they often did to each other. But
though he waited and waited, Timmy never showed up. He
left his hiding place and went in search of his friend, and
although he hunted over every nook and cranny and called
until he was hoarse, the construction site was deserted.
That's when he had run home and called for help.

Once Jason Crandall had been questioned, Dickerson and
the others assumed that he'd been hiding in the trees,
watching the boys — as he'd been doing since his backpack-
snatching days — and that when Kevin disappeared in order
to hide, Jason had approached Timmy and lured him away
on his dirt bike.

Because Timmy was the first victim, the officers reasoned
that perhaps Jason did not take him back to the Secret
Caverns, as he had the others, but killed him somewhere
else. The body might never be found, they told the boy's
distraught parents.

But Dylan had been there when they questioned Jason
about Timmy. His eyes shone as he described watching
someone he called the Troll Master argue with, then take the
life of, the troll. Up until then, he insisted, he had only been
stealing from the trolls. But he'd been growing increasingly
bored with that, and after watching the incident with the
Troll Master — who clearly got away with his crime and
stumped all the authorities — then he had realized how easy
it would be to take trolls back to the Secret Caverns for a
more challenging game — without being caught.

His story never wavered. Dylan tried to get Dickerson
and the others to question "Shadow" more fully about it, but
they refused to take his story seriously. "Guy's lost in

never-never land," Dickerson had said. "Nothing he says at this point makes a whole hell of a lot of sense, Tandy."

Sometime in the deep, dark hours of the night, as Dylan read the report over and over, she pushed the files aside, closed her eyes, and entered the labyrinth of reasoning that was the result of a tortured boy's escape from reality. For a good twenty minutes she quieted all thoughts of her own, forcing herself to think like Shadow.

The realization, when it came to her, was more horrifying than anything she could have imagined on her own. She tried to argue the idea out of her mind, but it wouldn't budge. In fact, it grew stronger with each passing moment, demanding attention.

She kept thinking of the Castillos, their hollow-eyed anxiety as each child had been found—one way or the other—but they were left with nothing but an empty room at home and no answers to their own agonized questions.

Dylan stepped out on the deck in the velvet night. The rains that had flooded so many people out of their homes, killed a dozen others, and kept the whole central Texas countryside hostage had thundered on out of the area and finally broken up somewhere in the Great Plains. Rubbing the back of her neck with one hand, Dylan stretched her spine. Cicadas droned. Wind ruffled the trees. The creek, still running high, rushed past in the dark. With no city lights to bleach the sky, the stars sugar-frosted the heavens with a breathless sweetness that made her melancholy.

Until Timmy Castillo was found, Dylan knew, the case would never be closed for her. And if the case were to be closed, once and for all, there was one more thing she had to do. Gazing up at the night's magnificence, she sent up a silent prayer for strength, then went back inside, to check once more to make sure her own children were safe and at peace.

• • •

Kevin Edwards's house was a modest brick tract house located in a housing development in which every third house on the block had the same floor plan. It was a young neighborhood; the houses were all fairly new, and most of the lawns had not fully grown in yet. The developers had apparently come in and mowed down every tree in the area; the only ones she saw were thin, freshly planted saplings. The construction site, she learned, was to be a new school. Most of the couples who resided in the homes worked all day and never really got to know their neighbors. The kids, however, were all well acquainted.

Brandon Edwards and his wife, Molly, were a handsome, hardworking couple who resented the word *yuppies* and did not consider themselves such. They were just a husband and wife, struggling to make a good life for themselves and their son. They were well educated and well informed. They knew who Dylan was and congratulated her on solving the Shadowland case. Their house was clean and sparsely furnished; Dylan suspected that most of their income went to mortgage and car payments.

She introduced the reluctant Sergeant Dickerson to them and asked if they would mind if she talked to Kevin a little while. They were glad to cooperate; everyone was saddened that little Timmy had not been found like the others. They wanted to do what they could to help.

Kevin was a good-looking, blond-haired, blue-eyed kid nearing his tenth birthday. He was well mannered and likable. Dylan asked him if he would mind explaining to her, again, exactly what happened on the day that Timmy disappeared.

As soon as she asked him, he began chewing on his fingernails. "Um, we went to play down at the new school," he said, his eyes darting nervously over to his parents. "We played hide-and-seek and stuff, and then Mike and Steve had to go home. Me and Timmy stayed."

Dylan gave him an encouraging nod.

He licked his lips. "We were playing hide-and-seek, and then this guy came up on a motorcycle and started talking to Timmy."

Dylan sat back in surprise. There had been no mention of a motorcycle or anyone else in the original report. "Where were you when this happened, Kevin?" she asked.

"Uh, I was up on top of a dirt pile."

"I thought you were playing hide-and-seek."

He glanced at his parents. "Yeah. Um, I was hiding, and then Timmy never did come."

"Did you see him leave on the motorcycle?"

"No."

"Where were you hiding?"

"Um, in one of those big barrels."

Dylan glanced over at Sergeant Dickerson. He gave her a questioning look. She leaned forward. "Kevin, honey, you told the officers at the time that you were hiding behind a stack of concrete blocks."

"I did?"

She nodded. "Kevin . . ." She made her voice as gentle as possible. "Tell me about the pile of dirt."

Kevin's voice began to shake. "It's just a big ol' pile of dirt we liked to play on. We'd play king-of-the-mountain, and we'd build roads and stuff for our cars and stuff. But we had to be careful because there was a big hole right next to it, and sometimes the dirt would slide into the hole. We had to be careful. . . ." His voice trailed off.

"Honey, I have to tell you; as soon as I was hired by the Scotts, I visited the construction site where you were playing. There were no big barrels there."

"I j-just got confused." His face flushed.

"Kevin," said Brandon Edwards in a stern voice. "You tell the truth to Ms. Tandy. If you'll just tell the truth, you won't get into any trouble. Were you and Timmy doing something you weren't supposed to do?"

A tear rolled down Kevin's face.

Dylan looked over at his parents. They had no idea. God,

there were times she hated her job. She reached out and took the boy's cold hand. "You weren't playing hide-and-seek, were you?"

He shook his head. More tears streamed down his cheeks.

"And you didn't see anybody on a motorcycle, did you?"

Kevin began to sob.

She glanced at his bewildered parents. Then she said, "Kevin, did you hurt Timmy?"

"I didn't mean to!" he blurted, tears choking him. The color drained from his mother's face. "I didn't mean to! We had a fight—" He ran and buried his head in his mother's lap. She looked over at Dylan with the horror-struck face of someone whose world is crumbling before her eyes.

"Kevin!" cried his father. "What are you saying, son?"

Face still buried in his mother's lap, the child cried out in a voice filled with anguish and too-long pent-up secrets, "I hit Timmy with a rock, and then shoved him into the hole. And I covered him with dirt. He made me so mad."

His mother covered her mouth with her hand.

Dylan said, "Kevin, you didn't try to help Timmy get out of the hole, did you?"

He shook his head and mumbled, "I was afraid I might get into trouble, so I just covered him up real good."

"And when the original search failed to turn up the boy—who was believed to be kidnapped—the construction crew returned and finished the job," said Dickerson bitterly. He looked at the stricken family. "I'm sorry, but I'm going to have to make some calls. I think this time we'll find him."

Brandon Edwards turned a gray face toward the officer and said, "Will you have to arrest him? He's just a *child*."

Dickerson sighed as though breathing were too heavy a job to handle just then. "I'm afraid I'm going to have to read him his rights," he said, "before we question him any further."

Kevin's mother enfolded her child in her arms and looked

on, mute with shock, while the police read the boy his rights.

As Dylan watched, she realized that the true Shadowland was a world in which kids killed kids, while the adults looked at each other helplessly and wondered *why*.

THIRTY-SEVEN

Dylan and Matt sat together on the deck on a warm afternoon, in the waning days of what had turned out to be the longest summer of their lives, watching their children splash and play in the tree-shrouded, sun-spangled stream behind their house. From the looks of things, horror might never have stalked their serene little world.

Except that so much had changed. The Shadowland case had brought not only a deluge of new business, but a firm book offer, opportunities on the lecture circuit, and even talk of a movie. It would be easy to get swept up in it all. Dylan, especially, was going to have to work even harder to make room for her children. They had already taken a couple of steps in that direction. They'd hired an assistant, and Dylan had instigated something she liked to call "Sunday Special Time"; an hour with each child exclusively, to be spent in whatever way the child chose. The assistant was proving to be a big help, and the Sunday Special Time was a smash success, but still she worried that it wasn't enough.

Children, it seemed to her, received so many conflicting messages from sources other than their parents in any given week: from peers, movies, and television. How well would she, as a parent, be able to compete? How could she be sure her messages were the ones getting through?

How could she teach her children the one lesson that Kevin Edwards and Jason Crandall had failed to learn: that human life is precious and irreplaceable?

How, too, could she protect her little ones from those tragic individuals who had *not* learned this powerful truth?

"I don't suppose I have to ask what you're thinking about, do I?" asked Matt, startling her.

She gave him a sheepish grin. "Just following that same old maze around and around. I wish I could understand what makes some people value life and some not. I mean, neither Kevin nor Jason came from abusive homes or were unloved. I just wish I could figure out what they wanted."

"I imagine they wanted what all kids want. Approval, a sense of belonging, a relative feeling of safety, maybe a sense of accomplishment."

Dylan nodded. This made more sense than any of her own mental meanderings. "I can see that. But I think there's more to it than that. After all, there are lots of ways for a kid to feel a sense of accomplishment besides murder and kidnapping."

He inclined his head in agreement.

"What is the one thing—above all else—that no kid ever has?"

Matt shrugged. "You got me, partner."

"A sense of control. Kids are totally powerless, dependent on adults who may or may not be capable of meeting their needs."

"Ergo, Shadow's peculiar quest," said Matt. "Not only did the media give him the attention he was not getting at home, but he was in complete control over the situation. At least, for a while."

"Makes sense to me. And it explains why he started snatching small, relatively helpless children, rather than luring someone his own age into the cave. So he could be in total control."

They sat quietly together for a moment, then Dylan shook her head. "But I still can't completely figure out Kevin Edwards, or other kids like him. I hear of new cases every day. There was a nine-year-old boy in Pennsylvania who shot and killed a seven-year-old neighbor girl because she taunted him that she was a better Nintendo player than he was. He used his dad's deer-hunting rifle. Just like Kevin's case, he nearly got away with it, too." She took a sip of her tea and swirled the ice around in her glass. "Kids are pulling guns on each other now, instead of pounding it out on the playground." She gazed toward the stream. "I guess I just wish that Ray Bradbury's fictional town of Green, where kids ran and played away a summer—that place of innocence—still existed. I feel such a sense of loss."

"I don't," said Matt. "There was a lot going on behind closed doors in those little towns back then that nobody knew about—child molesting, you name it. I'm glad times have changed. Anyway, you can't protect your children forever, Dylan."

She sighed. "Even when I try, I don't always succeed. Consider Chris Helmon. I thought he was a murderer, but in the end, he helped us find our daughter and looked after our son. And by the same token, I'd have let her play with Kevin Edwards anytime."

Matt smiled and started to say something.

Aidan emerged from the tree line just then and ran, shrieking, from her brother, who was chasing her with a squirming crawdad in his hand. "Look at her," said Matt finally, his voice swelling with pride. "Hasn't she been splendid through all this? Think how brave and resourceful she *and* Jeremy were in that cave."

Dylan, watching her kids with a smile on her face, nodded.

"Maybe the answer lies with the children," mused Matt.

Aidan came charging back, wielding a garden hose, laughing wickedly as she sprayed Caleb.

Matt said, "I think it's time that we learned to trust our children. Each one is an individual, you know. For every Kevin Edwards or Jason Crandall, there are a hundred Jeremy Scotts and Aidan Tandy-Armstrongs. Our future just might be in better shape than we think."

Caleb came tearing up onto the deck. *"Help!"* he cried, dripping water all over Dylan. His eyes were shining, his fair skin buttery from the sun. He plunked a hand into his mother's iced tea.

"Caleb!" she scolded.

He withdrew a large chunk of ice. "Emergency ammunition, Mom. This is self-defense!" With that, he flew off the deck and tackled his sister, who screamed and struggled as he stuck the ice down the back of her shirt.

Dylan removed her sunglasses and squinted at the warm shrieking bodies as they tumbled over the grass. Beneath the bright sunshine, it seemed to her as if they gave off a golden aura, like a sweet memory, so soothing to the soul on a cold rainy night.

She knew that, all too soon, these children *would* be a memory. Before her very eyes, they would fill out, grow up, and fade away into the misty journey of adulthood. She wondered if this would be one of the days they would take with them on that trip. Perhaps it would serve as a reminder, sweet and mellow as hot chocolate, to warm them on one of their own cold and rainy nights: a reminder that they were valued; they were loved.

But until that time came, she had the *now*. She had this moment, this day, this precious time. And as long as she recognized that in the here and in the now, then perhaps she was doing all she could to protect her children from an uncertain future.

"Heads up, guys!" she hollered and began pelting the scuffling youngsters with ice cubes. Immediately they joined forces and returned the attack. Dylan and Matt were forced to seek refuge behind a picnic table. When they ran out of ice cubes, a giggling Aidan, egged on by her brother, turned a garden hose on her beleaguered parents.

Matt responded by finding a twangy Country and Western song on the portable radio and turning it up extra loud. While the children screamed in agony, Dylan, shaking water out of her hair like a dog, gave him a dazzling smile.

"We can probably trust them with the future," he said, grinning back, "but we can't ever let them get one up on us."

ACKNOWLEDGMENTS

I sincerely hope the fine people of Kerrville, Texas, will accept my gratitude for their cooperation in the writing of this book, particularly the Kerrville Chamber of Commerce and Captain L. Scott Evans of the Kerrville Police Department. I hope they will not mind that I took a few geographical and meteorological liberties with their lovely city. For example, although there are numerous unexplored caves located on private ranches throughout the Texas Hill Country, I placed the Secret Caverns in a spot of my own choosing. Also, since Kerrville is located on the banks of the beautiful Guadalupe River, then floods do have to be a concern of the residents, so I hope they won't be too concerned that a flood does become an integral part of the story.

Residents will recognize a number of locations in the story; however, private homes and ranches, as well as Chris's Collectible Comics & Cards are fictional and not intended to resemble any existing places.

This story could not have been written without the wonderful cooperation of my friend, Garry Eckert, Dungeon Master extraordinaire. His expertise in the game Dungeons & Dragons and his suggestions for the manuscript were needed and appreciated.

Many thanks to my good buddy, Chuck Layer, of Charles Layer Private Investigations, for opening up to me the fascinating world of the real life PI, and for giving me some great laughs.

I would also like to thank Janice Sublett, a physician's

assistant who works exclusively with paraplegics at the San Diego Veterans' Hospital, for her patience in answering all my questions.

My deepest appreciation goes to my friend and mentor, Dean Koontz, for his guidance and encouragement. Hats off to you, Dean, for never forgetting.

And to my family: my husband, Kent (my love and my life), and my two great kids, Dustin and Jessica; my endless gratitude for putting up with the madness. You make me possible.